the thin space

Where Faith and Doubt Collide

endorsements

Dann Stouten is a master storyteller, alert to the ways every human story can intersect with God's story. In his newest book, *The Thin Space*, he weaves together stories of loss and grief—stories too familiar to so many of us—with a clear-eyed vision of God's seeking comfort. The result is a realistic vision of hope that acknowledges pain and acknowledges the God who carries us through that pain."

—**Aaron J. Kuecker**, Provost, Trinity Christian College, Palos Heights, Illinois 60463

Dann Stouten's skills as a storyteller shine in *The Thin Space*, a unique novel containing a story within a story. The theme of God's seeming silence in times of grief is a universal one and Stouten handles it with grace and sensitivity. A mysterious, delusional, homeless man adds to the wonder of God's gentle care for us.

—**Lynn Austin**, bestselling author of nearly thirty novels, winner of eight Christy Awards and one of the first inductees into the Christy Award Hall of Fame.

Dann Stouten is a master storyteller. He has the gift of capturing a heart, intriguing a mind, and changing a life through the art of story. In *The Thin Space*, he reminds us there is a real world all around us, but there is another world where God dwells and those who have gone before us live with Jesus. Dann helps us discover that, sometimes, these two places intersect.

—**Kevin G Harney**, author of the *Organic Outreach* Trilogy and *Organic Disciple*. founder of Organic Outreach International.

This is a story for all of us who have lost someone we love. It is incredibly poignant, especially interesting, and exceptionally real. In *The Thin Space,* Dann Stouten invites us along on a journey of discovery that explores the place between faith and doubt, life and death, brokenness and healing, what's real and the wonder of what's hoped for. Sometimes it's painful, sometimes it's comforting, always it's honest. In the end, *The Thin Space* provides each of us the encouragement and comfort we need to face life's most painful and challenging moments.

—**Tom Devries**, President CEO Global Leadership Network.

the thin space

Where Faith and Doubt Collide

Dann Stouten

ELK LAKE PUBLISHING INC

PUBLISHING THE POSITIVE
Plymouth, Massachusetts

Cover and Interior Design: Derinda Babcock
Editor(s): Peggy Ellis, Cristel Phelps, Deb Haggerty
Author Represented By: Credo Communications LLC

PUBLISHED BY: Elk Lake Publishing, Inc., 35 Dogwood Drive, Plymouth, MA 02360, 2021

Library Cataloging Data

Names: Stouten, Dann (Dann Stouten)
The Thin Space—Where Faith and Doubt Collide/ Dann Stouten

344 p. 23cm × 15cm (9in × 6 in.)

ISBN-13: 978-1-64949-223-4 (paperback) | 978-1-64949224-1 (trade paperback) | 978-1-64949-225-8 (e-book)

Key Words: Death of a spouse, homelessness, psychology, miracles, inspirational, mourning, delusion

Library of Congress Control Number: 2021939082 Fiction

dedication

This book is dedicated to the people I love, the people I've lost, and the God who has promised to prepare a place for us to all spend eternity together with him.

acknowledgments

I want to thank Kevin and Sherry Harney for their prayers, their encouragement, and for believing in my writing when few others did.

I want to thank Leroy Koopman for his theological insight, editing, and advice in the early stages of writing this manuscript.

I want to thank my publishing agent, Peter Ford, and Credo Communications for their representation as my literary agent.

I want to thank Deb Haggerty and the entire team at Elk Lake Publishing for investing in me and my writing.

I want to thank David VanOpstall and the congregation of Christ Memorial Church for their partnership in the gospel and for their willingness to listen to my stories.

And, finally, I thank God for his grace, my family for their love, and the way each has shaped my life.

Being confident of this, that he who began a good work in you will carry it on to completion until the day of Christ Jesus.

—the apostle Paul, Philippians 1:6

chapter 1

END TIMES

Remember Jesus of Nazareth, staggering on broken feet out of the tomb toward the Resurrection, bearing on his body the proud insignia of the defeat which is victory, the magnificent defeat of the human soul at the hands of God.—Frederick Buechner, *The Magnificent Defeat*

The summer I turned twelve, my older brother Seth started taking me steelhead fishing. One rainy day in August, the two of us were casting our lines off the breakwater near Front Street. The rocks can be slippery out there, so I kicked off my Birkies and went barefoot. Then things took a bad turn. I stepped on Seth's hook. He used a Mepps model B5, a large brass spoon lure with a treble hook. The pain dropped me to my knees. The barb punctured the soft tissue in the bottom of my foot, hooked around and stuck out the side of my arch. In that moment, our plans for the day ended. Pain blotted out all other thoughts. We tried to pull out the hook but the harder we pulled, the deeper the spur dug into my flesh. Eventually we gave up. We cut the lure from the line, and I limped home with my arm around Seth's shoulder—the longest two miles of my life.

Mom sat me down in a kitchen chair and put my foot in a galvanized washtub full of ice water. After my foot numbed, Dad tried to pull out the lure. Like a surgeon, he carefully laid out his instruments on a towel—a bottle of rubbing alcohol, two cotton swabs, chrome–plated tweezers, a Wusthof fillet knife, and a pair of needle-nosed pliers. Dad poked and pulled and prodded, but in the end, he didn't do any better than we did.

"I know you don't want to hear this," Dad said. "But I think the only way to get the hook *out* is to push it *through*."

Before I could protest, he grabbed the shank with the pliers, and with one swift twist, he pushed the barb through the skin. I yelled but it was too late. The deed was already done. When I calmed down, he cut off the barb, and pulled out the remainder of the hook. I limped for the rest of the summer. I still have the scar.

I tell this story because that's what happens when you lose someone you love. Grief hobbles you like a fishhook in your heart. Immediately you fall to your knees. All you can think about is the throbbing pain. Whatever plans you had are gone. Recovery won't be easy, but somehow, you must push through. For a while, you'll limp like a three-legged dog. Everything you do will be harder and heavier. Someday, you might walk normally again. You may even dance, but not now, not for a while. At least that's my story.

A year and a half ago, my wife Rachel and I spent the holidays in the oncology ward of Holland Hospital. Christmas cards and crayon drawings covered the walls of her room. A small green ceramic Christmas tree sat on the nightstand. One of the nurses wrote *Peace, Joy, Love,* and *Hope* in red marker on the whiteboard next to Rachel's bed. Wishful thinking. Slowly, our hope melted like a snowman in April. One by one, the people we loved the most came by to say their goodbyes, but nobody stayed long. Seeing Rachel like this was too painful. Eventually, the two of us were alone. I lay beside her in the dark, held her in my arms, and prayed for the coming of the Christ. He never showed.

The last thing I said to her was, "It'll be all right, honey." We both knew better. Rachel's body was a battlefield, and her scars were a reminder of every skirmish.

Three days after Christmas, my wife became another casualty in the war on cancer. What I thought would last forever was now forever lost. Her death tore my heart wide open. Emotions flew everywhere. Rachel was the victim. I was collateral damage.

Tired and angry and itching for a fight, I directed my comments toward God. I cursed. I yelled. I even questioned his integrity. Still, no matter what I asked, he did nothing. God remained painfully silent.

May I tell you something? Being mad at God is frustrating. The problem isn't he doesn't fight fair—in fact, he doesn't fight at all. I flung my words toward heaven like an angry fisherman casting his nets, but, every time, they came back empty. God continued to hold his tongue, and his silence spoke volumes.

Finally, reality set in. There would be no cavalry of angels, no coming of the Christ, and no Christmas miracle. Eventually, I did what I had to do—signed papers, made arrangements, and called the people I loved. Wounded, I soldiered on.

I had to talk with Lucy. I had to figure out how to tell a third grader her mother had died. Neither one of us were ready to have that conversation. I suppose you never are. Like a really good book, the best lives are always too short. They leave us wanting more. When we get to the last chapter, we're not ready for the story to end. That's our story. Maybe that's your story too.

I counted. God gave Rachel 12,231 days. If I could have given her some of mine, I would have, but God doesn't allow that. There are no gimmies, no do-overs, and no take backs. Every life is predetermined. Our days are recorded in the Lamb's book of life.

There is "a time to be born and a time to die," the Bible says. So, on the day of Rachel's birth, the recording angel made the following notation next to her name.

"Born into this world September 10, 1981, born into eternal grace December 28, 2015."

Thirty-three years, three months, and nineteen days was not enough time for me. I felt cheated. Emotionally and spiritually, I'd lost my way. After Rachel died, my faith and my doubts played kick the can with my soul. I went back and forth between belief and unbelief. Slowly, my trust in God eroded, and I fell into the inky twilight of doubt. I woke up one morning and realized I'd been living in the shadow of death for so long I'd become a permanent resident of the darkness. God seemed distant, aloof, as if he wasn't there or didn't care. I felt as abandoned as Christ on the cross.

Like it or not, life is full of little Easters. Somewhere along the way, we all get to play the role of Jesus. If you haven't experienced this yet, trust me, you will. You'll be crucified for something or someone, and in that moment, you'll feel godforsaken, gut shot, and left for dead. Somewhere, deep in your soul, you'll find yourself echoing the Savior's words.

"My God, my God, why have you forsaken me?"

Maybe your anguish will result from an illness or an addiction or a betrayal of some kind. For someone else, perhaps a lost job or a lost opportunity or a lost dream. My anguish resulted from the loss of the only woman I ever loved.

"Why, Lord," I asked, banging my angry fist on heaven's front door. "Why her, why this, why now?"

If he had one, God didn't share his answer with me. Like I said, his silence twisted like a fishhook in my heart. I began to lash out at the only one who could have comforted me. Little by little, my prayers turned to accusations. Each night, I mounted my case for his obvious unfairness.

"I don't deserve this," I said. "We don't deserve this. Certainly, she doesn't deserve all this pain. I don't know who you are anymore, Lord. There is no justice in this, no righteousness, no mercy, or compassion. There is only pain—relentless, unexplainable pain. You could have done something, but you didn't."

"How could a loving God let that happen?" I asked. "How?"

My prayers hung like helium balloons over my bed. Eventually, I met God's silence with a silence of my own. If he wouldn't talk to me, I wouldn't talk to him. I could be as stubborn as he was, even more so. For months, a wall of silence separated us.

In fact, the silence lasted one year, four months, and two days after Rachel's death. I waited that long before the answer to my unanswered prayers finally arrived. To my great surprise, the answer came disguised as a homeless vagabond in a polo shirt. He called himself Paul, and like most prophets, he hardly appeared to be the messenger from God. However, looking back now, I should have known better. After all, Jesus was clear about all this.

> "Blessed are you who are poor, for yours is the kingdom of God."

Paul was poor enough, that's for sure. Besides, God seems to enjoy coming to us in the people and places we'd least expect. Life is full of uncertainty—so is death. At least that's been my experience.

We found our rhythm. Every other Wednesday afternoon, Paul came and sat *Shiva* with me. Together, we practiced the sacred mourning period observed by Jews when they lose someone they love. Sometimes he talked, sometimes he listened, and sometimes he simply sat silently and joined me in an unspoken requiem of remembrance. Mourners have a way of finding each other, and over time, our broken souls began to bond in a way that's hard to explain. At first, I saw our relationship as one-sided. As a psychologist, I knew he needed help, and I was being paid to help him, so we met at my office twice a month. What I *didn't* know was he was there to help me.

When Rachel died, I had no idea what I faced. The frontier of my ignorance appeared vast and desolate. I simply didn't know what I didn't know. I knew what the Bible said about death, but I didn't know how losing her would mess with my soul. Knowledge and understanding are two different things. Knowledge is a matter of the mind, but understanding is deeper. Understanding happens in the soul. When Rachel died, my soul shattered like a window hit by a baseball, and the fragments of my faith lay scattered on the ground.

A year would pass before I realized my brokenness would drive me deep into despair but also deeper into understanding. What I didn't know, what I couldn't know, was my brokenness would draw me closer to God than I'd ever been before.

chapter 2

THE BEGINNING

Can you worship a God who isn't obligated to explain his actions to you? Could it be your arrogance that makes you think God owes you an explanation?—Francis Chan, *Crazy Love: Overwhelmed by a Relentless God*

My daughter, Lucy, didn't have school on Friday and had a sleepover at her friend Gracie Weaver's house. Gracie and her older sister Jackie were Lucy's closest friends—physically and emotionally. The Weavers lived two houses north of ours, and after Rachel died, I paid Mary Weaver to watch Lucy after school.

With Lucy at the Weaver's, I was in no hurry to get home, so I stayed at my downtown office and did some lecture prep. Just before five o'clock, Laurie from Judge Summerdyke's office called. She asked me if I could do an evaluation on a new patient in the psychiatric ward of Holland Hospital.

"He showed up yesterday at the Lighthouse Mission," Laurie said with a nervous laugh. "Get this, he thinks he's the apostle Paul."

She also said Dwight McKay, the director at the mission, feared he might be dangerous. Dwight's a little leery of paranoid schizophrenics. Two weeks previously, a guy named Charlie Lampen stood up during dinner and identified himself as an undercover agent for the FBI. Then he pointed across the table at Moses Hawks and accused him of being an ISIS terrorist. Things got ugly fast.

"Hawks leaped over the table like the quick brown fox," Laurie said.

"Hawks is a big man, over six feet and weighing in at two-forty. The fight wouldn't last long. But then, Charlie slapped him on the side of the head with a dinner plate, knocked him to the ground, and started stabbing him in the face with a fork. Three guys held Charlie down until the cops showed up."

"So anyway," she continued, "Dwight isn't taking any chances this time. He called Holland PD when this Paul fellow showed up. After they talked to him for a while, they brought him to the hospital. The man has identity delusion probably, but nobody's there this time of night to make the call. Can you help us out, Doc?"

"Sure," I said, "I can get over there later tonight if you want."

"That would be great."

When the courts are uncertain about someone's mental stability, they detain them on what's called a "seventy-two-hour hold." As a part of that, they usually have someone do an evaluation of the person's mental condition. That's where I come in. My job dictates I decide if the patient presents a danger to themselves or to others. The criterion is straightforward.

As always, I followed a five-step evaluation process. First, I looked at the patient's history.

As I entered the ward, Stan Martinelli, the night security guard, told me my patient was in room 732, then he handed me his chart. I checked to see if this patient, who calls himself Paul, had a history of instability, alcohol, or drug use.

The chart revealed little, but from what I could see he was clean.

I also looked to see if he currently was using any kind of prescription medication. Chemical imbalance in the brain is the root cause of a lot of delusion. When someone goes off their medication, simply reestablishing their protocol will often stabilize their condition. According to his chart, there weren't any presenting medical issues, so I moved on to step number two, observation.

I walked down the hall with Stan, looked through the small window in the door of room 732, and made a note of Paul's physical appearance. I studied the way he dressed, the way he sat, and I tried to see if his pupils were dilated.

Whenever someone feels anxious or threatened, their brain starts dumping adrenaline into the bloodstream. This causes their heart rate to go up and their pupils to dilate. Automatically, peripheral vision narrows, so they can focus on whatever threat is in front of them. I've learned to keep my distance if someone has large pupils. Paul didn't.

Third, I looked for an elevated heart rate. A person's blood pressure increases when their heart rate goes up. Often the higher rate is visible in a pulsing vein in their neck or an increase in perspiration. Sweaty patients are usually trouble, but this man seemed unusually calm and relaxed.

Next, I looked at Paul's shoulders. As any boxer can tell you, a person will often telegraph a punch by tightening their shoulders just before they strike. A balled fist and a deep breath also indicate increased agitation. When he stood and walked toward the window, I studied his posture and watched for signs of aggression. Anger isn't easy to hide. Strangely, this man seemed to be at peace with himself and his surroundings.

Finally, I moved from the physical signs to the emotional ones. I talked to the only staff person available, Stan Martinelli, to see if the patient seemed distant or distracted or paranoid. Did Paul exhibit signs of rage or aggression? Was he involved in reckless or inappropriate behavior? Once again, on the surface at least, Martinelli assured me everything appeared normal.

The more a patient is willing to engage in conversation, the more I'm able to understand their emotional stability, so I always ask a handful of introductory questions.

"Are you sleeping okay? How's your appetite? Is anything bothering you?"

These questions and more followed when I was on the other side of the door.

chapter 3

THE REFERRAL

It's still hard for me to have a clear mind thinking about it. But it's the truth even if it didn't happen."—Ken Kesey, *One Flew Over the Cuckoo's Nest*

The Ottawa County court system discounts my hourly rate by twenty percent, but I never have to chase them to get paid. Court referrals were easy money. When Rachel died, my client load increased. I saw her patients and mine. I made a rule not to take on any new clients, but with Lucy gone for the night, I needed to keep myself busy. Work helps mask the pain. Idle time is the enemy of anyone who has lost someone they love, so, I broke my own rule.

I've done these evaluations before, so I knew what to expect with this man who called himself Paul. Judge Summerdyke's referrals are all social misfits. They're a collection of lost souls, likeable rogues, paranoid schizophrenics, and petty criminals. Still, they add a little spice to my otherwise vanilla list of clients. Paul would prove to be no exception.

The chart identified him as Sha'ul Ben Andronicus, case number 1761-5SBA. We met the first time in his room in the psychiatric ward on the seventh floor.

The seventh resembles the other floors of the hospital, except all the doors stay locked. Access is restricted to those with a magnetized ID badge. An entry door just off the main elevator is staffed 24/7, and visitors are buzzed in and out during working hours. Otherwise, no one gets access without swiping their badge.

After peeking through the door and making my initial observations, I reached for my ID badge, but Stan already had his out and was about to let me in.

"This man says he has no ID, no money, no permanent address, and nobody to call," Stan said. "Kind of a sad case, really."

"Any problems?" I asked.

"No. So far at least he's been cooperative. Earlier today, we let him walk around the prayer garden for a while. The garden is peaceful and often has a soothing effect on the patients. He seemed to enjoy the walk. After looking at the tulips for a few minutes, he sat down next to Emma Higgins. He just started talking away as if the girl could hear every word he said. Emma is stone deaf. She dances to music the rest of us don't hear. I thought he might be a problem for her, so I drifted over in that direction.

"Talking to her seemed quite natural to him—no big deal—but talking to Emma *is* a big deal. She's a regular—one of Doctor Webber's patients. She can't hear or speak. She can sign, but often she chooses not to. For seventeen years, Emma has lived in her own little world, and rarely lets anyone in. When someone does something to upset her, she goes ballistic. That's usually how she ends up here."

"A regular. What usually brings her here?"

"Anger issues. This time was no different. Her parents live on the south channel out by the lighthouse. Emma's dad was one of the original investors in Intel, and he made a boatload of cash. Her family moved here a couple of years ago to be closer to Doctor Webber. The word is they've spent a fortune trying to help Emma. So far, Webber is the only one who gets through to her. Truthfully, he hasn't had much success either. She's a tough nut to crack.

"But like I said, your guy Paul sat in the garden and talked to her for almost an hour. And here's the thing, Doc. Emma nodded and smiled like she could understand every word he said. I'm telling you the sight was kind of weird. I mean who talks to the deaf?

"About an hour later, Paul went back up to his room. He's been sitting there in the recliner looking out the window ever since, waiting for someone, he said.

"There's something else you should know, Doc," Stan said in a serious tone. "This guy thinks he's the apostle Paul."

I smiled slightly to indicate I was aware of his condition, but he persisted.

"Seriously, Doc, I think he really believes he's the apostle."

"They always do." I said. "Just because someone *believes* something is true doesn't mean it *is* true. The world is full of lies and misinformation people swear is true. If they repeat the lie often enough, they start to believe it themselves. Politicians have the same problem."

Stan smiled, then swiped his ID badge through the slot in the door of Paul's room. When the lock buzzed, I knocked and then slowly pushed the door open a crack. The voice on the other side invited me in. Stan stationed himself outside for a few minutes in case of a problem. There wasn't. As he mentioned, I found Sha'ul sitting in an green vinyl recliner, looking out the window and waving to a teenage girl in the courtyard below.

As the door closed behind me, he turned and acknowledged my presence with a smile.

"I've been expecting you," he said. "I thought you'd be here earlier, but actually, your timing is perfect. Your delay gave me the opportunity to tend to a few things around here."

He slowly rose to his feet. The pained look on his face told me arthritis bothered him or perhaps something more sinister.

I extended my hand and introduced myself.

"Good evening," I said, "I'm Dr. DeVos. Is it okay if I call you Saul?"

"I know who you are," he said in a Middle Eastern accent, ignoring my outstretched hand. "And yes, Sha'ul is my given name, but my friends call me Paul."

"Paul it is then," I said, sliding my hand into my coat pocket.

Paul's words confirmed what Laurie, Stan, and the chart said. "Apparently the man has had a psychotic break and now thinks he's the apostle Paul."

We often encounter people who believe they're Jesus or the president or the king of England, but Paul and the other apostles also make an appearance on the psych ward every now and again.

As we talked, I took my MacBook from my briefcase and asked if I could take notes.

"I don't mind," he said. "In fact, I've done some writing myself. Maybe you've read some of my letters." Then he smiled as if he was proud of his writings.

"I've read all your letters," I said, hoping to win his trust. "Philippians is my favorite."

"Mine too," he said. "Mine too. I know how important good notes can be, so please feel free to write as much as you'd like."

He explained quite matter-of-factly that although the Creator told him to talk with everyone, he wanted Paul to talk specifically with me.

"Really?" I said. "That's interesting. Do you hear voices often, Paul?"

"Sometimes," he said with a smile. "I think we all have times when there are competing voices in our heads. The trick is figuring out which ones to listen to."

I returned his smile and tried not to look judgmental.

"I hear you had quite a conversation earlier today with a girl in the garden."

"Emma's a very misunderstood young woman," he said. "She feels isolated and insecure. Sometimes, she expresses her frustrations inappropriately, even violently, but really, she's a very tenderhearted person inside. I tried to reassure her that God and her family loved her. I also told her many of the great minds in the world have been misunderstood. Loneliness is often the companion of genius."

I didn't know what to make of all that, or how he learned the girl's name, but his observations about her were spot-on. I later learned from Dr. Webber that Emma was extremely intelligent, solitary, and sometimes violent. She tends to lash out at people whenever she feels threatened or is unable to communicate.

In my profession, I'm used to talking with people, who at least at times, can be insightfully delusional. Paul fit the protocol. To be honest, in a world full of phonies and pretenders, sometimes meeting someone who knows who they are, even if they're wrong, is refreshing.

Like I said, most of the Summerdyke court referrals have issues. Some are up for a felony of some kind. They often try to con me into helping them lay the groundwork for an insanity defense. Others have a chemical imbalance and are in need of medication. Still others have gone through a tragedy or trauma which caused them to have a psychotic break. I believe Paul fit in the latter camp.

My usual job with court referrals is to determine if they're competent to stand trial or if they meet the guidelines for parental custody. In either case, the patient is usually reluctant to open up and is skeptical of my findings. Some of them believe I'm part of some grand conspiracy that is out to get them. This makes for some interesting sessions. However, in the end, my job is simply to sift out the truth from what a patient says.

With my regular clients, I usually invite them to help me define the goals for their treatment regimen. I'll ask them what they want to accomplish or what they hope we're going to be able to do.

With court referrals, the judge sets the objectives, not the client. With the one, my goal is to help the client with a mental problem, self-understanding, or behavioral modification. With the other, the goal is to identify what's true and what's not about a specific situation.

Paul's case gave rise to two questions. First, what caused his delusion? And second, does he appear to be a danger to himself or others? As for the cause, I must determine if Paul's issue was schizophrenia, a bipolar disorder, or the result of trauma or guilt.

First impressions are usually a pretty good indicator of someone's sincerity. Paul presented himself well, but he wore the hardship of his life in the lines on his face. He kept his salt and pepper beard neatly trimmed and cropped close. Hair, short, dark as ink, and tightly curled, covered his head. A deep scar ran across part of his left cheek all the way to the helix of his ear. His chocolate brown, penetrating eyes and fixed gaze gave me the impression he not only concentrated on my every word, but also read my deepest thoughts. At times, I wonder who interviewed whom.

Paul wore well-worn Carhartt canvas khakis, coffee-colored Birkenstocks, and a faded pistachio green Mobaco polo shirt.

So which tribe are you from, Paul? Was the man from the Middle East? Was he well-traveled? The question was cause to dig a little deeper.

"Are you from around here?" I asked.

"I am from lots of places," he said. "I was born a Hebrew, a son of Abraham, of the tribe of Benjamin, in the town of Tarsus, on the plain of Cilicia, in what you now call south central Turkey."

"And you," he asked, returning my question, "where are you from?"

I wanted to say, "That's not the way this works. We only have a limited amount of time, and I want to spend those minutes learning what I can about you," but I didn't. The truth is we weren't in my office. There were no patients sitting in the waiting room ready to take his place. And with Lucy at the Weaver's, I really didn't want to go home to an empty house anyway, so I decided to humor him.

chapter 4

Growing Up

Twenty years from now you will be more disappointed by the things that you didn't do than by the ones you did do. So, throw off the bowlines. Sail away from the safe harbor. Catch the trade winds in your sails. Explore. Dream. Discover.—H. Jackson Brown Jr., *P.S. I Love You*

"I had a pretty great childhood," I said. "Growing up, my family owned a fruit farm on the east ridge of Michigan's Leelanau peninsula, a couple of miles north of Sutton's Bay. Each morning, I'd sit on the window seat in my bedroom, look across our orchards, and watch the sun rise over the waters of Grand Traverse Bay."

I told him more than I expected, and he proved to be a good listener.

"Our house, a neatly kept five-bedroom farmhouse, has white clapboard siding, green shingles, matching green shutters, and a big wrap-around porch.

I thought I might learn more about him by observing how he listened than by listening to what he said, so I kept going.

"A doublewide blacktop driveway expands in front of the garage and then veers off to the right. Past the fork, we use a small red tool shed as a blacksmith shop and a massive red post and beam building as the milk barn."

"Your home sounds quite wonderful," Paul said, "but what about your family?"

My family has a proud history, but I purposely left out some of the details. For example, in Dutch, *DeVos* means "the fox," so that became our logo. A huge weathered metal silhouette of a leaping fox hangs from the peak of the milk barn. Below the sign, large letters identify us as "Fox Farms."

Under that, in smaller letters is "S. P. DeVos and Sons." In truth, there was only one son, my father, Sebastian Peter DeVos, junior, who most people called Pete. My uncle Louis, a navy seal, died in the Korean War. Grandpa refused to change the sign in honor of his oldest son's memory. A stubbornly religious man, my grandfather vowed not to let this tragedy change what he believes or how he lives.

"My grandfather," I said, resuming my conversation with Paul, "is Sebastian Peter DeVos. Everyone calls him Sea Bass, Sea for short. Dad and I both carry his name. To avoid confusion they call dad Speck, short for Speckled Bass, because of his freckles. They call me Rock Bass, shortened to Rocky. As a kid, I tried to live up to the name. I wanted to be strong, immovable, rock solid.

"We all had nicknames growing up. Grandpa tagged my older brothers, Seth and Simon, as the Bull and the Bear. They live up to their names as well.

"We grew up blessed," I said, watching carefully how he reacted to my next few comments. "I used to say my brothers and I were born on second base because we started out in life ahead of a lot of people. Of course, what we do with what we're given determines our success or failure, but we were given more than most. We had the kind of mom and dad everybody wished they had. And we lived in a place grandpa always said was like *Mayberry R.F.D.* with snow."

Neither the baseball reference nor the seventies television show managed to bring any kind of visible response from Paul. He just smiled slightly and nodded, so I continued talking undaunted.

"Sutton's Bay is one of those little towns where everybody knows everybody. The population is listed at just a shade over six hundred. Our family is better known than most because my older brothers starred on the 1975 class D state championship football team. Like them, I played football for the Norseman, and I played a little college ball at Hope too. But my big brothers were the real deal.

I hoped talking about football would provoke a reaction or a comment. Didn't happen. Paul held his cards close to his chest.

"Please continue," he said, raising his right eyebrow and smiling.

"Seth worked the two hundred and fifty acres of orchards with Dad," I said. "Simon and Grandpa Bass started a cider house and winery in the old milk barn. Eventually the family was selling as much wine and cider as fruit. They had a good business, but I wanted something different.

"I had a prodigal heart from birth. I couldn't wait to leave home. That's probably part of the reason I moved out east and went to Rutgers after I graduated from Hope. Technically, I enrolled in a dual degree program offered by Rutgers and New Brunswick Seminary. While there, I began to distance myself from the faith and the family I once loved."

I surprised myself with all that. This might be the first time I'd ever told anyone about my spiritual journey. I guess I needed to talk, and I found Paul a good listener.

"A few years later," I said. "I earned both my Master of Divinity degree and my PhD in clinical psychology."

"My family hoped I'd pursue the ministry, but Rutgers gave me a teaching fellowship at the end of my junior year.

After that, I didn't look back. I joined the faculty full time after graduation. Three years later, I met Rachel."

"Is that your wife?" Paul asked.

I didn't answer, but smiled silently, and turned the conversation back to him.

chapter 5

HISTORY

You must pay the penalty of growing up, Paul. You must leave fairyland behind you.—L. M. Montgomery, *Anne of the Island*

I knew enough geography to know Tarsus was an ancient city in the heart of what's now central Turkey, with mountains to the north and the Mediterranean Sea a dozen miles south. The city, on the banks of the Cydnus River, perched on an artificial harbor—an ancient feat of engineering.

I shared what little information I remembered about Tarsus, hoping to catch a reaction from Paul. Once again there was none. He took my knowledge in stride, as if everyone was familiar with the ancient city's sordid past.

"Everyone knew about Anthony and Cleopatra," he said, "but their defilement of the marriage bed remained a secret only whispered behind closed doors. Octavian's soldiers made sure of that."

I minored in history at Hope. I knew Mark Anthony formed a military alliance with Caesar's nephew Octavian. Then he sealed the deal by marrying Octavian's younger sister Octavia. However, when Anthony had an affair with Cleopatra, the two former colleagues went to war. The final battle was a huge and costly naval engagement. After Octavian's victory, Anthony and Cleopatra fled to Egypt, where they committed suicide.

Octavian was so bitter he had any reference to Anthony's accomplishments struck from the official record. He even issued a decree which forbade people from mentioning his name. So, when Paul said people were reluctant to talk about Anthony and Cleopatra in Tarsus, his words fit with the facts. He might be delusional, but he'd done his homework.

Who was this man?

When I asked him how a family with such deep Jewish roots came to live in Tarsus, Paul responded in surprising detail.

"My grandfather was born in the town of Gischala," he said with some pride, "in the northern tip of Galilee. He and his neighbors took up arms in what is now called the first Jewish revolt. With Rome victorious, Grandfather had a choice between execution and expatriation. He chose the latter. He joined the Roman Legion and fought valiantly alongside Pompey when the latter conquered Cilicia. As a reward for his service, Grandfather received Roman citizenship, a section of prime grazing land, and the name Andronicus, Latin for 'the conqueror of men.'

"In time, he became a prominent businessman in Tarsus. His citizenship, wealth, and Roman name passed on to his son. Years later, my father did the same with me. At my circumcision, the rabbi announced I would have the name *Sha'ul* in honor of Israel's first king, but my citizenship papers carried my full Roman name, *Sha'ul Ben-Andronicus*. I was Saul, the first son of the first son of Andronicus.

"We all carry inside us the best and the worst of those who've gone before us," Paul continued. "What we do with

24

that is up to us. I made it my goal to honor the memory of those whose shoulders I stood on."

I waited for Paul to continue but he didn't. The complexity of his story surprised me. Usually those with delusions of grandeur take on the personification of someone famous with little or no knowledge of the intimate details of that person's life. Clearly, this would be an interesting case, especially for me.

I'd titled my master's thesis at New Brunswick "Following in the Footsteps of the Tentmaker." In it, I explored the historical roots of Saul of Tarsus. I knew he was a complicated man, with deep layers of faith forged in the fires of guilt and grace. Clearly, he was a brilliant theologian. He was also a passionate preacher whose life changed the landscape of religious thought. By all accounts, Paul was the most prolific writer of the New Testament. Without him, Christianity as we know it would not exist. However, what most people don't know is that he made a meager living with the awl and the needle.

The man sitting across from me had no way of knowing, but I knew the details of the apostle Paul's life better than most. As a young man, Saul of Tarsus tried his best to live up to his name and his heritage. Like Israel's first king, this Saul was also an overachiever who strove to be the best at everything he did. In athletics, academics, debate, and personal piety, his ambition was to conquer any and all competition. Also like his namesake, as a boy, Paul was probably tall, handsome, and athletically built.

As a young man, Paul's quick mind and ruthless ambition propelled him to the top of his class in Torah school. Clearly, like his father, he would go on to become a Pharisee, a rabbi, and a lawyer in the high circle of the synagogue. Also like his father, he would learn the family trade.

Sitting there, listening to Paul, I remembered how Rachel and I used to love to debate the unanswerable questions of Scripture. One of the things you discover when you study the Bible is the writers were stingy with their words. They were minimalists in details, so we're left to fill in the blanks with our imagination.

"Tell me," Rachel would say, "if Jesus's father Joseph was of the house and lineage of David, why didn't they stay with family when he and Mary traveled to Bethlehem on that first Christmas eve? Or, what was Jesus like as a boy? Or how long were Adam and Eve in the garden before the fall?"

Such questions would occupy our conversations on the long car rides between New Jersey and Michigan. On one of our trips, Rachel proposed a question about Paul.

"In the book of Acts," she said with a slight wink, "we read Paul was a tentmaker but the word used—*skenopoios*—is a bit nondescript. One meaning is tentmaker, but this same word can also mean leather worker. In your master's thesis, you said herds of goats with long, thick black hair populated the hills around Tarsus. Their wool was woven into strong strips of watertight cloth called *cilicum* and used for making cloaks and tents that were sold all over the Middle East.

"So, which is it, Rock Bass?" Rachel asked with a smirk. "Was he a weaver of wool or a tooler of leather?"

I took the traditional view, so naturally she insisted he was a leather maker. The debate ended like all the others, with little or no resolution. For this reason, I thought the question might be fun to see where Paul took the argument.

"Were you a tentmaker by trade?" I asked.

"Sort of," he said. "As a young boy, each day after school I worked in my family's business and learned the trade of my fathers. We were wool merchants, and the cloth made from the goats my family raised was exceptionally well-suited for making tents. Don't confuse the tents we made with the ones you take camping today. They were very different.

"In those days, tents were large sectional structures. When a family began to outgrow their old tent, they added on a new section. Tents were even passed down from one generation to the next. When a section of the tent's roof began to wear thin, rather than replacing the entire structure, a new section replaced the damaged portion. The old piece became a side curtain. In the Bedouin community, the women set up the tents, kept them in good repair, and replaced the worn sections as often as they could afford the cost."

"So, you did women's work?" I asked, hoping to provoke a response of some kind.

Without looking up, Paul slowly shook his head and squinted at me out of the corner of his eye. Then, in a tone expressing his disappointment, he spoke.

"The work was divided," he said. "Our women would gather up the sheared wool and weave the wool into large rectangular strips on their looms. The men either tended the herds or worked in our booth at the *Agora*."

I knew from my studies that the Agora was a large open market at the center of town.

"Early on," Paul continued. "My family exposed me to every aspect of our business. As an infant, my mother carried me on her back as she worked the wool on the loom. Sometimes I would go with my older cousins to tend the sheep. I spent my youth, however, working alongside my father in the family booth at the market. There, we displayed our wares, talked to potential customers, and cut leather into triangular pieces about the size of a man's hand. People sewed these triangles into the side curtains where the tent stakes were anchored, and into the roof where the center poles rubbed against the fabric."

Again, his knowledge of Paul's life surprised me. I noticed two small round scars on the top of his right hand between his thumb and index finger, and I decided to see to what lengths he would go to keep up his delusion.

"Did you get those scars from working with an awl?" I asked.

"No," he said. "I got them when a viper bit my hand on the island of Malta."

He spoke as if the incident was no big deal. In reality, according to the book of Acts, it was a really big deal—the snake that bit the apostle was extremely poisonous. The villagers were amazed Paul didn't suffer extreme consequences of some kind. Before I could press him for more details about the snake bite, he nonchalantly returned to his leather crafting explanation.

"If time allowed," he said, "we would also cut and tool leather sandals, breastplates, and belts. We made most of this work to order and sold to the Roman soldiers from the garrison outside the city. We also sold a few things to the public. This craft provided me with an income for most of my adult life.

"My father would often repeat a phrase he'd heard from the rabbis. 'Whoever does not teach his son a craft teaches him to be a thief.' For this reason, I spent my early years as his apprentice. I learned to cut and stitch leather from him just as he learned the craft from his father. As a reward for my accomplishment, when I completed my apprenticeship, he gave me a small leather satchel with the tools of my trade—an assortment of needles, awls, wooden mallets, sheers, chisels, punches, edge bevellers, and knives.

"'Always remember who you are,' my father would say to me, 'No matter what happens, no matter where you are, or who you're with, in your soul, you are a Benjamite. You are a Hebrew of Hebrews, a descendant of the great king Saul. Circumcised on the eighth day according to the law. Your Roman citizenship may win you favor, but your greatest inheritance is the blood of the king of the Jews that flows through your veins.'"

When Paul said those words, he looked down at his sandals again as a gesture of humility. However, his words and his tone betrayed a hidden confidence and pride that bordered on arrogance.

His historical accuracy, demeanor, and complete emersion into the character of the great apostle caught me by surprise. I barely noticed when he stood up and walked behind me. From there, he looked over my shoulder at the picture of Rachel I use as my screensaver. The picture was taken on the day of her graduation on the front lawn near what students called 'the Holy Hill' at New Brunswick.

"Is this your wife?" he asked.

Then before I could answer he answered his own question.

"Yes, of course," he said. "The way she looks at you, I can see the two of you are very much in love. I can tell by the way your arm rests gently on her shoulder that you want to protect her. But my guess is this is a woman who can take care of herself."

I closed my laptop as quickly as I could. To allow a patient too much access to your personal life is never healthy.

"At first blush, she is lovely," Paul said. "Delicate like a flower, but her eyes tell another story. The eyes are the windows to the soul, you know. This woman of yours has the eyes of someone stronger and wiser than her years. Her gaze tells me she is a person of depth and mystery. You can see she cares deeply and passionately about people. More than that, I believe she cares deeply and passionately about you. You are blessed. Loving such a woman can only make a man a better person. Am I right?"

"Yes, you're right," I said. But, truthfully, I wanted to shut him out of that part of my life as quickly as possible. "Unfortunately, I'm afraid we're out of time. If you agree, perhaps we might get together and talk again sometime soon?"

"Sure, any time," he said. "As I told you, God really wants me to talk to you. You and I have some unfinished business to tend to. So yes, I will meet with you whenever you like."

As I left the hospital, I thought his observations about Rachel were dead on. Hearing them poured salt in the wound of my broken heart.

Loving her did make me a better man, but losing her did the opposite. Too often now I'm moody and sullen, and both grow worse when the sun goes down. Most nights, sleep is sporadic. I lie in the darkness and drift through the thin space which fills the void between dreams and reality. The only saving grace is Rachel still lives in that space. Talking with Paul had pushed Rachel's memories out of the closet of my mind. As I drove home, I let the thoughts of what once was have their way with my heart. As always, remembering was painful. Still, loving her was worth the pain of losing her. Given the chance I'd do it again in a heartbeat.

chapter 6

SMITTEN

Too often we underestimate the power of a touch, a smile,
a kind word, a listening ear, an honest compliment, or
the smallest act of caring, all of which have the potential
to turn a life around.—Leo Buscaglia, *Love: What love
is—and what love isn't*

At night I'm always exhausted. Our bed calls to me like
a jilted lover. "Why do you not come and lie with me?" the
bed whispers silently. I resist.

I want to sleep. I need to sleep. I also know I need to
remember, and I do my best remembering at night. I promised
Rachel I'd never forget her, and I'm going to keep that
promise even if remembering kills me. Sometimes, if I think
other things will swallow my thoughts, I spray a little of her
perfume on the screen of our bedroom window. Then as the
night breeze blows in off the lake, her fragrance has its way
with me. That's what I did the night I met Paul. She doesn't
walk this earth anymore but she walks through my thoughts
whenever I close my eyes. When I finally fell asleep, thoughts
of her filled my dreams. I didn't know if I was reliving the past

or getting a glimpse of the future. Either way, I had Rachel with me again for a while.

Sadly, the only way we ever really know how much we love someone is to live without them.

The first time I had a conversation with Rachel she was an undergraduate student in my AAS class (Alzheimer's, Anxiety, and Schizophrenia). She came to see me after the semester to complain about getting a B+ on her final exam. Her demeanor showed unhappiness. As she leaned in to discuss her grade, her long amber hair fell casually down the sides of her face and partially covered the tortoiseshell reading glasses resting on her brow. Her perfume had the faint scent of vanilla ice cream.

The only makeup she wore was reddish-brown lipstick. The color matched the freckles spattered across her hands and face. Her hazel eyes grew with intensity as she spoke. Something different, something intriguing about her captured my attention.

Who is this spitfire, and how can I get to know her better?

I finally spoke when Rachel stopped pleading her case. "Tell me. Did you take my class for the grade or for the chance to learn?"

"That's not fair," she fired back. "Of course, I wanted to learn, but I wanted the grade too. I need a higher grade to get a teaching fellowship."

"You want to teach psychology someday?" I said.

"I want to help people. To do that, I need to graduate, and money's hard to come by. In case you hadn't noticed, tuition around here isn't cheap. Right now, I'm working part time as a CNA at the University Hospital, which doesn't pay much. I'd make twice as much next semester if I could get a teaching fellowship."

"Do you like working at the hospital?" I hoped to learn a little more about her.

"Sometimes," she said. "And sometimes situations make me angry, but mostly I enjoy working there."

"What do you enjoy?"

"The patients. I'm good with patients, especially terminally ill patients. Most people don't like being around them, but I don't mind. When sick people ask me to do something for them, I always try. I don't care if they want something little like fluffing their pillow or adjusting the blinds or listening to their stories or reading them a story. Serving them makes me feel good. I like doing what I can for people."

Rachel paused as if she was thinking about what she had just said. Then she started talking again. "I know this sounds funny. I like sick people. They like me too. Is that weird?"

"No, not weird," I said. "You're probably one of the few people who actually takes the time to listen to them."

Rachel nodded. "They tell me that all the time. I think everybody is so busy taking care of what's *wrong* with them they don't notice what's *right* with them. The nursing staff doesn't see the person behind the disease—like they're invisible or something."

"But you see?"

"Yes, I do. I see who they are, who they were, and who they wish they could be again. Take Mrs. Rodriguez," Rachel said, continuing to look deep into my eyes. "She's almost eighty years old and has liver cancer. I hear the nurses talking about her, but they never use her name. She's just 'the liver in 38B.' 'The liver needs her pain meds,' they say. 'Or the liver needs to be intubated. Or make a note about that on the liver's chart.'"

"And that bothers you?"

33

"Yes, their attitude bothers me. I don't think we should ever let other people define us. I swear, sometimes I want to yell, 'She's Esther; her name is Esther Rodriguez, and she used to be a dancer in New York City. That's where she met Leo—a trumpet player with Jimmy Dorsey, and for a while she sang backup with the band. They played in clubs all over out east.'

"She had this low lusty voice," Rachel said with a smile, "and he had that Latin charm. And well, you know, eventually the two of them fell hopelessly in love. They got married on a beautiful spring day in Central Park, and afterward, late nights, loud music, and lots of partying made up their lives. Everybody wanted to buy her a drink. So yes, sometimes she drank too much, but she was young—young and didn't know any better."

Rachel paused for a moment, and the tone of her voice shifted from defiance to disappointment.

"Esther's life story breaks my heart. Everyone who ever said they'd be there for her left, even Leo. He got drafted, and six months later a land mine in Korea killed him. That's when the drinking and the cocaine got bad. When their son was born, she named him Leo. Leo Raphael Rodriguez Jr., after his father. She tried to stay sober after that, but she couldn't. Eventually, Social Services took little Leo away from her, but she never stopped loving him, never."

"And before all that," she said almost apologetically, "she was a dancer. I saw the pictures."

When she stopped talking, Rachel looked around the room as if checking to make sure we were alone. With a sigh, she softly asked her question again.

"So, what about my grade?"

"I'm sorry," I said. "I admire your passion, but the grade stands."

She rolled her eyes, twitched her long, beautiful nose in disappointment, and slowly got up to leave. That's when it happened. A panicked voice began to whisper inside my head.

"Wait a minute, Rocky," the voice said. "Don't let her go. This is a rare opportunity for you. This is a woman of substance, passion, and grit. Someone like her doesn't come along very often, particularly to a guy like you. If you let her walk out of here, you'll be sorry."

The voice was right. I was smitten. So, as she walked toward the door, I clumsily offered her a job as my research assistant. She accepted, and I never stood a chance. I fell in love like I fall asleep—at first I resisted, but finally love devoured me. That summer I brought her back to Suttons Bay to meet my family. While we were there, I asked her to marry me. She messed with me for a minute or two and then said yes. A year and a half later, we were married in the New Brunswick chapel on Holy Hill.

Once, right before we got engaged, I asked her a question.

"If I give you my heart, will you promise not to break it?"

The question was one of those cutesy, clever things guys say to sound romantic. The thing is I meant every word. Even then I was afraid I'd lose her.

She promised she'd be with me forever—the only promise she ever broke—and I've been a broken man ever since. The pain comes in waves. Sometimes I think I'm doing okay, and sometimes I feel like I'm drowning.

This was one of those drowning nights. As I lay there in the dark, memories of Rachel continued to shuffle through my mind like a deck of cards. About five thirty, I finally got up, made a cup of coffee, and sat at my computer. I made some additional notes about my observations of the evening with Paul and sent Judge Summerdyke's clerk my findings.

"Dear Laurie, my initial diagnosis is that patient #1761-5SBA, Sha'ul Ben-Andronicus, aka the apostle Paul, does not appear to present any danger to himself or others. Still, I believe the prudent thing to do is to see him for a few more sessions. If he's allowed to return to the Lighthouse Mission, I could continue to see him as an outpatient at my downtown office."

Laurie responded the following day. I received approval for five one-hour sessions. She also requested a full written report be sent to the court upon their completion. We made arrangements for Paul to come by my office on the first and third Wednesdays, and she said she would inform him of the time, dates, and key code to get into the lobby of our building.

chapter 7

MARATHONS

The best way out is always through. —Robert Frost, *North of Boston*

Workweeks tend to follow a predictable pattern. Mondays and Fridays are bookends, and the stories of our working lives are sandwiched between the two.

Mondays are like the starting blocks of the week. On the way to work on Monday morning, we have a sense of bravado and confidence. The optimism of Monday assures us that, somehow by week's end, we'll be standing in the winner's circle.

On the other end of the workweek, we find Friday—the moment of truth, the weekly finish line. When we cross the line, whether we're in first place or in last, we have a sense of finality. For good or for bad, what's done is done.

Sandwiched in between, lined up like little books, are the monotonous routines of Tuesday, Wednesday, and Thursday. Too often, we coast our way through the middle of the week on autopilot. Our bodies might be there, but our minds are off somewhere else. You've been there, right? I was there, in the Wednesday of my grief.

Nothing was easy, especially relationships. People suddenly felt a need to do things for me. Neighbors and friends I'd hardly said hi to in months wanted to shovel our snow, get our mail, or show up at the door with lasagna. We got a lot of lasagna. For some reason, people seem to think pasta will make the pain go away.

Others did the opposite. They acted like death is contagious and avoided me like I was radioactive. If by chance they accidently ran into me at the grocery store or the gas station, they got this deer-in-the-headlights look on their faces and pretended not to see me.

There's an awkwardness to death that is hard to describe. Students, friends, coworkers, even family members all put their hands in their pockets and did this silent shuffle after Death came calling. If they said anything at all, it was usually "Sorry for your loss," or, "My heart goes out to you," or "You're in our prayers." I know most of them meant what they said, but after a while their words got heavy too. At some point, I knew things had to change, and only I could change them. I might never get over Rachel's death, but, somehow, I did have to get on with life, even if that meant pretending I was better than I was.

There isn't a formula for getting through death. There are books—good books—which talk about the stages of death and dying. They talk about going through periods of denial, anger, bargaining, depression, and acceptance as though we'd all roll through them sequentially. The feelings came at me like a swarm of angry bees.

The stinging was relentless, and I quickly realized I had lost control—if I had ever been in control. Maybe control is an illusion. Like nothing else in life, death exposes vulnerability. After a while, death wears you down. You leave the starting blocks of grief on a dead run, wanting to get through the process as quickly as possible. Eventually though, you realize this will take a long time, maybe forever. Like I said, I was in the Wednesday of my grief, and I had to learn to settle in and get comfortable with it.

Everyone who's ever run a marathon knows what Wednesday, what being in the middle miles of the race, feels like. We even have a name for it—hitting the wall. Fatigue nips at our heels like a junkyard dog, and we fight the urge to give up. In the middle miles, we often begin to think the whole thing is pointless, that we'll never finish. That's where racing and grieving connect.

By the time we reach the middle, we're tired. We're beginning to wonder if we have the endurance which we need to reach the end. At this point, the thought of winning slowly drifts into a fading hope of finishing. In short, we're too far from the start to turn back, and too far from the finish line to see the destination.

For some reason, we often think the most important part of our week is the beginning or the end. However, the part that tests us—the true measure of life—is the middle mile, the Wednesday, and here's the thing about the middle. The midpoint will always provide us with a wonderful opportunity to toss in the towel—the sweet spot for quitters. And you know what? Not quitting will always require doing what we don't feel like doing, so we live in that tension of the middle. We make or break our bones there, and that's where we often find the stories which are worth retelling.

This is one of those stories that happened on a Wednesday, which was surprising because Wednesdays by their very nature are generally ordinary. Like all Wednesdays, this one fell in the middle of the week and in the middle of a life that was wearing dangerously thin. Fortunately, my phone beeped, reminding me I had an appointment with Paul or I surely would have forgotten.

chapter 8

Fathers

I knew my father had done the best he could, and I had
no regrets about the way I'd turned out. Regrets about
the journey, maybe, but not the destination.
　　　　　　　　　—Nicholas Sparks, *The Notebook*

Paul walked into my office on Eight Street like he owned
it—proud and confident with an air of superiority. In his
mind at least, he was the great apostle, and he deserved to be
treated as such. The problem with people who are delusional
is they're convinced they're right. Rather than challenge him,
I accommodated him.

"Today is the day we are to begin our talks, is it not?"
he said, hanging a faded denim jacket and a tattered gray
Tiger's cap on the coat rack by the door.

"Yes," I said. "You're right on time, Paul. I'm honored you
agreed to come and see me. Please sit wherever you like."

He sat in a tall black leather wingback chair near the
north windows of my downtown office. I called the chair,
purposely taller than the rest of the seating in the room, the
power chair, because sitting there gave people the allusion
they were in charge. I knew Paul would choose to sit there.

"Where would you like to begin?" he said as if this was his meeting.

"Let's start at the beginning. Tell me how you think you ended up here."

"The beginning is a long way from here, both geographically and chronologically. However, time is of no consequence to me. As you know, I was born in Tarsus three years before Mary wrapped my Lord in swaddling clothes and laid him in the manger.

"The city was on the trade route that connected Asia Minor with the East. The amalgamated population consisted of Romans, Greeks, Egyptians, Africaners, and my tribe the Jews.

"Like my father and grandfather, I received the name Saul in honor of Israel's first king. As a young boy, the nickname Paul distinguished me from them. As you probably know, 'Paul' is Greek for little or small. During my formative years, the name fit. Little Paul was big Saul's shadow. I mimicked his every move. I walked like him, and talked like him, and I even copied the way he dressed down to the long leather laces of his sandals."

"Your father had a great influence on your life," I said. "He must have been very proud as he watched you follow in his footsteps."

Paul nodded. "I wanted to be just like him, but my father wanted more. 'My prayer is not that you would be like me, my son,' he would say. 'I pray that one day you will be far better than me.'"

"Every father's prayer," I suppose.

Paul's head swiveled between me and my daughter Lucy's picture sitting on my credenza. He smiled slightly. "She's a beautiful girl, Dr. DeVos. You are a man with many blessings."

I nodded in agreement but couldn't help feeling the sting in his words. Rachel died with the key to my happiness in her pocket. Since then, Lucy has been my only source of comfort.

"As I grew older," Paul continued, "I began to realize my father's words were not only his hope but also his expectation. He would settle for nothing less than my best effort in everything. Without coming right out and saying the words, he subtly demanded I run faster, do better, be stronger, and try harder than anyone else, including himself."

"As parents," I said, "sometimes we can place unrealistic expectations on our children. This will often result in feelings of inferiority, high anxiety, or a desire to run away from reality. Can you relate to any of this, Paul?"

"Sure. No matter what I did, he believed I could do more, and to my surprise, he was right. Things came naturally to me. As you pointed out the other night, some people are born with certain advantages which others don't have. I believe you called it "being born on second base.""

I nodded.

"By the age of twelve, I could run faster and farther than anyone in Tarsus. Each morning, I would rise with the sun and engage in a routine of rigorous exercise before going off to Torah studies.

"Linguistically, I learned from the best teachers of the day. My father made sure of that. In reality, he set the table for my learning. He expected me to become fluent in Latin—the language of Rome. I learned Greek—the language of commerce. I studied Hebrew—the language of Torah. I spoke Aramaic—the language of my people. Somewhere along the way, I also learned a smattering of Syriac, which, to my surprise, helped me later during my time in Antioch."

For a moment he paused, as if reliving memories of his youth. When he continued, he changed directions.

"Alexander of Cyrene was my father's most trusted slave. He would recite the key phrases of the day's business for me in his native language as we walked home from the Agora. As I worked beside him, he also made sure I learned the language of the Carthaginians, as well as a few phrases of Egyptian.

"'Do not waste an opportunity to learn something new,' my father would say. 'Knowledge is power.' He believed even the simplest of phrases might someday be useful for commerce or diplomatic communications or for safe travel within the borders of the Empire.

"'Even the barbarians have something to teach you, my son,' he would say. 'Your job is to listen and learn. Long ago, at the tower of Babel, the Creator scattered the collective wisdom of the world on the winds. He deposited wisdom randomly, bit by bit, among the nations, and now he brings their merchants to our booth in the Agora for your benefit. So, feast, my son, feast at the banquet table of knowledge.'

"I soon realized my father was right," Paul said. "Each of these communities had wise men and scholars who were more than willing to share their learning and their culture. Each day, when I finished my studies with the rabbi, I studied philosophy, rhetoric, and debate in the markets of Tarsus while I practiced my craft."

The app on my iPhone chimed on the hour, reminding me to end our session.

"Thanks for taking the time to meet with me, Paul," I said. "I'd like to hear more about your childhood in next session. I'm afraid, for now, our time is up."

"Yes, of course," Paul said, "whatever you'd like. As I said, God sent me to talk to you."

He quietly left the office before I could probe his comment further. He went out the back door, came around the corner onto College Avenue, and turned down Eighth Street. I watched him walk toward the mission from the open window at the north end of my office.

Who is this man? What kind of trauma has driven him to cling so tenaciously to his delusion?

As Paul walked by Tobin Welch, the strangest thing happened. He waved from across the street, and Tobin waved back.

"Hey, Mr. Paul," he said.

The thing is, Tobin Welch is blind as a bat, or at least, I always thought so. He wears thick dark glasses, and when he walks down the street, he taps his way along with a long white cane. On nice days, he sits on the bench outside the Clock Tower building with a paper cup and a cardboard sign that says, "Please Help."

Tobin is a Black man in his sixties or seventies—hard to tell. He sports a neatly trimmed salt and pepper beard. He's polite, always says "thank you," and "God bless you."

Tobin was one of Rachel's first clients when we moved to Holland, and for some reason, she took a shine to the man. She would bring him a sandwich sometimes or a cup of hot black coffee in cold weather. For her sake, I put a few dollars in his cup from time to time. I've bought him a few cups of coffee too, and discovered he was a con man hurt.

chapter 9

GENEROSITY

Hard is trying to rebuild yourself, piece by piece, with no instruction book, and no clue as to where all the important bits are supposed to go.—Nick Hornby, *A Long Way Down*

There's a small parking lot behind the building I share with the retail stores downstairs on Eighth Street. The rear entrance leads to a tiled foyer with three sturdy cherry-stained doors. One leads to Kilwin's Chocolates, another to a children's store called Tip Toes, and the third opens to the stairway which leads up to our office.

One night, a few weeks before we moved to Holland, Rachel spooned up behind me and said, "Rocky, I think God wants us to give something back. Gratitude doesn't come naturally—we have to work at it—and I want to be a grateful soul."

Spooning with Rachel was an act of intimacy. She would put her arm around me, slide her hand under my T-shirt and slowly run her fingers through the hair on my chest. I could feel her warm breath against the back of my neck.

"Sure," I said, "if you want to make a donation somewhere, I'm okay with that. You don't need to ask me. I trust you—just listen to your heart."

"That's what I've been doing," she said, "and my heart's asking if our practice might minister to the marginalized somehow."

"Kind of a leap of faith, but I'm open to the idea, I guess. With your salary from church and mine from the college, we don't need the money. You just keep praying, Rach—you'll get the answer."

When we moved to Holland, she'd decided we should try to limit our clients to those either the church or the court system referred. Reluctantly, I agreed.

I met with everybody first to do the initial psych eval. After that, we often shared clients, particularly those who'd been the victim of abuse, infidelity, or intimidation. I usually took the criminal cases and court referrals. She did most of the church work and marriage counseling. Sometimes we'd double team a client for a session or two, but more often we'd each take an individual session with the same client.

Rachel had a way of putting people at ease—she made them feel comfortable. They'd tell her things they'd never tell me. I concentrated on helping them identify their pain and make the hard decisions necessary to get back on track emotionally. Her goal was to listen. Mine was to help them get on with the rest of their lives. She joined them in the present. Together, we worked with clients from several area churches, as well as the district court system in Grand Rapids.

For the next eight years, life unfolded like a script. Everything fell into place. Rachel thoroughly loved her job at Christ the Redeemer. She was born to do pastoral care and counseling. When the phone rang, she acted like a firehouse dog listening to the bell ring. She'd get all excited at the possibility of helping someone or visiting someone or just doing some little thing like reading them a poem or some scripture.

The one thing losing her has taught me is grief is as unique as a fingerprint. No matter what they might say, no one else knows exactly how one feels. She's been gone almost two years now, but each morning the reality of her death still stings my heart. Time does not heal all wounds. For me at least, time has not dulled the pain—only deepened the agony. Walking into the office we shared often floods my mind with melancholy and memories.

I can see her touch everywhere, and I can feel her presence strongly in the room. Some days, the sensation is so real I can believe she just stepped out to get something from the candy store downstairs. Other days, her spirit is so much a part of this room I can almost smell a whisper of her perfume. This was one of those days.

I've done what she wanted me to do—soldiered on with the practice, but sometimes my heart isn't in my work. That was the case when Paul arrived for his second visit. I lit the fireplace to warm the chilly room and sat in the recliner to collect my thoughts. I asked myself the same old question.

"What do you do when you have everything you ever wanted, but no one to share your riches?"

I sat there feeling sorry for myself when Paul knocked on the office door.

chapter 10

PAIN

Pain insists upon being attended to. God whispers to us
in our pleasures, speaks in our consciences, but shouts
in our pains.—C. S. Lewis, *The Problem of Pain*

Somewhat startled by his arrival, I tried to gather my
thoughts as Paul walked into my office. He wore a pair of
faded jeans, brown Birkenstock sandals, and a wrinkled gray
cashmere turtleneck sweater. Everything looked well worn.
Still, Paul had an eye for quality. I'm surprised at what one
can find at the mission thrift store. Mindful of a deadline for
my evaluation, I decided to press him a little bit harder today.

"Paul," I said, as he sat again in the wingback chair. "One
thing has always puzzled me. Most scholars believe there's
a gap of almost a dozen years between your encounter with
Jesus on the road to Damascus and the beginning of your
missionary travels. What happened? What were you doing
all those years?"

"As I'm sure you know, I was blinded by my encounter
with the Christ. For three days, I neither ate nor drank. With
tears of repentance day and night, I laid my sin before the
Lord. Finally, one of the brothers named Ananias came to me.

"'Brother Saul,' he said. 'The *messiah*, Yashua, the one who appeared to you on the road, has sent me so you may regain your sight.'

"Immediately," Paul said shaking his head slightly, "something like scales fell from my eyes, and I could see. As you can imagine, I was quite shaken. At first, I didn't know what to do. Then after a small meal of dried fish and dates, I went to the Damascus Synagogue. There I began to preach about the one I once hoped to persecute.

"To my great surprise, my words were met with both resentment and resistance. Some in the synagogue even threatened to stone me for blasphemy. They angrily promised to wait for me outside the city gate. For three days, fear kept me inside—I was afraid to leave Damascus or to show myself on the city streets. Finally, under the cover of darkness, some friends lowered me over the wall in a fish basket. From there, I scurried off into the darkness like a frightened mouse.

"I left Damascus quite shaken. My own people wanted to kill me. The irony of that did not go unnoticed. The hunter had become the hunted. I knew how relentless the soldiers of the Sanhedrin could be. I had trained them well. Fear and anxiety dogged my steps. I trusted no one. Finally, I fled to Arabia, to the Mountains of Midian. I knew no one would look for me there. Like Elijah, I found my way to Mount Horeb, a jagged and desolate peak.

"I made my home in a small cave—so small I had to bow to enter. For almost three years, I lived liked a recluse. A few days a month, I worked in the local bazaars among the *Goyim*, the non-Jewish population, making whatever I could with my needle and awl. Then I bought a bag of grain, a few dried fish, a flask of wine, and returned to my rocky perch. There I spent my days sitting in front of a small fire reading my scrolls and Scriptures and questioning everything I ever thought I knew about God.

52

"Each night, the wind whined through the canyon below as the sun fell slowly behind the adjacent ridge. Then, like Elijah, I stood in the mouth of the cave, wrapped my face in my mantle, and listened for the voice of the Lord. Most nights, he said nothing. But sometimes, sometimes, he whispered to me in a voice so silent only I could hear it.

"When the voice stopped, I retreated to my stony tomb. There, by lamplight, I meticulously reread every messianic text in the Torah. I left no room for doubt. I sifted everything I had learned about this Yashua of Nazareth through the ancient words of Micah, David, Jeremiah, and Isaiah. Finally, I was convinced he was, in fact, the one they had all written about.

"God forgive us," he whimpered in a low, uneasy voice. "We crucified the Christ."

Paul paused as if the thought were still too horrible for him to believe. Then he slowly continued.

"After three years of soul searching, I decided to go directly to the supreme council of the Sanhedrin to reason with them from the book we love. They were, after all, the ones who had originally sent me to Damascus, and they had jurisdiction over all religious business.

"The Great Sanhedrin consisted of seventy elders, the youngest of which was my brother-in-law, Ariel. The high priest was Joseph Caiaphas, the son-in-law of Ananias. At the time, Ananias had been unseated for his unscrupulous behavior. He would later be reinstated, but in this assembly, the beaked-nosed Pharisee had no authority to speak. Like an eagle on its nest, he sat in the balcony with his arms angrily folded across his robe. He wanted to speak, but he was under a sentence of silence. All he could do was watch the proceedings through squinting eyes and turn his head back and forth like a hungry bird of prey. I never liked that old man.

"On the other hand, I had always looked up to Caiaphas. He was square-jawed, handsome, and purposeful. His neatly trimmed, graying beard contrasted with his long unruly locks of ink-black hair. Like his father-in-law, the man was a force to be reckoned with. When he spoke, people listened. He had a brilliant mind, a love for his people, and an ability to quickly sift his way to the truth. The total number in the Sanhedrin assembly was seventy plus one. Caiaphas was the plus one. In the event of a tie, his vote was the deciding factor. He presided over the meetings that took place each day in the temple at Jerusalem. When he saw me standing in the gallery, he waved me in and immediately gave me the floor.

"I bowed before the High Priest and the assembly," Paul said as if he really remembered the moment. "Then I addressed them with the dignity they deserved.

"'My brothers,' I said, with all the respect I could muster. 'I apologize for my lengthy delay. I know you expected me sooner. Three years have passed since you sent me to Damascus on a mission of urgency and orthodoxy. I must apologize. I am long past due in presenting my finding to you. Like you, I love the Torah. When I heard followers of the rabbi Yashua were blaspheming holy words, I went with great haste to put an end to their activities.'

"With that said, the assembly of the seventy nodded in agreement. Caiaphas sat stone still, reserving his judgment until I finished.

"'I am after all a Pharisee,' I said, with conviction and pride. 'Like many of you, I only have tolerance for the truth. So here it is. I went to Damascus to denounce this would-be messiah, but I return to you baptized in his name.'

"Immediately the marble halls of Israel's high and holy court erupted in anger and outrage. Ananias stood and shouted, 'Blasphemy' from the balcony. Then he tore his tapestry tunic. As the word crossed the old man's pinched lips, the temple guards seized me. They stripped me of my robes, dragged me into the courtyard, and gave me the dreaded forty lashes minus one in thirteen sets of three, according to the letter of the law. This was the first of five such beatings I eventually received for my devotion to Yashua."

As Paul spoke, he stood and turned around. He lifted his sweater, revealing the horror of the beating he had endured. His back, shoulders, and left upper arm were covered in a series of crisscrossing crimson welts. His flesh looked like the lattice on the top of a cherry pie.

"Flagellation is painful," he said in an eerily calm voice. "Each crack of the whip cuts deeper and deeper into the flesh. Some have been injured so severely by such beatings they lost all feeling in their hands and feet. Not wanting to lose the ability to work or to write, I tried to shield my right arm by twisting my body to the left. The turning cost me part of my ear and some of the feeling in my leg, but in the end, I accomplished my goal. The pain was excruciating. At some point, by God's mercy, I passed out. When the wounds finally healed, I had these ropes of raised scars across my back and cheek. They are a constant reminder of what happened that day."

The sight of Paul's disfigurement caused me to wince, and the words of Isaiah echoed in my head. "He was wounded for our transgressions, he was bruised for our iniquities: the chastisement of our peace fell upon him; and by his stripes we are healed."

Even though his wounds had long since healed, the thought of such brutality made me sick to my stomach. I wanted to look away, but for a moment I held my breath and forced myself to witness the man's agony. Clearly something horrific had happened to him. I wondered if perhaps the only way he could deal with the memory of the trauma was to take on the persona of the apostle Paul.

He wasn't the first person I'd ever met who tried to escape the pain of the past by slipping into the sandals of someone else's soul. He was, however, the most convincing. At the very least, his disfigurement added credibility to his story.

Paul pulled down his sweater and returned to his seat. There, he picked up his story as if nothing had happened.

"When I was unshackled from the whipping post, my brother-in-law, Ariel, picked me up from the cobblestone courtyard. He carried me like a rag doll through the streets of the city to his house. We both cried.

"'If he is the Christ, then he doesn't need you to defend him,' Ariel whispered as I started to regain consciousness. 'And if he is not, then there are no words to defend him.'

"I said nothing in return. Two weeks later, Ariel made arrangements for me to go by caravan to Caesarea, and then, finally, back home to Tarsus."

The tale Paul told was so fascinating and so historically accurate I got lost in it. Too soon, my iPhone chimed the hour.

"Paul," I said, trying to end our session by getting back on track, "why do you think Judge Summerdyke sent you to me?"

"The judge is a nice man, but he is not the one who directs the affairs of men like us." Paul spoke with his typical air of confidence. "Like I told you before, we are subject to a higher power. Your judge didn't send me. The One who judges the hearts of humanity sent me."

The details of his story were unlike the ramblings of most of the schizophrenics I'd met. His story was logical, reasoned, and historically accurate.

Who was this man? My mind played with the possibilities. He might be a historian or a theologian or even an author researching a book on the great apostle. The possibilities were endless. I would learn the truth in time. The next day, I asked Judge Summerdyke's clerk Laurie to check missing persons for anyone with Paul's approximate age, height, ethnicity, and knowledge of history.

A couple of days later, she reported they ran Paul's profile through the FBI's Missing Persons Register and one name was a possible match, a forty-eight-year-old Lebanese immigrant by the name of Gabriel Shalhoub, a green card holder, who has lived and worked in Dearborn, Michigan, since 2007.

Before coming to the US, Shalhoub lived north of Beirut in a Maronite monastery. The Maronites are the Eastern branch of Catholicism and have remained faithful to the Vatican despite immense persecution. Even today, they make up almost a fourth of the population of Lebanon.

My internet research on Shalhoub revealed that, for seventeen years, he had been the historical curator of the Maronite Catholic Church. His job was to preserve, store, and exhibit the church's historical documents and relics. He also maintained the computerized database of the sacred artifacts and archives.

The church's namesake, Saint Maron, was a seventh century monk who would spend months at a time fasting, meditating, and praying alone in the mountains of Lebanon. Whenever anyone asked the holy man why he chose to live such an austere life, he would simply say he was following in the footsteps of the apostle Paul.

Few Christians realize many of the life-changing moments of Paul's life happened not in Israel, and not where he planted churches in modern-day Turkey and Greece, but in and around Lebanon and Syria. His conversion was on the road to Damascus. He spent three years in the mountains of Arabia, where Jesus revealed himself and his gospel to

Paul. He began his teaching ministry with Barnabas in Antioch. He stayed in Tyre on his way to Jerusalem to visit with Jesus's brother James. And finally, on his way to trial in Rome, Paul was chained to the centurion Julius. He had developed such respect for him that he allowed Paul to meet with his friends at Sidon.

I felt my pulse quicken as I continued to research Shalhoub and the Maronite church. A man like this would have immense knowledge of the early Christian church.

Laurie's email revealed Shalhoub and his family were in the Rafic Hariri International Airport in Beirut, Lebanon, on July 13, 2006. They intended to celebrate their son's recent graduation from college by going on a US holiday. They planned to visit Gabriel's brother Mikha'il in Dearborn, Michigan. Gabriel is a big Tigers fan and looked forward to taking in a baseball game. Unfortunately, the vacation never happened.

"They were walking across the runway to board their plane," Laurie said, "when suddenly, their world exploded in a ball of flames."

According to newspaper reports, the assault was Israel's retaliation for Hezbollah rocket attacks three days earlier on the village of Zar'it in northern Galilee. Six civilians died and a dozen more were wounded.

On the day of the Hezbollah attack, Israel's prime minister Ehud Olmert issued a public warning. He promised the consequences would be "swift, painful, and far-reaching." The wholesale slaughter of life was so common along the Israel/Lebanon border that Gabriel ignored Olmert.

The prime minister's words proved to be prophetic. The Israeli Air Force, Artillery, and Navy launched more than a hundred attacks on Lebanon. One of these was an airstrike which destroyed the runways and fuel depot of Rafic Hariri Airport. Forty-four civilians died. One of them was Shalhoub's wife, Hoda. His daughter Aya died three days later. Gabriel and his son Alaxandre received severe burns.

They were transported to Beirut's Clemenceau Medical Center. For months, they slowly recovered from the burns on their backs, chests, necks, and arms. Ultimately, the Shalhoubs returned home to Bekrke, but their lives were never the same.

Before the accident, Alaxandre had received his Bachelor of Science in Nursing—BSN—from The American University of Beirut. With his accreditation, he could find work anywhere in the world. He convinced his father to move to America. They sold the family villa and bought a modest three-bedroom home two blocks from Gabriel's brother in Dearborn. He took a job as the assistant curator of The Arab American National Museum. Alaxandre became an emergency room nurse at Beaumont Hospital about three and a half miles away. On most days, the two of them rode to work together.

Two years later, Alaxandre—a Lebanese Muslim— met and married Jada—an African American Baptist, but somehow, they made their marriage work. A year later, Jada gave birth to their daughter Aya. She was beautiful, and Gabriel doted over her.

On the surface everything was going well, but occasionally, on a weekend or a holiday, Gabriel battled with bouts of depression. He called them "the darkness." When the darkness hit, he'd often disappear for days, even weeks at a time. Later, when Alaxandre would ask him where he went, all Gabriel would say was that he spent some time with the dead.

He disappeared again a couple of months ago. Ten days later, the Dearborn police put out an APB, but so far no one has seen or heard from him.

"He sounds like he could be our guy, don't you think, Doc?" Laurie asked.

"He could be," I said, remembering Paul's gray ball cap with the Old English D. "He very well could be."

chapter 11

FRIENDS

The friend who can be silent with us in a moment of despair or confusion, who can stay with us in an hour of grief and bereavement, who can tolerate not knowing, not caring, not healing and face with us the reality of our powerlessness, that is a friend who cares."
—Henri J.M. Nouwen, *Out of Solitude: Three Meditations on the Christian Life*

Lucy and I came downtown later that week to watch the *Volksparade*, the kickoff to the annual Tulip Time Festival in Holland. Lucy loved the parade, and I hoped we would have a chance to talk. Something bothered her, but so far she kept the problem to herself. You don't trust your secrets with people who don't take the time to listen. Today was about taking time.

The parade began the same way. The mayor of Holland donned his white gloves and ceremoniously went out to inspect the cleanliness of the city streets. After publicly declaring they were in desperate need of scrubbing, scores of residents gathered to accomplish the task. They all wore colorful traditional Dutch costumes and wooden shoes, and the tourists loved the spectacle. The scrubbers started at College Avenue and made their way down Eighth Street toward River Avenue, armed with buckets of water and long bristle push brooms.

I hoisted Lucy onto my shoulders as they began to douse the streets with water. We then stood on the curb with the hundreds of others who lined the streets to watch the event. The governor was there, as well as a couple of congressmen and some local TV personalities, but the one person who caught my eye was Stewart Overbrook.

He was dressed in the traditional *Achterhoek* costume, a replica of the fashion worn by residents of the eastern section of the Netherlands which juts out into Germany. The costume has a blue and white striped collarless shirt, a bright red scarf, a black double-breasted vest, and blousy black trousers. Like all Dutch dancers, Stewie also wore wooden shoes.

The costume was totally out of character for him. Stewie always wore the same thing—a plaid, button-down, short-sleeved shirt, stone brown khakis from JCPenney's and polished black Doc Martens with the signature yellow stitching. He had been Rachel's client. She had me meet with him five times, and he wore five different plaid shirts, but otherwise his costume never changed. Seeing him dressed as a Dutch dancer caught me by surprise.

Stewie was a man in a boy's body. He was twenty-seven, but looked much younger—most people with Down syndrome do. He was about five foot, six inches tall with brownish hair and ruddy cheeks. His boyish appearance bore some of the characteristics associated with DS. He had a short neck, a smooth facial profile and nose, and his hazel brown eyes slanted upward slightly. There was a handsome innocence to the man.

Like Paul, Stewie was also one of Summerdyke's referrals. He came to us a few years ago after being arrested for stealing a case of cigarettes. The driver said he saw Stewie take the case off the back of his truck in the parking lot next to the Back Door party store. Truthfully, I always suspected someone put Stewie up to the theft. but he refused to rat them out, so I never knew for sure.

With no bottle returns and cold weather on the way, he found his way downtown to the Lighthouse Mission where he's been ever since.

The other thing about Stewie is a very private person. He hates crowds, but there he was, smack dab in the middle of one. When I looked a little closer, I saw Paul in his faded gray Tigers cap walking along the edge of the parade route cheering him on.

"You can do this, my friend," Paul kept shouting. "You're doing great. Your dad would be so proud of you, Stewie. Dwight and I are proud of you too."

Dwight McKay is the director at the mission. He's a good man with a good heart, and he has worked with a lot of people in Stewie's situation. He felt what Stewie really needed was a place where he was valued and belonged.

I agreed. Patients with Down syndrome are extremely sensitive to changes in their environment. Stewie struggled with some depression issues related to that. The great thing was Dwight not only could see his pain, but he also heard his silent cries for help—a rare thing. Only those who really care can hear us even when we're quiet, and Dwight always listened.

He agreed to give Stewie a job in the kitchen. This not only gave Stewie a little spending money, the work also reinforced the idea the mission was his new home. I lost touch with Stewie after he seemed to settle into the program.

Lucy and I watched the rest of the parade. Then we got a hotdog, an elephant ear, and an ice cream cone. We talked about everything except what bothered her, and then we went home. Sometimes a parent must be patient. The currency for those kinds of conversations is time, so for now all I could do was wait.

In the meantime, I made a point to reconnect with Stewie. I called Dwight, who set up the meeting. The two of us met for coffee a few days later at the Windmill Restaurant.

"I didn't do anything wrong, Doctor Rocky," Stewie said nervously as he sat down at the table. "Really, I didn't."

"I know, Stewie," I said. "I just wanted to tell you how proud I am of you. I saw you in the parade the other day, and I told my daughter how great you looked in your Achterhoek costume."

For a moment, Stewie lit up like a glow-stick.

"My friend Paul helped me," he said.

"Really?" I said, "what did he do that was helpful?"

"I don't know," Stewie said. "Nothing really, or maybe everything, at least it was everything to me. Explaining friendship with words is hard. Paul just does what friends do. He sits with me at mealtime and in chapel. He listens to me when I need to talk. And he tells me I can do stuff I'm afraid to do, like walk in the parade. I don't know why, but I'm a better person when I'm with him. Paul says that's because iron sharpens iron. Do you think that's true, Doctor Rocky?"

"I do," I said. "I really do."

I talked with Stewie for about a half hour, and he kept bringing the conversation back to his new best friend Paul.

"I think we all have these scary monsters that live in our heads," he said, looking down at the floor. "But real friends don't let the monsters win. They listen to us even when we're silent, and they protect us from the monsters and from ourselves. Do you know what I mean, Doctor Rocky?"

I said I did. Sometimes wisdom shows up in the most unexpected places. 'Only those who really care can hear our silent cries for help.' I scribbled Stewie's words on the back of my napkin and shoved it into my pocket. For the next several minutes, I listened as he raved about how good God was, and how good life was, and how good it was to have a friend like Paul. After a while, he went back to his job at the mission, and I went off to teach my Intro to Neuroscience class at Hope.

chapter 12

BULLIES

Schoolboys are a merciless race, individually they are angels, but together, especially in schools, they are often merciless.—Fyodor Dostoyevsky, *The Brothers Karamazov*

For good or for bad, a child begins to form relationships at a very young age. They quickly learn to trust or not to trust in the first few years of life. The lucky ones receive unconditional love and support by their parents, and they grow up to be emotionally healthy adults. In Lucy's case, that love and support would come only from me.

I know that children who are forced to deal with prolonged grief are more likely to have long-term emotional problems, and I could see something bothered Lucy. When she refused to talk to me about the problem, I decided I'd talk with her teacher, Mrs. Vandenberg, a kind woman who loved each of her students like they were her grandchildren. Lucy loved her back. If she would open up to anybody, it was Katherine Vandenberg.

We met after school at The Klutz. After the usual small talk, we got down to business. I told her Lucy was probably going to need some extra attention. She was struggling. Something was bothering her. I suspected the problem had to do with her mother's death, but I couldn't be sure. I asked Katherine to keep a close eye on her, to watch for things like mood swings, poor academic performance, or long periods of self-isolation or silence. Any of those could be a sign of a problem.

Kids who are grieving can sometimes feel lonely or afraid or like they don't belong. They can easily become withdrawn and disconnected. You must work at including them. Most important of all, you must let them talk out their feelings. They may want to tell you what happened or where they were when something happened or what the incident felt like for them. Telling their story is part of the healing process. They need to tell their story, and they need people to listen. And they need to feel safe.

A few weeks later, Katherine Vandenberg reported she'd witnessed the kind of behavior we talked about.

"Is there something you want me to do?" Katherine asked.

"No," I said, "I'll handle the situation, but I really appreciate the call which helped confirm what I already suspected."

That night at dinner, I hinted around at things with Lucy, but I couldn't get her to open up to me. Later that night, after she said her prayers, I tried again.

"Is everything all right at school?"

"Yes." she said.

"Anything you want to tell me or anything I can help you with?"

"No," she said.

I bided my time. A few days later, while we were out for a walk on the beach, she finally was ready to talk.

"Daddy, do they have 'roni in heaven?"

I assumed she asked the question because she knows Rachel loved macaroni and cheese.

"Sure," I said, "they have anything you want in heaven."

"So, if I were in heaven, I could have whatever I want for dinner?"

"Yep."

"What if I just wanted candy?"

"Well," I said, "if that's what you want, that's what you'd get."

"That's what I'd want," she said. "Milky Ways and Mallo Cups."

"No vegetables?"

"Nope."

"No fruit?"

"Nope."

"No 'roni?"

"Nope, just candy."

"How about cookies?"

"Okay, candy and cookies, but nothing else."

Ever since Rachel's death, Lucy had asked a lot of questions about heaven. I always did my best to answer them in language she could understand. Some questions were just curiosity, but others revealed certain fears she had about death.

"Is Mommy happy there, Daddy?"

"Yes, she is very happy. The Bible says there is no pain, no sadness, and no tears in heaven."

"So, there aren't any mean people there?"

"No," I said, "mean people aren't allowed."

She furrowed her brow and got a stern look on her face as if she was silently processing what I said.

"Is somebody being mean to you?" I asked.

"Well," she said, "sometimes Emma Davis says stuff."

"What kind of stuff?"

"Oh, just stuff about Mommy being dead," she said softly.

My heart broke. I was angry. Lucy already had more than enough on her plate and now she has to deal with this playground bully. I wanted to call Emma's mother and read her the riot act but that might only make things worse, so I didn't. Sooner or later, Lucy would have to learn how to handle people like this, and now was a good time to start.

"Emma's the chunky one, right?" I said.

Admittedly this wasn't my best moment as a parent but a part of me wanted to hurt the kid who hurt my kid.

"Ya," Lucy said, laughing. "She says she's big boned."

"When I was your age, I had a friend named Ronny," I said, trying to redeem the moment. "He was big boned too."

I told Lucy more about him. "His dad would tell Ronny he was fat, and he should stop eating so much. But Ronny did the opposite. He'd go to his room crying, but as soon as he could, he'd sneak out of the house with a bag of chips or a pint of Rocky Road or a box of Jujubes. He'd eat them all by himself.

"In catechism class when the teacher asked, 'what's your only comfort in life and in death?' Ronny said, 'ice cream.'

"Sometimes the other kids in class would tease him. Kids can be mean sometimes. They hurt Ronny really bad when they said things about him being fat."

"Did he cry?"

"Yes, he cried, and he'd want to run away and hide, and sometimes he'd get mad too. When unhappiness bubbled up inside him, he exploded. One day Ronnie went ballistic when Michael Miller teased him. He socked Michael right in the nose. He kept hitting him and hitting him. After that everybody stopped teasing Ronny. In fact, they were afraid of him. And guess what."

"What?"

"When Ronny went from feeling powerless to feeling powerful, he started bullying other kids, which was horrible.

He'd shove them or threaten them or called them names, and he was always looking for a fight. Sometimes in class, he'd just look at someone, shake his fist, and snarl for no reason. He became the kind of person he used to hate. Ronny was now the class bully, and whenever he'd tease someone, the other kids would laugh."

"One day I said to him, 'Ronny, why are you acting that way? That's not like you. You used to be nice.'

"You know what he said?"

"No, what?"

"He said being nice only brought him pain. He didn't care who the kids were laughing at as long as they weren't laughing at him. But the truth is they were still laughing at him. Behind his back, they were all laughing. They laughed at him and they laughed with him, and like Ronny, they were happy as long as they weren't the one being laughed at. Isn't that sad?"

"Ya."

"Do the kids in your class ever laugh at Emma behind her back?"

"Sometimes."

"We all must decide what we're going to do when something like that happens, but I try real hard not to join in the laughing because I always wonder when they're going to start laughing at me. Jesus said, 'Do not judge, and you will not be judged. Do not condemn, and you will not be condemned. Forgive, and you will be forgiven.'"

Lucy nodded and we walked on down the beach.

Again, she furrowed her brow and got that stern look on her face like she was contemplating our conversation.

chapter 13

Observation

You know my method. It is founded upon the observation of trifles.—Arthur Conan Doyle, *The Boscombe Valley Mystery*

Two weeks later, we had hardly started our third session when Paul walked over to the bookcase. He looked intently at a small fragment of brown papyrus framed in varnished cherry. Two years ago at Christmas, Rachel had given me the numbered, limited edition print of a two-thousand-year-old letter called *The Petros Fragment*. In her mind, at least, the first line of the old letter was kind of a veiled reference to me.

The document was faded, badly damaged, and written in a type of early Aramaic that was Judea's *Lingua Franca*, the language of the day, at the time of Jesus. In this letter, the writer used a sub-dialect similar to one seen in some of the Dead Sea scrolls. This made translation difficult with any certainty. Only a dozen or so people in the world could translate the sub-dialect with accuracy. They would have to be fluent in both Hebrew and Aramaic, and, also, somewhat of a New Testament scholar. That way, they'd be able to recognize little bits and pieces of Peter and Paul's personal lives referenced in the writing fragments.

One such person is a friend who spends his summers in the Middle East. Dr. Bob Coffman is the professor of Old Testament studies at Western Theological Seminary. Each year, he works alongside a distinguished group of scholars which includes people from Harvard, Yale, Rutgers, and Brown. They gather after the May term for a joint archeological expedition. Two summers ago, while working in northern Syria, Bob unearthed this small piece of papyrus. One of the world's leading paleographers dated the fragment to be from the latter half of the first century.-What set this piece apart was it appears to be an early first century Christian correspondence.

This fragment begins by identifying the sender. "*Petros*," or as we might say "Peter, the rock." He then describes himself as "a servant of Christ Jesus." Unfortunately, much of the rest of the letter is so badly damaged only a few words and phrases can be deciphered with accuracy.

"Simon Petros never should have written this," Paul said peering intently at the papyrus fragment. "He knew better. I felt like he'd sold his soul to make peace with the brethren. After that, I took any advice from the Jerusalem council as a suggestion, not as the law. In the end, this was one of the reasons Barnabas and I decided to go our separate ways."

"Are you familiar with this letter, Paul?" I asked, somewhat surprised.

"I should be," he said. "Peter wrote the letter to me."

He then shifted his attention to a picture of Rachel at the farm in Suttons Bay on a beautiful fall day. She and I had gone up to help with the apple picking. She had on my mom's faded red barn coat as she sat on a bale of hay drinking a cup of hot cider. The cold had put a rosy blush in her cheeks. I snapped her picture with my phone.

"Your wife has a smile which could capture a man's soul," he said, sitting back down in the black wingback chair. After that, we talked about love and loss for a while, dredging up old bones for both of us. By the time Paul left my office, we felt a little sorry for ourselves. Grief doesn't *change* who we are, it *reveals* who we are. As I thought about Paul and his faith, I began to realize how shallow mine was. Honestly, there were days when I wondered who was helping whom.

The next day, I went to see Bob Coffman. When I arrived, he sat in his office talking to a student about an assignment.

"When you get a minute, I'd like to meet with you," I said.

"Sure," Bob said. "Come on in. Brian here is one of my brightest students. He and I were talking about next year's Israel trip. You should come with us."

"Maybe Brian would be interested in seeing this as well," I said and pulled my copy of the Petros fragment from my briefcase. "I need a little help translating something—the exact words."

I didn't really need to bring my copy of the fragment. The twin sat on the shelf of Bob's bookcase. His copy was also framed in glass and had a brass plaque identifying the discovery date with a boast. This was copy number 001. Bob knew the fragmented letter as well as anyone.

"We all have trouble with this fragment," Bob said, leaning back in his chair and gesturing toward number 001. "Although badly damaged, we can make out bits and pieces. The rest is only an educated guess.

"Here, for example," he said, pointing to a line in the text. "This says, 'the faith of you.' And this word means 'we have obtained an inheritance.'"

Slowly sliding his finger down the frame's glass, he traced the frayed edge of the papyrus. Bob continued to say the words in Aramaic, and then translated them into English for my sake. "This one is 'obedience.' This is, 'circumcision.' And this one is 'boasting.' Here we read 'for the salvation of your soul.'

"The writer appears to be trying to make a case for why all first century Christians needed to continue to keep the Torah laws, including circumcision. Christianity was still in its infancy at the time, and circumcision became an issue when more and more Gentiles started following Jesus."

"Perhaps one of the most fascinating lines is this one," said Brian, eager to join in the conversation. "The papyrus is badly disintegrated due to water damage. The letters are smudged and almost illegible, but the words appear to identify the letter's recipients as 'Paul and Barnabas.'"

"We can't say for certain," Bob added, "but that's our best guess, at least for now. The most exciting thing about the letter is the possibility of it being correspondence between the apostles Peter and Paul."

"If only we had a little more to work with," Brian interjected. "I guess we're lucky to have this fragment. Still, if we had a little more information, we could piece this puzzle together a lot easier."

We chatted about the fragment for a while. Again, they invited me to go on next summer's dig. I said I'd think about it, but probably not. Eventually, I thanked them for their time and went to teach my afternoon class.

chapter 14

CALLED

Behind every specific call, whether it is to teach or preach or write or encourage or comfort, there is a deeper call that gives shape to the first: the call to give ourselves away—the call to die.—Michael Card, *The Walk: The Life-changing Journey of Two Friends*

Rachel and I were part of a dual master's degree program in theology and psychology at New Brunswick on the campus of Rutgers. After graduation, I took a teaching fellowship and pursued my Ph.D. I always thought Rachel would do the same, but she surprised me. Instead, she chose to pursue a career in the ministry. As she got closer to graduation, she began applying for several open ministry positions.

I always enjoyed the study of religion. For her, religion was less a subject to be studied, and more a passion to be lived. She was a truly spiritual person and she had a heart for the poor, the marginalized, and the broken. Because of that passion, a month later, she received an offer for an associate pastor position at Christ the Redeemer church in Holland, Michigan. Suddenly we had a decision to make.

"I don't know what I was thinking," she said on the Saturday night she received the call. "I never really thought I had a chance of getting that job. I only went on the interview because we were visiting your family in Michigan. I foolishly thought being an associate pastor might be a good learning experience for me. We can't leave New Brunswick. You love your job too much. I'm going to call Pastor Ben on Monday morning and tell him I can't take it."

Ben Boonstra had been the senior pastor at Christ the Redeemer for fifteen years. He was the kind of man you'd want at our back in a fight. Ben was six feet two, and two hundred and fifty pounds. They called him the wedge in college, and he still looked like a fullback. He was strong, dependable, and someone you knew you could count on. Maybe most important of all for me, he was pragmatic and somewhat liberal theologically. Ben's messages were always upbeat and affirming, so I knew he would be a great mentor for Rachel.

"You're right," I said. "I do love my job, but I can get a teaching job in west Michigan. That would be a great place to start a family too. Listen, Rach, if you feel God is calling you to Christ the Redeemer, we better take a leap of faith. Besides," I said with a smile, "the change will be an adventure."

I'd always thought a calling was more of a vocation than a location, something we do, not the place we do the job. A question of gifts, abilities, strengths, and compatibility. No matter what anyone said, I never bought into the idea God somehow mysteriously manipulates the events of our lives to get us to his chosen destination.

Holland seemed like the kind of place where we both could flourish—small-townish, like Suttons Bay, but not too small, and Hope College provided a little sophistication. Cottages and year-round homes dotted the nearby shores of

Lake Macatawa and Lake Michigan. Seasonal residents came up from Chicago and helped bolster the local economy with some added culture and tourist dollars.

"Oh, Rocky," Rachel said, "I really felt the Spirit whispering in my ear about moving to Holland and taking this job, but I didn't dare let myself listen. Would you really think about leaving Rutgers?"

"The truth is I've been thinking about leaving for a while. I kind of want to teach part-time and maybe start my own practice. So, you pray about the position. If you think God wants you there, that's good enough for me."

"Do you know how much I love you, Rocky?" And then she started crying.

"Why are you crying?"

"A family," she said, "You said we're going to start a family."

"We are a family," I said, pulling her up from her chair and into my arms. "But now we're going to start making babies."

"Let's start tonight." she said, kissing me passionately.

Jesus taught us that true love always involves sacrifice and that the truest words of love are "thy will be done." The surprising thing is when those words are spoken from the heart, both parties are blessed. Nothing brings us more joy than bringing joy to those we love. So, for me, doing what Rachel wanted was easy. The truth is, from the moment I met her, all I wanted to do was to make her happy.

A month later, Two Men and a Truck unloaded our stuff at the small craftsman-style house we'd bought on the boardwalk by the beach. The three bedrooms upstairs had their own dormer with a window. From up there, one could watch the sun slip into the blue waters of Lake Michigan each evening.

"This is it," I said to myself when we first saw the house. "This is where I want my children to grow up."

I took a teaching job at Hope College, and we set up our practice two blocks away, in an upper-level office condo. The front window overlooked Eighth Street, the main drag of downtown Holland. The back-deck provided a panoramic view of the college campus. This office was where most of my meetings with Paul would take place.

chapter 15

SELF-AWARENESS

I believe there's a calling for all of us. I know that every
human being has value and purpose. The real work of
our lives is to become aware and awakened to answer the
call.—Oprah Winfrey

Two weeks later, Paul walked in and I realized, even
though this was his fourth office visit, in many ways he's
still a mystery, a walking enigma. The more he told me
about himself, the less I knew about the man. With his
usual swagger, he hung up his jacket and the Tiger's cap
and took a seat in his regular chair. He looked at me with
raised eyebrows as if to say, "What's next?"

"Early on, you had a growing sense of who you were and
what God expected of you," I said. "Some people receive the
call in a moment. They can point to a certain time and place.
For others, the realization of their personal destiny is more
of a gradual process. Talk to me a little about your journey
of self-discovery."

Paul spoke with his customary confidence. "A couple
of years before my *Bar Mitzvah*, I started to rise like cream
on milk. I separated myself from my peers. I was preparing

myself for a seat on the Sanhedrin, and even though I didn't realize this at the time, God was preparing me for something more."

Once again, Paul sounded a little like the prep-school crowd I met in my first year at Rutgers. Ordinarily that sense of entitlement is a byproduct of second-generation money. Daddy was a driven, type A personality who made sure his children had the best. In return, he demanded the best from them as well. That's part of the pressure that goes along with being born with a silver spoon in your mouth. I decided to probe the issue.

"Did you want this?" I asked. "Or was this something that someone expected of you?"

"Both," he said. "My father would often say 'you are a Pharisee of Pharisees,' and each time he did, I knew what he expected of me. But I wanted the success as well."

"So, let me ask you, Paul, do you think your father's expectations led to you becoming an overachiever? Did you become one in the hope of winning his affection?"

"Perhaps," Paul responded. "Still, thinking back now, I believe learning and teaching were my destiny. We have that in common, you and I. God invented the alphabet so through his words, we'd have a way to listen to his voice and to teach others what we've learned. After all, what good is knowledge if we don't share what we've learned? Am I right?"

I nodded and smiled politely.

"I learned this from Rabin Mordecai," Paul said. "Teachers are the guardians of the nation's wisdom. They have the burden and the blessing to educate. If teachers fail to teach, the world will quickly become filled with fools."

He paused for a moment and gazed off into the distance as though remembering his time as a student and, also, as a teacher. He was deeply engrossed in his own story, which may not have been real, but was real to him. I hoped his own words would somehow help him build a bridge back to reality. Until then, I decided to let him talk. Besides, his story fascinated me.

"While others could hardly wait for the rabbi to let them out of class, I could hardly wait for class to start again. I was like a sponge soaking up knowledge. Nothing satisfied me more than learning something new. As the *chazzan*, the headmaster of the school, so often said, 'I asked questions my classmates hadn't even thought of.' Like a fox on a rabbit, I would leap at the chance to learn something new.

"The day after my sixth birthday, I started attending *Bet Seper*, the house of the book, to begin my Torah study. The goal was not just to study Torah, but also to commit the first five books of Moses to memory. I completed the task in less than three years. By my Bar Mitzvah at twelve, I had also done the same with the *Nevi'im*, what you call the Prophets. For me, reading the sacred writings of my people was like being invited to join in a conversation with the greatest theological minds of all time. I couldn't get enough of it.

"So, I was not surprised," he said with a little grin, "after serving a two-year apprentice with my father, I received an invitation to continue my education at Jerusalem's *Bet Midrash*, the house of learning, the school adjacent to the Temple."

I knew this was the equivalent of saying he'd been accepted at Harvard Law or John Hopkins or Julliard. Paul would have no way of knowing this, however, unless he'd done some graduate time studying theology or Middle Eastern History. The more he talked, the more convinced I became that this man, whatever his identity, had spent considerable time poring over the dusty journals of an antiquities library of some kind. I must admit at times I lost track of reality. I'd so get caught up in the details of his story I'd forget I was there to help him, not just to listen. Not ready to prick the bubble of his illusion, I fueled his imagination with another question.

"That sounds like a very demanding course of study. Tell me, exactly what was the curriculum like there?"

"For the next three years," Paul said, "I would spend my mornings memorizing the *Ketuvim* and the *Mishnah*, the historical and legal writings of Israel. Then in the afternoon and evening, we would discuss and debate what we learned with our teachers, and anyone else who might have come to Temple that day. Sometimes these didactic sessions could get quite confrontational. Still, they served to help us think theologically and to hone our skills in debate, so I enjoyed the banter.

"Gameliel first noticed me there," Paul continued. "Eventually, at his invitation, I pursued the final leg of my education in *Bet Talmud*, the doctoral school of the rabbis. For the next fifteen years, I walked in his dust, ate at his table, and listened to his every word. He became my spiritual father. In time, I grew to love him like one as well."

Once again, the chime on my iPhone signaled our time had ended. As he was leaving, Paul handed me an envelope.

"You were curious about the letter," he said. "I wrote down what I could remember. I hope my translation is helpful."

I put the envelope in my sweater pocket, and after he left, I made some additional notes in his file.

I realized Paul talked at length about his father but not his mother. I put a post-it-note on his file to remind me to explore the women in Paul's life in our next session. Then I hung my sweater on the door and went off to my afternoon class.

chapter 16

Anger

The root of anger is the perception that something has been taken. Something is owed you, and now a debt to debtor relationship has been established.—Andy Stanley, *Enemies of the Heart*

On Sunday night, I started looking over some of the proposals for advanced research papers, but my heart wasn't in it. After making some notes on a half dozen or so, I put down my red pen and walked out on the front porch where I sat in a wicker rocker and looked at the big lake. There's something hauntingly beautiful about watching the sun slowly sink beneath the waves of Lake Michigan. The orange, red, and yellow rays streaked across the horizon in a luminous glow. For a few brief moments, twilight danced gently on the swells while a bawdy crowd of seagulls sang their vespers. Darkness slowly swallowed the dusk.

Metaphorically, darkness has always been a place of uncertainty and death, so it is no wonder watching the sunset has tugged at the soul of humanity since the beginning of time.

The ancient Egyptians saw sunrise and sunset as symbols of life and death. Ra, the sun god, rose in the east each morning and descended into the darkness of death each night. He sacrificially gave his life each night while they slept the little sleep of death. He then made his way through the underworld to be triumphantly reborn again the next morning. Thus, Ra gave humanity what they wanted most, the gift of immortality.

As the tip of the sun slid into its watery grave, my hope sank, and my thoughts turned a little melancholy.

In times past, we wore a black armband when we lost someone we love as a sign of our mourning. After Rachel's funeral, I chose to do my mourning in private. In one-eighth-inch high black block letters, I had her name, birth, and death tattooed in Hebrew characters on my left arm—my secret armband hidden beneath my sleeve. Lucy is the only one who knows about my tattoo. I don't advertise my grief, but those Hebrew characters remind me I'll carry a piece of Rachel with me for the rest of my life.

"Oh God," I thought, half praying and half muttering to myself, "I don't understand any of this. How could you let this happen? I'm an emotional wreck. Life doesn't make any sense without her. It's not fair. It's not right. When you took Rachel, you took my faith in the fairness of life. And you know what, I'm really mad at you for that."

As always, God remained silent. Under my breath, I yelled, I cursed, and I questioned God's integrity, but no matter what I did, God did nothing.

In the book of Micah, the old prophet asks, "What does the LORD require of you?" Then he answers his own question. "To act justly and to love mercy and to walk humbly with your God."

Until then, I always assumed that was a two-way street. I thought we could require the same thing from God. You know—what's good for the goose is good for the gander.

I'd always believed life held a certain fairness, a kind of Christian karma in play. If that were true, then eventually good things happened to good people, but my reality spoiled my belief. When Rachel got sick, God didn't keep his end of the bargain. He neither acted justly nor showed mercy, so I stopped walking with him the day she died.

My decision didn't mean I stopped believing in God—I just stopped believing he rewarded goodness. That's when I decided to go alone for a while. Of course, we can't really run away from God. He's there whether we want him or not, but we can turn our backs on him, and that's what I did. I didn't care if he'd fight or not. I had enough fight in me for both of us.

God and I were no longer on speaking terms, and if I did speak, my words didn't sound much like a prayer.

"This isn't fair," I'd say, in the cold awareness of my empty bed. "I don't deserve this. We didn't deserve this. Certainly, Rachel didn't deserve to die so young."

In the privacy of my thoughts, I whispered those words again and again, and through the endless night, God remained silent.

Don't misunderstand. I'm not naïve. I know there's evil in the world. I also know no one goes through life without testing and tragedy, but not this. This was too much.

The God I believed in simply would not, could not, let that happen. So, until December 28, 2015, I refused to believe he'd allow Rachel to die so young. I just knew that, at some point, God would show up and do what only he can do, and miraculously Rachel would be all right. I guess that's what you think is always going to happen when you've led a charmed life. Until then, that certainly had been the case for me.

So, like I said, when Rachel died, I stopped walking with God. I wasn't public about it. In fact, I was quite private. My daughter Lucy needed to believe in a God of mercy, kindness, and love who, for reasons I couldn't explain, took her mother to be with him in heaven. So, we went to church periodically. We prayed at mealtime and bedtime. We read *Jesus Calling for Kids* each morning before she went to school. As best I could, I kept my anger in the closet of my heart. Until I met Paul. He had a way of picking the scab off old wounds like no one I'd ever met.

chapter 17

WOUNDED

He was pierced for our transgressions, he was crushed for
our iniquities; the punishment that brought us peace was
on him, and by his wounds we are healed.—Isaiah 53:5

I walked back into the house as the patter of raindrops
began pelting the tin roof of our front porch. A glance at the
clock revealed the time was a few minutes after seven o'clock.
Rachel and I always watched *60 Minutes* together on Sunday
night. In a way, the ritual connected me to her. In some ways,
I suppose I really didn't care what program I watched. I just
wanted to be distracted from the demons raging in my head
for a while. So, I quickly got lost in the story when the tick-
tock of the stopwatch went silent and Scott Pelley appeared
on the screen. The subject of his report—the ancient practice
of self-mutilation—was still being practiced in hidden corners
of the Catholic church.

"We recorded this story several months ago," Pelley said
in the introduction. "But now, in light of yet another round of
accusations of sexual misconduct within the Catholic church,
we decided tonight is the time to run the story. Before we air the
report, we will issue a word of caution. Parents, please be advised.

We do not feel the content of this story is suitable for younger viewers. Some of the material is quite graphic."

A huddle of hooded monks appeared on the screen walking across the crowded campus of the University of Notre Dame. The golden dome of the administration building loomed in the background, and the statue of the Virgin Mary kept a watchful eye. The scene looked harmless enough, but the ominous tone of the violin music served as a second warning to usher the children out of the room. I made sure Lucy was studying in her room. Once again, I turned my attention to the television.

"Self-mutilation," Pelley said, continuing his story "was once common practice among the monks and mystics, particularly for those who wanted to escape the enticing temptations of the secular world. Self-mutilation fell out of favor in the last half of the nineteenth century when Sigmund Freud suggested any form of mortification was a veiled attempt to repress one's secret sexual desires. His comments cast a suspicious eye on their policy of celibacy. Eventually, the practice of self-mutilation fell out of favor with Vatican authorities. However, in certain circles, this habit is still in practice underground.

"Many dedicated disciples and mystics," Pelley said in his dry Texas drawl, "are still secretly mutilating themselves as an act of penance. Their goal is to share in Christ's suffering by suffering themselves."

At this point, the scene of Jesus being flogged in Mel Gibson's movie *The Passion of the Christ* appeared briefly on the screen. The more gruesome details—shown for only a few seconds—was enough to cause most viewers to wince.

After a pause, Pelley commented psychologists formerly believed young people used cutting themselves to obtain attention. Now, some psychologists suggest this is a kind of coping mechanism to deal with their negative thoughts and feelings. Hurting themselves gives a sense of being in control and the rush of adrenaline distracts them from the pain.

Like most *60 Minutes* stories, this one used the familiar interview format. A dim strategically placed light exposed the figure of a hooded monk sitting on a stool, but a dark shadow hid his face. He spoke with an electronically altered voice, but I could hear his Mediterranean accent.

"You are a Jesuit priest in the diocese of Toronto," Pelley asked, "and a member of Opus Dei?"

"Yes," the priest said.

"And privately you sometimes practice self-mortification as a form of penance?"

"I do."

"Tell me about that."

"I fast. I kneel for hours on the monastery's marble floor. I pray and practice self-denial."

"And like Silas in the movie *The Da Vinci Code*, do you also sometimes wrap a small hobnailed chain around your upper thigh to inflict pain?"

As he asked the question, a short clip of the movie flashed across the screen. The albino monk raised his brown robe and tightened the chain around his thigh with a grimace of pious satisfaction on his face.

"Yes," the priest said, "I have sometimes used the *cilice*."

Pelley explained the current belief people sometimes deal with inner pain by cutting themselves and then asked, "What do you think about that?"

"I speak only for myself, but, yes, easing inner pain is part of my reason. Guilt and pain are part of being human. No one is immune to struggles with demons of some kind. I do whatever is necessary to cleanse my soul when I've wandered away from the heart of God."

"Do you wander away from God often?"

"Too often, I'm afraid," the shadowy figure said, dipping his head slightly.

Pelley paused to study his notes, then asked, "Have you used the whip as well?"

"As a young boy, I learned the importance of living an examined life, to face my inner demons head-on. So weekly, I enter the confessional, but sometimes the penitent man requires more than a cleric's absolution. On these days, I sometimes use the whip. As you say, one pain can distract a person from another. Agony can be a great teacher. My back bears the scars of my sinfulness."

"I'm curious. What has pain taught you?"

"The importance of forgiveness," the priest said. "The church is full of sinners, and some of the worst wear robes. A few, and I must emphasize it is only a few, have used their position to prey on the young, the vulnerable, the innocent and the voiceless. But now the victims have a voice. Some of those who were once the prey are now priests themselves, and they will not be silenced. The truth must be told, all of it. Only then can we learn to forgive.

"This seems very personal for you," Pelley said.

"The best warriors in any battle are always those who have a reason to fight."

"So, tell me, Father," Pelley asked, "how do you deal with the pain?"

After a nod, the priest spoke softly. "As Cardinal Francesco Giuliani once said to me, 'When Satan reminds you of your past, you must remind him of his future.'

"Do you think the church is finally free from its past?"

"No, but we're working at it.

"And by 'we' you mean the leadership of the Catholic church?"

"Yes."

"There is rumor that even some of those who work closely with the Holy Father himself know the pain we speak of.

Remember, Satan is good at what he does, and he's been in business for a long time."

Again, Pelley paused as if he were letting the thought that such activity even penetrated the walls of the Vatican sink in with his listeners. After a moment, emboldened by the shadowy priest's willingness to share, he quietly asked an even more probing question.

"Sister Tobiana Sobodka," he said slowly, "who worked in John Paul II's private Vatican apartment, has said sometimes late at night, she would hear the Holy Father flog himself. Does that surprise you?"

"No, no, not at all. John Paul was a very devout, very pious man. Like all true believers, his sins weighed heavily on his soul. I'm sure he sought forgiveness wherever he could find relief. Sometimes, even for a pope, sanctification can be a painful process."

For a moment, the priest paused as if his own sins were weighing heavily on his soul. Then after a long, heavy sigh, he continued.

"Many of us believe hardship and hunger will help us overcome the weaknesses of the flesh. As the great apostle himself once said, 'I strike a blow to my body and make it my slave so after I have preached to others, I, myself, will not be disqualified for the prize.'"

As with most *60 Minutes* stories, the interview ended as abruptly as it started.

As I shut off the TV, I couldn't help but make the connection between the scars on the back of the shadowy priest and the scars on Paul's back. *Were they one and the same?* After a few minutes of wild speculation, I went back to the task at hand. Again, I started making notes on the research paper proposals stacked on my kitchen table. After a couple of hours, I finished and went to bed—exhausted but unable to fall asleep. At about three o'clock, more out of frustration than faith, I mumbled a halfhearted prayer under my breath.

"Why don't you talk to me, Lord? Explain yourself if you can. Certainly, you have a good reason for wreaking such havoc in our lives. What's the matter? Have you no word of wisdom to offer? Has the cat got your tongue?"

chapter 18

BRAVERY

"I wanted you to see what real courage is instead of getting the idea that courage is a man with a gun in his hand. It's when you know you're licked before you begin but you begin anyway, and you see it through no matter what. You rarely win, but sometimes you do."
—Harper Lee, *To Kill a Mockingbird*

The silence of God is a horrible thing.

"Word," John said, "and the Word was with God, and the Word was God."

The voice of God set the world in motion. Words are powerful. Before the first word there was nothing. No light, no birds, no fishes, no animals, no vegetation, no humanity. God hovered over a formless, empty, darkness of silence. That's where I am. I lay there in the empty darkness of silence waiting for God to speak.

"Say something, Father," I pleaded, "anything. Tell me that you're listening. Tell me you love me. Tell me you're disappointed in me. I don't care, but for God's sake, God, say something."

If John is right—if the Word was God—then the absence of words is the absence of God. I lay there wrestling with the silence for a couple of hours until, finally, I got up and went back into the living room. I sat down in my chair, turned on the lamp, and reached for the TV remote. That's when I saw Rachel's NIV study Bible lying on the shelf under the table. Without thinking, I picked up her Bible and began randomly thumbing through it. I fanned the pages like a dealer shuffles cards and stopped at each of the passages she'd highlighted. I guess I was hoping to reconnect with her, and maybe with God too.

In Timothy, smeared with a pink marker, were the words, "be prepared in season and out of season."

"Well," I muttered, "Sorry, honey, that ship has sailed. Nothing has prepared me for this. I'm lost. I'm just wandering aimlessly. I've been making life up as I go along ever since I scattered your ashes off the south pier over a year ago."

She asked, and I couldn't say no.

"Bass," she had said, using the shortened form of my given name, which telegraphed the seriousness of what she was about to say. "I want to be cremated. Sprinkle my ashes in Lake Michigan. I don't want people looking at what's left of me lying in a coffin. Let them look at pictures of what our life was like instead. We had a great life. I don't have any regrets. Really, I don't. I don't want you to carry me around in an urn, either. I want you to carry me around in your heart."

She whispered the words one night as we lay in bed on our backs, holding hands. For a few moments, I was trying to forget she was dying of cancer. She would not let me forget.

"Pour my ashes off the end of the pier at the state park," she said. "We've had so many great days there. I don't want Lucy going to visit me at the cemetery. That's just morbid. Sick and wrong."

"Let's not talk about that right now," I said. "There's still hope. The treatments might work, you don't know."

"I don't know, but I want to be prepared either way. You know I've been thinking a lot about dying lately, and death doesn't scare me anymore. The end of this life used to, but then I decided I don't want to be so afraid of dying that I stop living."

I put my arm around her and pulled her close. Then as she gently laid her head on my shoulder, I kissed her cheek. Like me, she'd been crying, and the salty taste of her tears broke my heart.

I know you need to talk about this, but I don't know if I can. I'll hold you, I'll cry with you, but I've got no words for this.

For the past few months, all the things I busied myself with before suddenly seemed unimportant. My work, my writing, my friends—none of them mattered. What mattered was Rachel. All I wanted to do was to squeeze every ounce of joy we could out of the time we had left together. While I tried to make more room for her, she tried to make more room for God. She spent more and more time reading her Bible, meditating in solitude, and praying.

A part of me understood that. The closer she came to meeting God face to face, the more she wanted to prepare for meeting him. What caught me off guard was most of her prayers were litanies of praise and gratitude.

The depth of her spirituality exposed the shallowness of my own. Already, a little bit at a time, I was losing her to God and there was nothing I could do.

The problem wasn't that I didn't pray. I prayed all the time, but my prayers were more selfish. I wanted him to give her back. What can I say—the soul wants what the soul wants.

Mercifully, she broke the silence.

"When you get cancer, you get to practice being brave," she said, regaining her composure with a sniffle.

"You try to be brave when they give you the diagnosis. Later, when you look up cancer on the internet, you try to be brave all over again. Then you try to be brave when you get chemo, and when you get sick, when you lose your hair, when they tell you they've done all they can do, and everything is in God's hands now. Then one day you realize everything has been in God's hands all along. After that, death isn't so scary anymore. You wake up one morning and realize you've just sort of gotten comfortable with the thought of dying. The next thing you know, everybody's telling you how brave you are."

"I'm not comfortable with the idea," I said. "I'm not brave either. Death scares me to death. In fact, the only thing that scares me more than death is the thought of you dying. So, here's the deal. If somebody gets to die around here, it's going to be me, okay?"

"Okay," she said laughing slightly. "Have it your way. You can do my dying for me."

"I would if I could," I said. And I meant every word.

But I didn't get to have my way with her life, and now her death is having its way with me. Two days after Rachel's funeral, I asked her dad, Gunny, how he ever got over losing Tika.

"I've never did get *over* it," he said. "I just try each day to get *through* it. Some days are better than others. Other times, a man just has to cry his way through things in silence. At least that's what I try to do."

I began paging through her Bible again and found one of her favorite verses highlighted in yellow. The words were from the pen of the prophet Isaiah. She'd ask me to read them to her while she was getting chemotherapy. We'd be sitting in a room full of people hooked up to IVs, playing preacher.

"Read out loud," she'd say. "That way everyone can hear."

How foolish we were.

At the time, I had convinced myself the words were true. I read the words with a naïve gusto. Like a carnival barker

98

in his striped-pink sport coat, I invited everyone to join us. I was a preacher addressing his dying congregation. How hollow the words seem to me now. I wept when I stumbled across the faded yellow highlighting.

> "[S]ay to those with fearful hearts, 'Be strong, do not fear; your God will come, he will come with vengeance; with divine retribution he will come to save you.' Then will the eyes of the blind be opened and the ears of the deaf unstopped. Then will the lame leap like a deer, and the mute tongue shout for joy."

I kept turning pages, and in Galatians, this time in pale green, she had marked "Do not lose heart, for in due time you will reap the harvest."

"Oh, Rachel, we're too late," I whispered. "I lost my heart to you a long time ago, and I'll never get it back again."

I flipped back a few more pages and found where she'd underlined part of Paul's love poem from first Corinthians.

"[Love] always protects, always trusts, always hopes, always perseveres. True love never fails." Then, next to it, she had scratched the words "Stand firm, and do not wander or waver," in red.

Dear, sweet Rachel, if only you knew how weak-kneed I am without you. My mind wanders into so many places it shouldn't go. And what's worse, my faith wavers between the dimly lit candle of my convictions and the smoldering wick of doubt. At night I lay in the silent darkness of the bed we shared, and my mind flutters back and forth between the two like a wounded hummingbird.

Again, I pushed my way through the pages of her Bible until I stumbled across a verse she'd highlighted in blue at the end of the book of Colossians.

"See to it that you complete the ministry you have received from the Lord," Paul wrote.

Once again, the fact that she marked those words burned in my soul. The Lord didn't let her finish the work he gave her. Her work at Christ the Redeemer is unfinished, her work with the patients in our practice is unfinished, and her work as a wife and mother is certainly unfinished.

Now her work is my work. All I can do is try to carry on what she started. I owe her that. In some ways, keeping it alive keeps her memory alive. So, even though my heart isn't always there with the same passion, I try my best to minister to the marginalized, to be Jesus to the broken. And then, Lord knows, I'm trying to be both a father and a mother to Lucy. But I can't begin to fill Rachel's shoes.

Eventually, I went back to bed. Faint thoughts of Rachel haunted my restless dreams until I finally slipped into the silent emptiness of exhaustion.

chapter 19

INTEGRITY

Our lives say much more about how we think than our books do. The theories we preach are not always the ones we actually believe. The theories we live are the ones we really believe.—R. C. Sproul, *Lifeviews: Make a Christian Impact on Culture and Society*

The next morning, I woke up surly. I didn't really feel like making breakfast for Lucy, so I took her to deBoer Bakery instead. Over oatmeal and eggs, we made the usual small talk. She was handling life better than I was. Whenever she laughed, I saw a reflection of Rachel in her smile. My child was growing up right before my eyes. I wished Rachel could see her. Maybe she can, I don't know, I hope so. I dropped Lucy off at Gracie Weaver's house, and Mary came out to say hi.

"You doing all right, Rocky?" she asked. "You look a little tired."

"I am tired," I said. "But Lucy and I are going to kick back and relax over the Fourth. I think we're just going to walk the beach, watch the fireworks, and eat too many hotdogs."

"We're going to have a few friends over from church on Sunday," Mary said. "You know you're welcome if you guys want to come over for a burger."

"Thanks," I said. "Lucy might come down and play with Gracie and Jackie, but I'm looking forward to a little alone time."

Another lie. I hated being alone, but I hated having people feel sorry for me even more, and I knew her church friends. They'd be all over me like syrup on pancakes. There is a group of them that gives me that, "Oh, you poor dear" look at church. I can't stand their expression.

Mary and I chatted a little more until I had to be in class. Today was the final session of my behavior disorders class for the June term. I collected the exams and walked across the campus to my office, hoping to catch a catnap before my afternoon appointments. I must have dozed off for a bit because, when I woke up, the orange afghan covered me, and Paul sat across from me in the black wingback chair.

"You were sleeping soundly when I arrived," he said, smiling, "I decided not to wake you."

"Sorry," I said, "I was up late last night. Family issues."

"Your daughter?" he asked.

"Yes," I lied. I sat up and turned the conversation toward Paul.

"Tell me about you family," I said.

"Much of who I am," Paul said, "was shaped by my father's perception of how the world worked. He loved diversity. He thoroughly enjoyed meeting new people, going new places, and learning new things. Naturally, he passed that love on to me. But there were checks and balances as well."

As always, Paul told his tale with such detail that he drew me into his delusion.

"'The world wants to teach you its ways, my son,' Paul said, mimicking his father. "'But you must always filter everything you learn through Torah.'

"That's exactly what I did," Paul said with a slight smile. "From age six to twelve, I went to the synagogue in Tarsus each morning to study the Torah with the *chazzan*, Mordecai. He was an old man, gauntly thin with high cheekbones, squinty deep-set gray eyes, and a long pointy nose like a fox. Age weathered his face, and his long silver hair was wispy thin and wild.

"Mordecai wore the same costume every day, which was rarely, if ever, washed. The musty smell of incense embedded his long black wool tunic, which dragged behind him in a train as he walked. He always wore a prayer shawl around his shoulders. The shawl, made of coarse white wool yellowed with age, had two thin blue stripes woven into the hem. Knotted ornamental tassels, the length of an outstretched hand, hung from the edges. These indicated both his station and the depth of his holiness. His well-made ox-hide sandals had two corded straps that crisscrossed up the old man's bony legs and tied in a neat bow just below the knee.

"Mordecai's demeanor was distant and aloof. Most of his students considered him unapproachable. Even though I was his most prized student, or as he might say, his most gifted *talmidim*, he never once invited me to call him by name. Instead, like all his students, for six years I called him Rabin, Chazzan, or the Teacher. We all knew his name, which we'd say in jest behind his back, but never did we utter his name in his presence.

"Learning with him was a two-sided coin," Paul continued. "First we learned by observation. We followed the teacher to the market, to visit the sick and the suffering, and when he sat in the city gates where people would seek his counsel. They wanted him to judge their disputes. While Rabin Mordecai sat settling their differences with a rigid impartiality, we stood straight as sticks, just a few feet away. We listened carefully to his words, questioned his reasoning if we dared, and responded to any question he might ask.

"'What are we to learn from this, master?'" we would ask. Or 'why did you take us here?' Or 'how are we to apply this teaching to our lives?'

"Sometimes the answer was simple.

"'You are to learn when a man is hungry, he must eat,' the teacher would say. 'The word of God provides bread for your soul, but the baker rises early to provide bread for your stomach. Both are necessary if you intend to live a righteous life.'

"Other times, the answer to a question might require both time and a more mature spirit to be fully grasped. For example, one day, while we were walking through the marketplace, an old woman snatched the loaf out from under the teacher's arm and quickly disappeared into the crowd. As I set out to catch her, Mordecai ordered me to stop.

"Frustrated and angry because Mordecai did not allow me to help him, I said 'I do not understand, Rabin. Your behavior makes no sense to me. Clearly, she took what belonged to you. I could have caught her easily. Why would you let the old woman go unpunished?'

"'First,' Mordecai said softly without looking up. 'Everything I have belongs to God. And second, am I the judge of right and wrong? For all I know, God decided to use this to feed the old woman. Or perhaps this is what he will use to condemn her to hell. Either way, this was his decision, not mine. He is the judge of such things. Perhaps the Lord felt she needed the bread more than I.'

"But what if you go hungry tonight?" I protested. "What if you starved to death?"

"'When you knock on the door to heaven, 'tis better to have a full heart and an empty stomach, than a full stomach and an empty heart.'

"At the time, I felt more chided that instructed," Paul said. "But the more I thought about his words, the more I began to appreciate the old man's wisdom. Learning is often that way.

"According to Mordecai, a good rabbi never says, 'do what I say.' Instead, he will always say, 'do what I do.' So as his *talmidim*, we watched him closely. We observed how he lived his life, and we tried to emulate everything he did. Over time his words, his mannerisms, his prayers, and his beliefs became ours as well. This is the way of the student. Our job is to do what our master would do if he were there. In that way, his thoughts, his values, and his ideas will live on after he's gone.

"For this reason," Paul continued, "many times I have written what I have been taught. 'Follow my example as I have followed the example of Christ.'

"You would do well to give the same instruction," Paul said, motioning toward Lucy's picture on my bookcase. "It is a powerful thing to know others are trying to imitate our every move."

Like any parent, I was vaguely aware that Lucy watched me. But Paul's words reminded me that, for now at least, I was probably the most influential person in her life. I was glad Lucy and I were going to spend a few days together. They would be good for her, and probably even better for me.

chapter 20

LONELINESS

All alone! Whether you like it or not, alone is something
you'll be quite a lot!—Dr. Suess, *Oh, the Places You'll Go!*

Holidays can be hard. The Fourth of July was no exception.
Rachel's fingerprints were all over our activities. She loved
the beach, the boat, and the fireworks, and each would trigger
memories for Lucy. I knew she'd be full of questions, but I
vowed to make the best of the situation. We got up early and
went to deBoer's for breakfast. She had her favorite—sugar
bread with strawberries. I had pancakes with candied lemon
zest, ricotta cheese, and caramelized blueberries—deBoer's
never disappoints. Back at home, we took a leisurely walk
down the beach—already a swell of humanity—toward the
state park.

The parking lot was full at a quarter to ten. People were
everywhere. The smells of bacon still hung like a cloud over
the campground. Kids riding bikes with red, white, and blue
streamers wove their way around people walking their dogs.
Cars lined the beach road, waiting for their turn to get into
the park.

Boats of all sizes and shapes came and went through the channel. Lake Michigan was choppy, and several smaller boats were having second thoughts as they approached the end of the pier. Fishermen lined the edges of the pier, and as we made our way toward the lighthouse, we stopped periodically to talk to them.

"Catching anything?" I asked. A teenage boy and his dad smiled and nodded toward a bucket full of bluegills and yellow perch. Everybody we talked to had a similar story. The fish were definitely biting. Lucy took her turn at asking when we got a little closer to Big Red, the lighthouse at the mouth of Holland harbor.

"Are you catching anything?" she asked a girl with headphones and pink streaks in her hair. At first the girl ignored her. Before I could tell Lucy not to bother her, she bent over, made eye contact with the girl, and asked her question again.

"Are you catching any fish?" Lucy said, even louder this time.

The girl looked up at her, smiled, and slowly shook her head no.

Lucy smiled back and then quickly moved on. A few feet further down, she walked up to an older guy in a faded orange Hope College T-shirt and asked her question again.

"Are you catching anything, mister?"

He chewed on his cigar for a moment, smiled, and nodded to a plastic pail full of flopping perch.

"Fish for dinner tonight," he said.

"We're having hotdogs," she said, "and we're roasting marshmallows too."

"Well, that sounds good too," he said, and Lucy was off asking her question to the next fisherman down the line.

We sat on the end of the north pier watching the boats parade in and out of the channel. Across on the south pier sat Big Red, Michigan's most photographed lighthouse. Since 1907, the scarlet sentinel has stood guard over Holland harbor where the river empties into Lake Michigan.

The square light tower is bright red. The matching Queen Anne Victorian-style keeper's house has two steeply sloped gables, each with a weathered-gray shingled roof. The structure is imposing at three stories high, and the light reaches twenty miles on a clear night.

A freckled-face girl stood at an easel, sketching the lighthouse in charcoal. Next to her, a round-faced woman snapped photos with her phone. Others looked across at Big Red through the passing boats.

"Beautiful," said a mother to her daughter, "just beautiful."

"I never get tired of looking at Big Red," said an older man leaning on a cane.

Total strangers chat freely with each other on the pier. Here, Lucy talked to anyone who'd listen. Like her mother, she is gregarious and engaging. Soon she was best friends with everyone out there. After making the rounds with the crowd on the pier, she came back and sat down next to me again.

"Do you think we could take *The Four Angels* out today?" she asked.

The wind had died down a little, but the lake was still choppy.

"The water will be a little rough out there," I said.

"I like it rough," she said, sounding like her mother, "and I'll wear my lifejacket."

"We'll see," I said, knowing full well she'd already won.

We walked back up the beach, and as usual, Lucy jabbered all the way home. After a lunch of yogurt and fruit, we put on our swimming suits and went back to the beach to build a sandcastle—Lucy's idea and a good one. We built drizzle sand towers with stick flag poles and a wall with a popsicle stick drawbridge gate. Afterward, we dug a moat around the outside that filled with every wave. Just as we were finishing, the Weaver girls walked over to admire our work.

"Your sandcastle is beautiful," Gracie said, and Jackie agreed.

"I want to live in a castle someday," Jackie said.

"Me too," Gracie added.

"This is what my mom's house looks like," Lucy said. "She lives in heaven."

"How do you know what her house looks like?" Gracie asked. "You've never been there."

"Don't have to go to know," Lucy said. "They sing about heaven all the time at church."

"What?" said Gracie, looking at Lucy suspiciously.

"They sing about ivory palaces, and pearly gates, and mansions on hilltops, and that sounds like castles to me."

Gracie and Jackie slowly nodded in agreement and looked at me to affirm what Lucy said.

"That sounds about right," I said, which settled the question.

"Do you want to come over and play at our house?" Jackie asked. "We're going to have a party, and my mom says you guys can come."

"Thanks," Lucy said, "but my dad and I are going sailing, right, Dad?"

"Yes," I said, "that's the plan."

"Okay," Jackie said, "but if you change your mind, you're welcome." With a wave, they walked up the beach back to their house.

A few minutes later, we took our eighteen-foot Hobie out for a sail. The hulls were white, and the sail and webbed tramp were navy blue. Rachel had named the boat *Four Angels* because of Revelation chapter seven. "After this I saw four angels standing at the four corners of the earth, holding back the four winds."

When we bought the boat, Rach had the name lettered in a calligraphy style script along each hull. Behind the words she added the silhouette of four dancing angels, creating a beautiful design.

Lucy loved to sail the boat almost as much as her mother did. Rachel started taking her out as soon as she was old enough to wear a lifejacket, and by now Lucy was a pro. She had a feel for being out on the water and would shift around the tramp and duck under the boom based on the direction of the wind without me saying a word.

"Faster, Dad," she'd yell, as one of the hulls lifted out of the water. "I want to fly higher."

On days like this, I remembered she was gutsy like her mother.

The wind was strong, about fifteen knots, and Lucy loved riding on the trapeze. She'd hike out on the windward hull, clip into the wires that hung off either side of the mast, and start flying.

The Hobie is a simple boat to sail. That day, I let Lucy hold the tiller. Eventually we sailed north toward Grand Haven, and then came about a couple of miles past Pigeon Creek. Our route was a long sail in a catamaran, but we had nothing better to do. Lucy was quiet on our way home. Both of us were a little blue. Without words I knew that, like me, she was missing Rachel. Being out on *Four Angels* will do that to you, so quiet, so peaceful. Old memories haunt your thoughts.

As we drifted past Tunnel Park, I decided we'd felt sorry for ourselves long enough, so I changed the mood.

"Lucy," I said, "instead of just roasting marshmallows, I think we should make s'mores."

"Yay," Lucy said gleefully. "They're my favorite."

I know, I know.

The previous night, after Lucy had gone to bed, I got things ready for our Independence Day dinner. One by one, I checked the necessary items off my list. Hotdogs, buns, catsup, mustard, pickles, paper plates, potato chips, dip, drink boxes, marshmallows, graham crackers, and Hershey bars. I put some of the items in an old green Coleman cooler with some ice. The rest of the items went into a cardboard box with two stainless steel extendable hotdog forks, some lighter fluid, and a box of matches.

At home after our sail, we changed out of our swimsuits, and I took the cooler and the rest of our gear down to the beach. I put kindling on some crumpled paper and lit a fire. When Lucy joined me on the beach, we sat in a couple of old, weathered, red Adirondack chairs and began roasting hotdogs. Dinner was simple—hotdogs, kettle chips, and blueberry drink boxes.

As the sun started to set, boats of all sizes began to claim their spots at the mouth of the harbor. People often say the best place to watch the fireworks is on the water, but Rachel and I believed our beach was better. As the fire died down, Lucy and I began roasting some marshmallows for s'mores—a gooey mess, just like they're supposed to be.

"Daddy," Lucy said, wiping the chocolate off her cheek, "how far away is that sailboat out there?"

"A long way," I said, standing up to get a better look. "About three miles maybe."

As the boat made its way north along the horizon, the silhouette of the sail temporarily blocked the setting sun.

"Could we sail *Four Angels* out there, Daddy?"

"We probably could, but I don't think we should."

"Pleeease," she said in a voice that usually got what she wanted. "I don't want the day to end. Come on, Daddy, let's go chase the sun."

"I wish we could. We all wish some days would never end, but life doesn't work that way. We have to learn to be thankful for today and hope God will give us an even better day tomorrow."

I wasn't sure which one of us I was trying to convince, but she seemed to buy what I was selling.

Lucy slowly reached over and grabbed my hand.

"I love you, Daddy" she said.

"I love you more," I replied trying not to get emotional.

Every year, the Van Andel family puts on a huge fireworks show. They shoot the exploding rockets over Lake Michigan, and we can see them clearly from our house. The fireworks show began as the last rays of the sun faded in the western sky. As always, they were spectacular.

"Best seats on the beach," Lucy said.

"No doubt about it."

As the fireworks went off, we oohed and aahed as each seemed more amazing than the last. About ten minutes in, Lucy asked a question.

"If heaven is up there on the other side of the fireworks, just beyond the stars, do you think Mommy is watching them too?"

"Maybe," I said. "Maybe she is."

After the fireworks, we went back to the house and to bed. Like Lucy, I didn't want the day to end, mostly because I faced another long, lonely night.

chapter 21

MENTORS

Every once in a while, you'll run into someone who is eager to listen, eager to learn, and willing to try new things. Those are the people we need to reach. We have a responsibility as parents, older people, teachers, people in the neighborhood to recognize that.—Tyler Perry, *Don't Make a Black Woman Take Off Her Earrings*

An old Dutch proverb says one hundred percent of what a child learns in their first five years is from their parents. From ages five to ten, the number drops to seventy-five percent. From ages ten to fifteen, the parents' influence is reduced to fifty percent. Finally, from fifteen to twenty, their influence dips to twenty-five percent. After that, our children become the teachers of our grandchildren.

Paul would have agreed. In the first of our now monthly sessions, he said that as he grew, more and more of his learning came from teachers and mentors. Early on, chief among them was the *chazzan* Mordecai.

"Each day." Paul said, taking his usual seat, "the old schoolmaster drilled and disciplined us in the dialect, accent, and rhythm of the Hebrew scriptures. When we could recite every jot and tittle perfectly, then and only then, could we begin to commit the sacred text to memory.

"I always suspected I was the old man's favorite," Paul said with a smile. "My suspicions were confirmed one day when Mordecai invited me into his private living quarters—a stark and windowless little room attached to the main chamber of the synagogue. A straw-filled mattress lay on the tile floor filling much of the space. A table with two sturdy chairs occupied the rest. A lit clay lamp eerily illumined the room. Mordecai's shadow danced across the far wall as he made his way to one of the chairs. Then, with a long bony finger, he motioned for me to sit in the other chair, which I did.

"For a few moments, I sat silently listening to the teacher breathe, until he spoke again.

"'Just as you have followed me,' Mordecai said, 'so too I have followed you. In the afternoons, when you leave me, you go about your father's business, learning the ways of the world. This troubles me. Your father is a good man, a man of wealth and power, but he tells me he wants more for you than that, and I believe him. This is the reason he sends you to me each morning. However, there will come a time when you must choose between his ways and mine. You are almost a man, and you can't live in both worlds much longer, so listen closely. After much prayer, God has given me these words for you. 'You must be willing to sacrifice your life for the Lord. The world will try to get you to conform to their ways. You must choose instead to be transformed by the word of God. That way his will and yours will become one.'

"The two of us sat in silence for some time," Paul said. "Then without saying a word, the old man blew out the lamp, and I followed him out of his little room. As we reentered the main chamber of the synagogue, the contrast of the two rooms struck me. One is concealed in darkness—the other in light.

"Sunshine flooded into the assembly chambers through many windows. Ornate carvings of grapevines, stalks of wheat, pomegranates, sheep, cattle, and a beehive covered the plaster walls. Five rows of wooden benches lined three of the walls around an open area in the middle. Most mornings, we sat on these benches as Mordecai paced back and forth in the open space. He waved his skinny arms wildly as he walked, and he instructed us in the words and the ways of our ancestors.

"Two massive wooden doors with heavy, hammered brass hinges stood in the east wall of the synagogue facing Jerusalem. On the north side of the doors stood a golden menorah, which remained lit day and night. On the other side, a purple curtain hung to the floor. The *Aron Kodesh*, the Holy Closet that housed the Torah scroll, was hidden behind the curtain.

"As we entered," Paul said, remembering the room as if it were yesterday, "Mordecai immediately retrieved the sacred scroll from the shelf. When he returned, he instructed me to sit under the window on the last row of benches with my back against the wall. When I sat down, the teacher did what he had done many times before. He gently laid the parchment in my lap as if the scroll were a newborn child. Methodically, he unrolled the document to the words of the prophet Jeremiah. His fingers moved swiftly but still he was careful to touch only the wooden handles of the sacred scroll.

Paul continued in a soft voice, "After whispering a prayer for wisdom, Mordecai picked up the *yod* which had been resting on a pillow on the readers table. The yod was a long silver stick capped with a small ivory hand with the index finger fully extended used as a pointer. I always thought the yod looked like a miniature version of old Mordecai's own twisted, arthritic hand. As always, for a few moments, he regally cradled the pointer against his chest, as if the yod were a king's scepter. Swiftly and precisely, the teacher wielded the yod like a sword and pointed to the words he wanted me to read.

"'The word of the Lord came to me saying, "Before I formed you in the womb, I knew you; before you were born, I set you apart. I appointed you as my prophet to the nations.

"'This is your verse,' Mordecai said in a hushed and holy voice that only I could hear. 'This is God's word for you. He told me he preserved these words all these many years for your eyes to read. The verse speaks of his plan for your life. If you will let him, God wants to speak not only *to* you, but *through* you to all the nations of the world.'

"He returned the scroll to the hiding place behind the purple curtain. I knew the verse, of course," Paul continued with a bit of bravado. "Like every line of the sacred writing, I'd committed those words to memory, just as Mordecai had instructed me.

"'Read each line out loud,' the Rabin would say. 'Close your eyes, nod your head back and forth, and silently whisper the words over and over until every jot and tittle is a part of your very soul.'

"The method worked so well," Paul said, "that years later, as an old man, whenever I close my eyes, my head starts nodding up and down, and immediately I see the words of the ancient scrolls unfold before my mind's eye."

With a growing sense of credibility, he continued to tell his tale as if he had lived it. I had to remind myself constantly that he was delusional, or I would get lost in the story. Truthfully, at times I did.

"By the time of my Bar Mitzvah," Paul said, puffing his chest out with pride, "the student had outgrown the teacher. For the next two years I continued my study alone, at night, by candlelight. I tried not to show my presentiment, but I was not surprised when the invitation finally came for me to study in Jerusalem. After all, I had earned the privilege."

Not wanting to seem too eager or impious, Paul said he did what was expected of him. He spent three days in cloistered prayer and meditation, but never once did he consider declining the offer. After the three-day waiting period, Paul accepted the appointment, secured the necessary travel funds from his father, and he and his young bride made the long and difficult journey to Jerusalem.

"By now," he said, "little Paul was not so little anymore. Like my namesake, I stood head and shoulders above my new colleagues, both physically and mentally."

Paul told me that Gamaliel and the other teachers of the law marveled at how his mind would comprehend every nuance of the text. He devoured his prey with the efficiency of a hungry lion. Even then, people whispered one day Saul would sit in one of the seventy seats of the Sanhedrin.

When our session ended, to my surprise, Paul said he was going to the beach. "The winds and the waves are nourishing for my soul."

I agreed, and without thinking, offered to give him a ride.

"I canceled my afternoon class today," I said. "I'll be headed home after this. I can drop you off on my way rather than have you take the bus."

"I intended to walk."

"Five miles?" I asked, thinking the distance might change his mind.

"What is five miles to a man who walked from Jerusalem to Rome?" Paul responded and bid me farewell. "May the grace of the Lord Jesus be with you."

I responded in kind as he stepped out the door. "And also with you."

I filled out an online evaluation report for Judge Summerdyke's office. I started by recapping my first encounter with him in the psych ward at Mercy Hospital, and then, I detailed the subsequent sessions we'd had in my office.

"Case number 1761-5SBA, Sha'ul Ben-Andronicus, hereafter referred to in this report as Paul, does in fact believe himself to be the first century apostle. I have tried, unsuccessfully, to discover his identity. He still holds stubbornly to his delusion. There are indications his psychotic break was the result of some as yet unspecified personal tragedy or trauma. One can never be sure about such things, but I hope to explore this further in subsequent sessions.

"Despite his condition, Paul is a charismatic individual. He presents himself well and appears to be well educated. In my sessions with him, he repeatedly demonstrates an extraordinary knowledge of the apostle Paul's personal history and ministry. This I find fascinating, and I hope his knowledge may help us piece together the puzzle of his past.

"Once again, I want to reiterate—in my opinion, Paul does not appear to present any danger to himself or to others.

"On another note, I was disturbed to discover his body is covered with severe scarring. They appear to be the result of multiple injuries. Perhaps more could be learned from an extensive medical exam. I recommend the court order the exam and share the findings with my office.

"Finally, I believe I have gained Paul's confidence, and I'd like to continue to meet with him monthly in hopes of helping him reconnect with reality."

I reread the report and hit send. On my way out of the office, I grabbed my coat and hung my sweater on the door. An envelope fell out onto the floor—the envelope Paul had given me after our fourth session. I slipped the envelope into my coat pocket to read later.

chapter 22

TRANSLATION

The word 'translation' comes, etymologically, from the Latin for 'bearing across.' Having been borne across the world, we are translated men. It is normally supposed that something always gets lost in translation; I cling, obstinately to the notion that something can also be gained.—Salman Rushdie, *Imaginary Homelands: Essays and Criticism 1981-1991*

Later that evening, I tucked Lucy into bed and listened to her prayers. Then I grabbed a bottle of Summer Apple cider, sat down in front of the fire, and took Paul's envelope from my coat pocket. Inside, I found a handwritten document in unusually large letters scratched out crudely with a fountain pen.

"I was in Damascus with Barnabas," the note read. "We were staying in the house of Ananias when Phoebe arrived with Peter's letter.

Petros, an apostle of Jesus Christ, along with James our Lord's brother, and the rest of the faithful in Jerusalem. To Paul and Barnabas, our beloved brothers in the Lord, peace be with you.

We trust that you both will do what is right and what the council has agreed upon here in Jerusalem. As you are aware, we have obtained an inheritance passed down from Moses that sets us apart as God's chosen people. The very sign and the seal of this promise is circumcision.

For this reason, we were grieved to hear you have abandoned this sacred treasure. It has been reported to us that in your preaching among the Gentiles, you have inferred such things are no longer necessary for salvation. We welcome the Gentiles as brothers in the way of our Lord, but we also must insist they also follow the laws of our fathers. Remember, Jesus himself also freely followed the Torah.

We are therefore asking that you both refrain from preaching unless you are willing to amend your message. As those chosen by the Lord Jesus himself, we urge you to join us in affirming our inheritance of salvation both as children of the covenant and followers of the risen Christ.

"At the time I was greatly angered by his words," Paul wrote. "Despite Barnabas's efforts to calm my spirit, I was deeply wounded by his accusations. I saw no other option but to discuss the situation face to face with the fisherman. For this reason, Barnabas and I left for Jerusalem immediately with the intention of settling the matter once and for all.

"In the end," Paul continued, "my differences with Peter were short-lived. I asked for, and received, his forgiveness for the anger in my heart. In kind, he responded generously to my rebuke. For a time, sharp words went back and forth as we debated the mandatory requirements of salvation among the brothers in Jerusalem. Eventually he and John even came to my defense. In the end, we all agreed. The only thing that could trump God's law was his grace.

"There were reports our differences were a long-standing debate, but this was not the case. Seeing his note in your office momentarily brought back the pain which those words initially caused me, but until then I had long since forgotten it."

Almost as an apologetic post-script, he wrote the following words at the bottom of the page.

"My memory is not what it once was. I fear I may have omitted a phrase or two from the original correspondence. Even so, I believe this is a fair representation of the letter's intent, if not its exact words."

For a few minutes, I sat in front of the fire sipping my cider, somewhat stunned at what I'd just read. A swarm of thoughts filled my head like bees.

Could it be? Of course not. Don't be ridiculous. But how else could Paul possibly translate the ancient Aramaic manuscript? I must admit his scars had fueled my imagination for some time now. Still, in my more rational moments, I know there's no way this man is the apostle. That isn't even possible. Is it?

Even so, the words of Jesus kept echoing around in the back of my head. "With man this is impossible, but with God all things are possible."

Using my MacBook, I researched the words 'Petros Fragment' and compared what I'd found with Paul's note. My Hebrew is sketchy. I hadn't done much with the ancient language since seminary. Aramaic is closely related to Hebrew, but there are numerous differences, so I struggled. Despite my linguistic limitations, the words I could translate seemed to correspond with Paul's note.

"How could he know what the letter said?" I questioned. "Who is this guy?"

I could think of only one answer—Paul had been telling the truth all along. But that couldn't be, could it? I finally closed my computer after a couple minutes of telling myself

I was letting my imagination get the best of me. I swallowed the last mouthful of cider and went to bed. As I lay in the dark, I promised myself I'd bring a copy of Paul's translation of the Petros Fragment to Bob Coffman in the morning.

The next day I found Bob sitting in his office grading papers.

"I have something I want you to see if you have a minute."

"Sure," he said, "what is it?"

"I hope you'll tell me what you think of this," I said and handed him a photocopy of Paul's note. I'd blocked out all his personal correspondence with me, leaving only the translation of the letter fragment.

He read the translation like a pharmacist reads a doctor's handwritten prescription. With each line, Bob's eyes squinted, and he tilted his head as if he wasn't sure what he read. The look on his face confirmed what I'd suspected. There was something to this. That was for sure.

"Where did you get this?" Bob asked, almost bouncing in his chair.

I had never seen him so excited. "A friend of mine saw the Petros Fragment in my office and gave me this a few days later."

"I can't say for sure without doing a comprehensive word-by-word comparison with the original letter," Bob said. "But at first glance, I'd say this is a brilliant combination of translation and speculation. This is something which would ordinarily take months or even years to postulate. Who is this friend of yours anyway?"

"I'm really not sure," I said. "And even if I did know, I couldn't say because he's a client. The whole thing is complicated."

"Well, he's either a savant, or he's an extremely gifted linguist and historian. This is an amazing piece of work. I'd really like to meet him if there's any way to get around this client/patient confidentiality thing."

"Sure. Maybe. I don't know. I don't think so, but I'll see what I can do."

"Do you mind if I make a copy of this? I'd really like to do a comparative study of it with the original. If it's okay with you, I'd like to show it to some of my colleagues too."

"All right," I said. "If you want. Let me know what you find out."

With that said, he duplicated my copy of Paul's note. I thanked him for his time and left. To be honest, I secretly hoped Paul's translation was a hoax, but Bob's comments fueled my imagination with more questions.

chapter 23

MONSTERS

We can easily forgive a child who is afraid of the dark;
the real tragedy of life is when men are afraid of the
light.—Plato, *The Republic*

That Sunday, after Lucy went to bed, I sat in a green
wicker rocker on the front porch. My mood matched the
weather—brooding. There's something hauntingly inviting
and forbidding about watching a storm roll in across Lake
Michigan. Billowing black clouds filled the western horizon.
Lightning momentarily flashed across the sky. Then the
muffled rumble of thunder boomed like a distant drum.
Occasionally, the sweeping beam from Big Red pierced the
rapidly darkening sky. The fierce wind blew through the
trees around the house with such force the branches chafed
against the siding. Heavy rolling whitecaps crashed into the
beach. I knew this would be a big one.

As a boy, Grandpa Sea would often quote from the book
of Job in a thunderstorm.

"Listen." he'd say, slowly putting his bony pointer finger
to his lips with a grin.

"Listen to the roar of his voice, to the rumbling that comes from his mouth. He unleashes his lightning beneath the whole heaven and sends it to the ends of the earth. After that comes the sound of his roar, he thunders with his majestic voice. When his voice resounds, he holds nothing back."

Again, the thunder grumbled in the distance, and lightening flashed for a brief second, exposing the foamy surf pounding the shore. The wind drove the rain through the screens with such force I went back inside. For a while, I sat at the kitchen table with my MacBook and tried to grade some papers online, but I couldn't concentrate. Random thoughts flittered through my mind like a honeybee in a field of flowers. I finally put the grading aside. On a whim, once again I tried to research the words 'Petros Fragment' on the internet to see what I could find.

I clicked on a picture of Bob. He was at the dig site with an Israeli archeologist named Dr. Avrehim Laubstein. The two men were facing each other. Bob was showing Laubstein the fragment which rested on a large oval metal tray. Laubstein had a beard, and a hat partly covered his face, but from what I could see he bore a striking resemblance to Paul.

Could this be my patient? I couldn't get the possibility out of my mind.

When I researched Laubstein, I discovered that a year and a half after finding the fragment, he received serious injuries in an accident when an IED, an improvised explosive device, went off at a shrine in southern Syria.

ISIS had put out a propaganda video claiming they had hidden IEDs in several ancient Jewish, Christian, and even Muslim holy places. Their intent was to intimidate the local population and instill fear in their hearts. They succeeded. The locals refused to help, but Dr. Laubstein and his wife, Marta, ignored the warning and joined a large United Nations task force to preserve the ancient sites and prevent their destruction. The decision would prove to be costly.

One of the targets mentioned in the video was a statue still under construction in Syria near the town of Heena, where Jesus reportedly appeared to Paul on the road to Damascus. The statue was a bronze figure commemorating the conversion of the apostle Paul. While the UN team was examining the site, the IED exploded, sending a hail of shrapnel and mayhem into the air.

Dr. Nasser Hawassi from Jordan was the one who stepped on the device. He, Rebecca Fienberg, a graduate student from London, and Marta Laubstein died instantly. A low stone wall partially shielded Dr. Laubstein, who stood a few feet away from the blast. The shrapnel, however, had unmercifully slashed through the flesh and bone in his back, shoulders, and left arm. He also had superficial, but significant lacerations on his neck, cheek, and ear.

After he was stabilized at nearby Dar Al Shifa Hospital in Damascus, he went to the University of Michigan hospital in Ann Arbor to be treated by Dr. Arnold W. Hatfield, an army colonel who completed his vascular surgery fellowship at Mayo Clinic in 1997.

The article said after six months and several surgeries, Laubstein was sent to Mary Freebed Hospital in Grand Rapids, Michigan, for rehab. I checked with a doctor I knew who works there. She said Laubstein recovered physically but continued to struggle emotionally. A little less than a month ago, he left the hospital unexpectedly without telling anyone.

"We haven't heard from him since," she said. "We really have no idea where he is now."

I have an idea. I needed to know more before I shared my suspicions with anyone. Besides, I still hadn't ruled out Gabriel Shalhoub, the former historical curator of the Maronite

Catholic Church. My patient could easily be either of them or neither of them. At this point, I couldn't reach a decision.

As I sat there, I remembered something Dr. Finkbinder, one of my psychology professors, once said, "Sometimes you have to go a little crazy before you can begin to make sense of tragedy."

Maybe he was right. If Paul was, in fact, Laubstein or Shalhoub, then Finkbinder's comment might be an accurate description of what happened to him.

I sat at the table with a warm cup of Earl Gray and turned the teabag with my spoon. The storm raged outside, and I raged inside. In my head, I picked a bone with a comment Paul had made a couple of days earlier.

"There are times," he said, "when the winds and the waves are good for your soul."

There are also times when they are like an undertow that takes your mind into the depths of despair. This is one of those times. Not only am I not sure who Paul is, I'm not sure who I am either.

One of the things I've discovered is fear and doubt are nocturnal. They often come out after sunset to haunt our idle thoughts. That happened to me as I listened to the thunderstorm sweep across the lake.

"I didn't sign up for this," I whispered, under my breath, half praying and half complaining. "I always expected Rachel to do the bulk of the parenting with our children. She'd be the compassionate one, the understanding one, the one with all the right answers. I'd be the fun one. She'd do the heavy lifting, and I'd be the frosting on the cake. I could do frosting, but not this. This is too much to ask."

Then, as if God had read my mind, I was roused from my wandering thoughts by a loud crack of thunder and the sound of Lucy's voice calling to me from her room.

"Daddy," she said in a trembling little voice. "Daddy, are you there?"

"Yes, I'm here," I said, making my way to her bedroom. "Did the storm wake you up, honey? Did you have a bad dream?"

"I think I heard something under my bed."

I wanted to say, "Oh, Lucy, there's no reason to be afraid. The scariest monsters live in our heads, not under our beds," but I didn't. Instead, I did Rachel's job. I sat beside Lucy and lied. I told her there was no such thing as monsters. There's nothing hiding in the darkness that isn't there in the light.

"The sound is just the wind from the storm blowing through the branches of the trees," I said.

Then I turned on the light and closed the window in her room.

"If you'll feel better, I'll check under the bed and in the closet."

She nodded, and I kept my promise. I got her a glass of milk and some Chessmen shortbread cookies and tried to make her laugh.

"Uh-oh, Lucy," I said apologetically. "You were right. I've taken a second look, and there *is* a monster under your bed—a monster dust-bunny. I'm so sorry. Daddy's not very good at cleaning."

We laughed, but the levity didn't last long.

"Daddy," she said as the lightning flashed outside her window, "I miss Mommy."

"I miss Mommy too," I said.

"I know," she said, burying her head in my chest with a bear hug. "Sometimes I hear you crying at night. I know you want to be with her, Daddy, but don't go. I don't think I could stand losing you too."

I guess I've been so angry about losing her mother I never thought Lucy might be worried about losing me. Grief can be a self-absorbing monster. We can easily wrap ourselves in a cocoon of anger and self-pity and ignore the cries for help from the world around us. That had happened to me. Thankfully, Lucy's words opened my eyes to her fears.

"Don't worry, Lucy," I said, looking her in the eye. "I'm not going anywhere. I'll always be here for you. I promised Mommy I would take care of you, and I will. *I will*."

Then I squeezed her really hard as tears streamed down my face.

"I love you, Daddy," she said softly.

"I love you too, honey," I said, trying not to let her see me cry. "Why don't I stay here with you until you fall asleep. Would that be all right?"

"That would be great," she said. Twenty minutes later, after the storm had passed, I quietly slipped out of her room and sat down in the living room and turned on the TV.

chapter 24

Secrets

> If you want to keep a secret, you must also hide it from
> yourself. You must know all the while that it is there, but
> until it is needed you must never let it emerge into your
> consciousness in any shape that can be given a name.
> — George Orwell, *1984*

I took the time to record the upcoming episode of *60 Minutes* with an intriguing trailer. The tick-tock of the stopwatch counted down the seconds. Scott Pelley's voiceover said the shadowy priest he interviewed six months earlier had suddenly disappeared. Three weeks after shedding light on the dark secrets of the Roman Catholic Church, Father Paul Andrew Aboud mysteriously vanished without a word. According to a spokesperson for the Toronto monastery, one night he retired to his sleeping quarters as usual and the next morning, he was gone.

"What's happened to him," Pelley said, "and maybe even more disturbing, why? This story and more tonight on *60 Minutes*."

The ad did what it was supposed to do—piqued my curiosity. I had seen the earlier episode, and like many others, I wanted to know what happened to the priest who called out the Catholic Church. A part of me also wondered if the mysterious disappearance of Paul Aboud might somehow be connected to my Paul's appearance at the mission. When I turned on my VCR, my suspicions grew even stronger.

"Paul was not concerned for his own safety," Pelley said. "However, for his protection we chose to keep his identity hidden during our last interview. In his absence, that's no longer necessary. In fact, now by revealing his name and photograph, we hope someone will come forward with information that might help solve this mystery."

A grainy black and white picture of a young priest flashed across the screen with the identification as being from Aboud's ordination twenty years before. I could see a slight resemblance to my patient. This Paul was a slim man, with middle eastern features, short, curly hair, and a neatly trimmed beard—perhaps in his mid-twenties. A scar on his left cheek caught my attention. My mind soon ran down the rabbit hole. I found myself wallowing in the wonderland of conjecture, innuendo, and wild speculation. I started connecting the dots like a kid with a puzzle book.

"His name is Father Boulous Andreas Aboud," Pelley said. "Everyone calls him Father Paul. *Aboud* is Arabic for God's Servant, and according to those we talked to, he lived up to his name."

"Boulous was born to Ouseph and Rabka Aboud in 1979," Pelley said. "They lived in a middle-class suburb of Hama, a city on the banks of the Orontes River, forty-nine miles north of Damascus. His parents were part of the Syrian Catholic church. Ouseph was an electrical engineer, an outspoken supporter of the new political regime in Syria. Rabka worked part-time as an elementary school teacher."

A map of Syria and pictures of a bombed-out village began to shuffle across the screen.

"For months," Pelley said, "tensions had been escalating. The political unrest was a concern for the Abouds, but they believed government troops would keep the rebels in check. They didn't realize they were about to be caught in the crossfire of competing Islamic ideologies. On one side were the Sunni extremists, most of whom were members of the Muslim Brotherhood. On the other side was the more secular Ba'ath Party which controlled the government of Syria.

"Random acts of terrorism occurred in neighboring towns and villages, with both sides accusing the other of instigating the violence. By spring, no one was safe, least of all non-Muslims. The sound of gunfire and mortar became commonplace. Ouseph and Rabka began to wonder if they should relocate to Turkey.

The Abouds realized their worst fears one moonlit night in May. Masked gunmen kicked in the door of their home. Ouseph tried to defend his family with a kitchen knife but met a hailstorm of automatic weapons. Moments later, Rabka met the same fate as she tried to shield her baby with her body. In the final act of terror, one of the insurgents fired three rounds into the baby's crib.

"Blood splattered everywhere. A bullet pierced the child's shoulder, another miraculously missed, and a third tore open the child's cheek. To this day, he carries the scar."

Middle Eastern descent, I thought, with a scar on his cheek. That certainly fits.

"An hour later," Pelley continued, "neighbors found the infant unconscious and hardly breathing in his bloody crib. They brought him to the house of Cardinal Gregorio Schaphini, Archbishop of the Syriacs."

"Cardinal Schaphini and his personal aide, Father Francesco Giuliani, set up a makeshift medical clinic in the rectory, and they tended to the boy's wounds as best they could. Eventually the Archbishop smuggled the child out of the country on a plane chartered by the Vatican for the evacuation of the remaining Syrian clergy. The Archbishop made sure his staff left the country, but he refused to leave his small congregation.

"Instead, he gave Father Giuliani the necessary paperwork and instructed him to bring the infant to the home of his parents in Rome. Though in their late sixties, Dr. Lorenzo—a retired pediatric surgeon—and Sophia Schaphini—his OR nurse—were qualified to tend to the child's medical needs temporarily.

Dr. Schaphini and his wife adopted young Boulous and changed his name from Arabic to Italian and that's when Boulous became Paolo, or as we'd say in English, Paul. As they had with Gregorio, they provided him with the best education money could buy.

"Paolo attended Rome's famed Massimiliano Massimo Institute, a Jesuit school considered one of the most prestigious and exclusive schools in the country. Thereafter, Paolo attended the Pontifical Biblical Institute for his university work in linguistics. While there, both Sophia and Lorenzo died leaving Paolo the totality of their estate. The following spring, he graduated summa cum laude, took a vow of poverty, and donated the bulk of the inheritance to the Jesuits before being ordained. He later officially changed his name to Paul and received his Ph.D. in Biblical Linguistics. He is fluent in Italian, Greek, Hebrew, Latin, Arabic, and English.

"Paul served as a teaching fellow at the Seminary of the Latin Patriarchate of Jerusalem in the town of Beit Jala, Palestine. Five years later, he became the Augustine Professor of Linguistics and served in that role for nine years. His academic prowess, humility, and charisma earned him the prestigious posting as the assistant to the prefect of the Vatican Secret Archives."

The dominos are falling faster than I can process them. I need to write all this down.

As Pelley continued to talk, photos of the schools scrolled across the screen, ending with a picture of the Secret Archive's exterior. No photography is allowed inside the walls except by the archivists themselves.

"Anything housed in the Vatican Secret Archives," Pelley said, "is the exclusive property of the Pope. He has complete control over any access to this treasure-trove of documents. Still, according to church officials, the situation is not quite as nefarious as we might think. A true understanding of the Latin word 'secret' might better be rendered 'private.' However, parts of the archives remain classified and off limits even to most members of the clergy.

"Among the materials actively prohibited for outside viewing include documents relating to contemporary personalities and activities. This includes the private records of any members of the clergy for the last seventy-five years.

"Father Paul Aboud worked with this material during his time in Rome. In fact, the rumor was he was working on a 'secret' paper for the Holy Father when he was abruptly transferred to his post in Toronto."

Once again, the priest's grainy black and white ordination picture appeared on the screen. My mind was spinning with possibilities and justifications of who this man might be today—Father Paul, Gabriel Shalhoub, or Laubstein maybe? I didn't know, but I had my suspicions.

"So, what exactly happened to Father Paul Andrew Aboud?" Pelley asked. "Where did he go and why? Is he being held somewhere against his will? Is he running away from whatever trauma haunts his past, and if he is, does he want to be found?"

Once again, a picture of the Toronto monastery appeared briefly on the screen.

"Some of those we talked to suggested he was mysteriously called back to the Vatican for some secretive assignment. Is that the case or was his return something more sinister? Was he about to share something embarrassing he uncovered while working in the Vatican Secret Archives? And if he was, is Paul being cloistered somewhere to keep him silent?"

Pelley paused to let the listeners ponder the possibilities.

"We have lots of questions," he said, "but no answers yet. We aired this episode hoping some of you might be able to help us. If you have any information about Father Paul Andrew Aboud, please contact us here at *60 Minutes*. We promise to share any new information we might learn in the coming weeks."

I turned off the TV and tried to make sense out of what I'd heard. I wanted to call CBS and have a talk with someone in Pelley's office, but to do so would be unethical, a clear breach of confidentiality. Besides, I had only a hunch at this point and even that was a stretch. There was no proof, no reason to go jumping to conclusions.

"This is ridiculous," I said, somewhat frustrated that I'd allowed my mind to tumble into this fantasy in the first place. "What am I doing?"

For a few minutes, I sat there quite disgusted with myself. I turned the TV back on and tried to get lost in an episode of NCIS. For a little while, at least, the program was my escape from reality. Finally, after watching the weather at eleven o'clock, I went to bed hoping to fall asleep before I fell apart. I didn't. The escape proved only temporary. As I lay in the dark, old thoughts and questions came calling again. My mind played ping-pong with the possibilities of Paul's identity. I mulled the mystery over in my mind until thoughts of him gave way to thoughts of Rachel.

If only she were here, I could spoon up behind her and sleep. God knows I'm a wreck without her. My running argument with God was on again.

Why did you take her from me, God? Never mind. I don't even want to hear your reasons anymore. In fact, I don't want to hear anything from you. I've made my peace with the silence, so I'll tell you what. I'll make a bargain with you, God. You stay out of my business and I'll stay out of yours.

Even as I thought those words, I realized I was making a one-sided contract. God never agreed to the deal. He simply sat silently in his heaven and watched me struggle.

chapter 25

Marriage

What right had I to imagine that she would wish to unite her life with mine? Who and what am I? A man of no account, wanted by no one and of no use to anyone.
—Leo Tolstoy, *Anna Karenina*

The email had arrived two days earlier from Summerdyke's office.

"As you indicated, a medical examination confirmed the client was the victim of a severe physical trauma, the exact time or cause not revealed. The resulting scar tissue, however, indicates the incident did not occur in the patient's immediate past. Perhaps the scarring is the result of an old combat injury or an automobile accident or even prolonged physical abuse. There's no way to be certain, but we also suspect the injuries might have something to do with his psychotic break. We would encourage you to probe this further, if possible. Once again, we ask you to submit a follow-up report upon completion of your final session."

Paul arrived early for our one o'clock appointment. He was in the waiting room when I came back from lunch. He walked into the office with me and took his usual seat.

"I hear you're talking to God again," he said, smiling. "You've taken the first step in a long journey, but you're on your way now, and that's what matters."

His meaning eluded me, so I let it slide. However, I knew where I wanted the conversation to go in this session. I knew better than to try to unmask his delusion directly or to force him into a confrontation. I'm paid to help him root out reality, though, and I would do my job. With the recent revelations of the *60 Minutes* report, I started our session with a question.

"Have you ever been to Canada?" I asked.

"No. Why do you ask?"

"No reason, really," I said, "I was thinking about going there sometime."

Internally, I chastised myself for being so direct. What was I thinking? Did I believe mentioning the maple leaf would cause his story to come spilling out of him? Mentioning Canada was a foolish thing to do. As we went forward, I promised myself that I'd be less obvious.

I knew Laubstein lost his wife in the explosion in Syria. With that in mind, I took the opportunity to pose a question to see if I might expose a chink in the armor of his presumed identity.

"Paul," I said. "The other night, I seemed to recall you said something about your wife. I went back through my notes, and they confirmed my memory. I realized you'd never mentioned your marriage, and I wondered why."

"The marriage bed," Paul said without hesitating, "was a prerequisite for a seat on the Sanhedrin. Since that was my ambition, I married my second cousin, Shamir, before leaving Tarsus for Jerusalem. My father and his cousin Elazar, a wealthy merchant, made arrangements for us to be married while we were both small children. Ten years later, two days after I accepted the invitation to study in Jerusalem, my father and I met with Elazar to pay the 'bride price.'

"We sat on a mat under an awning in the courtyard of their house while Shamir, her sisters, and her mother listened from inside the front doorway. A servant brought us a small bowl of figs and some wine, and after extending the obligatory hospitality, Elazar spoke.

"'The price for replacing this daughter will be extremely high,' he said, looking down at the ground and shaking his head slightly. 'I'm not sure you'll want to pay it. Like her mother, my Shamir is a woman of rare beauty. Perhaps you would do better to consider one of her older sisters. We do not normally give away the younger daughter before her older siblings. Salome and Shiphrah are both strong and well mannered, and the price would likely be much more reasonable for either one of them.'

"Then Elazar raise his eyebrows, tilted his head, and looked at me with a long, silent, awkward pause.

"Like Laban with Leah, Elazar was hoping to substitute his older daughter for his younger, but I would have none of it. I shook my head in defiance, and then my father spoke."

"'We came for Shamir,' he said, 'and we will not be persuaded otherwise.'

"'But you know Shamir has always been my favorite," Elazar continued. 'And to be honest, her mother and I are having second thoughts. We're not ready to let her go. If you are unwilling to accept one of her sisters, perhaps you should come back again in a year or two.'

"Every father says these kinds of things," Paul said, "but with Elazar it was true. He and Shamir were always very close.

"'My kinsman,' said my father in a firm and deliberate tone, 'we made these arrangements many years ago while our children were both still young. If you'll remember, you approached me. You suggested the engagement, you set the

143

bride's price, and when I agreed, we sealed the troth with an oath. These things can't simply be undone.'

"My father continued. 'Since their betrothal, your daughter has blossomed in both form and appearance. My son is fortunate to have such a woman as his bride, and surely the men in our village will rise up and call him blessed. No one is denying that, but the balance scale tilts both ways.

"'My son is not only strong and handsome, but his reputation as a scholar is unsurpassed. He is the only student Mordecai has ever had who has been invited to study with Gamaliel in Jerusalem. In the highest circles of our faith, they are already whispering that one day he will sit with the elders in the Sanhedrin. So, you must be careful not to test my resolve, my cousin, lest I start asking you to renegotiate our contract.'

"Eventually," Paul said, "my father paid the originally agreed-upon dowry. With the negotiations complete, Shamir and her mother joined us on the mat. Slowly my father poured out the drink offering and handed the cup to me. I then turned to Shamir, offered her the wine, and said the words of promise.

"'This cup is our covenant,' I whispered as I held out the cup. 'I offer it to you with this promise. From this day forward and forever, I give you my life and my love.'

"To my surprise she was tentative. For a moment, she froze like a startled deer in the forest. She glanced at her mother, who quietly nodded her approval. Then the slightest hint of a smile crept across Shamir's face. With that, she accepted the cup, and without saying a word, took a long, slow sip. The sun shimmered off her wet lips. By drinking the wine, she accepted my offer and was offering her life to me as well.

"Smiling broadly, Elazar then put his hands on our shoulders and offered his blessing. The wedding date was set for two weeks from that day.

"Our custom is for the groom and his father to begin construction of an addition on the family compound, but in our case, construction was not necessary. There were many rooms in my father's house. Besides, I knew I would soon leave my father and mother, and my new wife and I would be on our way to the city of David. What I didn't know was that our union would be so difficult at first."

She was both a very charming and a very challenging woman. With one seductive glance from her eye, my heart would explode into unquenchable flames of passion. But with another, she could drive a thorn deep into my soul.

Every time Paul said her name, his speech would slow. He would drag out each syllable with a gentle sigh of tenderness. The pendulum of my mind had now swung fully away from the Canadian priest to either Shalhoub or Laubstein. I was almost sure. This is a man who knows what it was like to love a woman.

"Shaa-meeir," Paul said, "had an unparalleled beauty. She was tall and graceful, like a palm tree swaying in the wind. Her coal black eyes could capture your gaze like a young fawn on the edge of the field. Her head was crowned with a forest of raven-colored curls that danced across her shoulders. Her almond-colored skin was as smooth and delicate as Arabian silk, and her lips were like the seeds of a pomegranate drizzled in wild honey.

"As she walked," Paul said as if he was remembering, "the hem of her robe swept the desert sands with such an ethereal enticement, a righteous man had to force himself to look away. Ah, but despite her haunting beauty, she could also be quite prickly at times.

"You see," he said, "my Shamir was her father's favorite and quite used to getting her own way. Spoiled she was—I must admit I was as well. Neither of us had ever had to develop a taste for compromise, so when we disagreed, the flint would spark an argument, and we would fight like hungry jackals.

"Ah, but when we made up," Paul said with a grin. "Then this same heat and passion would manifest itself in other ways. Before long, I would be holding her trembling body close and whispering my apology in her ear. Then our love would burst into flames of passion. Making love to such a woman is extremely addictive."

He paused for a moment almost as if he'd forgotten how sweet her kiss could be. Then he proceeded slowly with the trace of a smirk on his face.

"I soon learned," he said, "winning an argument with Shamir paled in comparison to drinking in the sweet taste of her affection. So more often than not, she got her way. Shamir held my heart in the palm of her hand.

"On more than one occasion, my brother-in-law Ariel would witness her fiery temper.

"'Paul,' he would say, 'you must learn to control your woman.'

"'Can the wild lion control the lioness?' I would ask. 'No, he can only marvel at her beauty and try his best to avoid her claws.'

"Such was the agony and ecstasy of my first year of marriage.

"Passion was always a part of our lives," Paul said, pausing slightly. "But as our love grew deeper, so did our respect for each other. In our second year of marriage, we only argued about one thing. I wanted children. She wanted to see the world. However, about six months after we settled into our living quarters in Jerusalem, this maternal desire to nest began to blossom somewhere deep in the depths of her soul."

For a moment, a peaceful smile came across Paul's face. Then he continued.

"We had rented an apartment from Ariel," he said. "Shamir spent her days shopping the markets and bazaars of Jerusalem with my sister Phoebe. They almost always brought my ten-year-old nephew, Benjamin, and Phoebe's fourteen-month-old twins. Perhaps seeing the joy which the two toddlers brought their mother caused Shamir's change of heart, because suddenly, she was the one talking about having children. A newfound passion was aroused in her. At her bidding, we nightly engaged in the business of making a baby—perhaps the sweetest year of my life."

"Yes," I whispered in my heart. "Nothing brings more joy to a man's soul than the love of a good woman. She completes him—makes him whole. There is no way a priest could know such things."

For a few moments, I was so lost in thoughts about Rachel, I almost didn't notice the tears chasing down the laugh-lines of Paul's cheeks.

chapter 26

BROKEN

The less you see your own brokenness, the more broken you are.—Kyle Idleman, *The End of Me*

"Are you all right, Paul?" I asked. "Is something wrong?"

He paused and turned his head toward me. His eyes glistened as he tried to blink back his tears. Paul took a sniffling breath, wiped his cheeks with one hand, and slowly continued.

"A little less than a year later, my joy turned to torment and tears," he murmured softly. "Shamir and the child were both taken from me as she labored to give the boy birth. Sometimes, I still hear her screams in my dreams. The only thing worse was the silence that followed. Death blew in like the winter wind and chilled my heart to the bone. I could feel his presence. Somehow, I knew he was coming for her, but I refused to let her go without a fight.

"You cannot have her," I shouted, as Death circled the two of us like a hungry jackal. "I was wrong. Even as I held her in my arms, I could feel her life slip through my fingers. Death is a relentless bully, and he will not stop until he gets what he wants. As the Spirit of God had his way with her soul, Death had his way with her flesh, and she grew cold and lifeless in my arms. Hers was a life too short, and the unfairness of it still burns in my heart.

"Still," Paul said with a sigh, "the depth of love, not the length, matters. Our love was a bottomless pit. I knew I would never love anyone like that again. For all these years, I have carried that thought like a thorn in my flesh. Yet somehow, by God's grace, I've learned to live without a woman's embrace.

"Like a fox in a vineyard," Paul continued, regaining his composure, "Death devours everything he sees. Too many times, I've seen Death take those I love, and each time he comes with the smug confidence of a conquering hero. Like a Roman general in his *trimphus*, his crimson cape flutters behind him in the wind. And the sight of him always dredges up memories of my Shamir. Death and sadness have a way of piling up.

"Nine days later, my brother-in-law Ariel came to see me with a letter from my old mentor, Mordecai.

"'I regret to inform you,' the Rabin wrote in a shaky hand, 'that your father went to bed two nights ago and never awoke from his sleep. Your brother Yaakov is taking good care of your mother, and he is making sure the family business continues. Your father was a good man, well respected and well loved, and he lived a full life. No one can expect more from this life. You and your family are in my thoughts and prayers. I trust that God's grace will comfort your troubled soul.'

"The letter was simply signed 'Mordecai,'" Paul said. "I took his signature as his way of acknowledging the student was now the peer of his old master."

After a long silent pause, Paul spoke in a solemn tone.

"The news of my father's death only deepened my grief. The weight of the tragedy pushed me deeper into the pursuit of meaning. Methodically, I picked my way through the ancient words of my ancestors. I knew meaning, if it was to be found at all, would only be found in the study of Torah."

The pain of remembering genuinely seemed to shake his confidence. Rarely had I seen someone so delusional talk and act so rational. Real or not, he felt the pain of the memory. I'd learned long ago never to question anyone's feelings. Whether real or imagined, the pain *felt* real to Paul, therefore, in his mind at least, the pain *was* real. Even now, reliving the pain was agonizing for him.

"How did you deal with the pain of such significant losses?" I asked. For the first time, I realized that, on some level at least, this man and I were brothers. We both had loved and lost, and the pain was a part of us now.

"Not very well at first," he said. "Sometimes, the only thing I could do was to get lost in prayer."

His words startled me. His pain caused him to pray more? How could that be? Mine did the opposite. Delusional or not, Paul was a holy man—his depth of faith obvious. Now more than ever, I wanted to hear what else he had to say.

"I'd sit for hours with my eyes closed," he said in a voice as smooth as a breeze. "Slowly, I rocked back and forth, as I'd been taught, softly chanting the psalms."

A touch of vulnerability and disappointment crept back into his tone.

"David once wrote 'God is near to the broken hearted,' but truthfully if he was there, I never saw him. I never felt him either. Only Gamaliel came to sit with me on the mourner's bench. When I couldn't look on the bright side of life, he came and sat with me in the dark. At the time, I wondered why he bothered. Who knows, maybe God sent him. At least I like to think so now."

"'You need to talk about this, Sha'ul,' the great teacher would say, but giving language to my pain was difficult."

For a few moments, Paul closed his eyes and silently rocked his head back and forth very slowly.

"No, wait, don't stop here," I whispered somewhere deep in my soul. "I need to hear more. Speak to me. I need to know how you handled the pain." Right on cue, Paul continued.

"The loss drove me to silence," he said so softly I could hardly hear him. With his eyes closed, he continued to rock ever so slightly. His bobbing head made him look like a man drunk on his own memories.

"I learned as a boy to keep my emotions to myself," Paul said as if he regretted the advice. "Strong men hide their feelings. At least, the old men in my village told us.

"The most shameful thing a man could ever do," they said, "was to cry in public.

"I knew if I spoke of her," Paul said, "I would immediately start to weep uncontrollably. So, I masked my brokenness in bitterness. Otherwise, I would have been emotionally naked, unacceptable in a man.

"I now know the only shame in mourning the loss of someone we love is to keep our emotions buried inside. When we do that, we are no help to ourselves or to others. Sometimes a prayer of lament is an act of faith, but instead of facing my pain, I ran from it. Instead of inviting God into my broken heart, I blamed him for what happened. Bitterness will feed on your soul if you let it."

Once again Paul closed his eyes and began rocking his head back and forth.

"*Kaphar li, Avinu*," he whispered.

He said those words over and over again. From what I could remember of my Hebrew, he was saying, "forgive me, my Father," or more literally, "cover over my guilt, my Father."

In that moment, I could only think a long time had passed since I asked God to cover over my guilt with his grace. However, before I could talk to God about it, Paul continued his story.

"I told Gamaliel," he said again, making eye contact with me. "I could not worship a God I could not trust."

"'Then I will just have to trust him enough for both of us,' the old man replied.

"And after that, the two of us regularly sat together on the mourner's bench following our evening meal. We rarely said a word. We didn't have to. Most of the time I was confused, bewildered, and angry. Like David 'my bones wasted away through my groaning.' Shamir's death lay heavy on my heart like a stone."

Once again, Paul closed his eyes and sat quietly. He looked to be pondering his own thoughts as if reliving Shamir's death in his mind. Delusion or not, the loss was reality in his head. I had to fight my desire to take his words at face value. The clinical side of me knew extreme trauma can play tricks with the mind, which is what amnesia, delusion, and schizophrenia so often have in common. Something so terrible has happened in the patient's past their mind does whatever is necessary to block out the trauma in the present.

"As we sat silently together on the mourner's bench," Paul said, looking up with a reassuring smile. "People didn't quite know what to make of us. Usually, they had one of two reactions. They either thought we were lost in a heavenly trance or trying to rid ourselves of a demonic curse. In truth, both were probably right. There's a fine line between inspiration and insanity. Who whispered in my ear—God or Satan? Often, I did not know. I only knew the angels and the demons had taken up their places in this tug-o-war of lament, and they constantly pulled me from one side of the line to the other."

Paul's observation was astute. Without reacting, I made a note in his file.

I wish I had a mourners' bench. I wish even more someone would join me there. But then, as my thoughts turned melancholy, Paul's voice brought me back to the moment.

"I think that's why Gamaliel sat with me so often. He was simply living up to his name. Gamaliel means 'God's recompense,' or as you might say, 'God's compensation.' Sometimes, after someone has lost a child, they name their next child Gamaliel. In this way, they honor God with their grief. As Job said, 'the Lord gave, and the Lord has taken away; may the name of the Lord be praised.'

"Having the one doesn't make up for the loss of the other, of course," Paul said as if he was reading my mind. "But the joy of the one mingles with the grief of the other. This doesn't make everything right, but we remember even in our grief, some things are right. Does that make sense?"

I nodded slightly, and for a few minutes, we sat together in silence. Then Paul smiled, got up, and walked out the door. When he left, I sat in my office for an hour and cried. I cried for his loss, I cried for my loss, and I cried for anyone who'd ever lost someone they loved. The Bible says Jesus wept as he stood outside Lazarus's tomb. There was a part of me that knew exactly how he felt. Sometimes all you can do is cry.

chapter 27

CHOICES

Two roads diverged in a wood, and I—I took the one less traveled by, and that has made all the difference.— Robert Frost, *The Road Not Taken*

"A good teacher worries about his talmadim, his students," Paul said, walking into my office and sitting down in the wingback. "In my case, there was good reason. Bitterness, uncertainty, and anger dogged my steps relentlessly like a fox chasing a frightened mouse."

A part of me wondered if he was talking about me, but no. Paul had the uncanny ability to pick up a new session exactly where he left off in the last one. A month had passed since our last meeting, and to be honest, I missed the man. A part of me worried maybe we were getting too close, and another part of me was glad we were.

"After Shamir and the boy died, any mercy I might have had evaporated in the flames of the refiner's fire," Paul said, slumping in the chair. "Pain is often the path one takes to becoming a zealot, and I was well on my way.

"One night," he said, following a deep sigh, "as the sun dipped like a dying candle behind the horizon, Gamaliel broke his silence.

"'You have grieved long enough, my son,' he said. 'Now you have a choice to make. This kind of pain either sends a man running into the arms of God or running away from him. You need to pick your direction. I've done all I could do to help you find the right path. Now you must decide. Will you embrace God's law and his love, or will you reject him? Choose wisely, my son. Forever is a long time to be wrong.'

"To be sure, I was lost," Paul said. "For a while, I didn't know which way I would go. Grief is a dark chasm, a bottomless black hole, and when you fall headlong into it, you spend your days groping for something to hang on to. Some days, I turned my back on God. Partly, I suppose, because he seemed to turn his back on me. Other days, I ran to him like a prodigal son, hoping to find some comfort in his fatherly embrace. Through it all, Gamaliel held me like the arms of God and silently tried to inhale some of my pain. His embrace made the unbearable a little better.

"I once told him I didn't think I could stand the pain.

"'You can't,' Gamaliel said. 'But thankfully when you've reached the end of yourself, you've arrived at the beginning of God, and he will walk with you through this whether you want him to or not.'

"With Gamaliel's help," Paul said with a slight smile, "I gradually immersed myself in the scrolls and scriptures. Day and night, I looked for a rational explanation, some absolute truth which could explain my situation. Finally, eleven months later, I emerged from my sorrows with the conviction the world was awash in a sea of unfairness and cruelty. Life, and any joy it brings, is fleeting. 'We brought nothing into this world, and we'll take nothing with us when we go.' But the one constant, the only thing that is the same yesterday, today, and forever, is the law of God.

"After that," Paul continued, "the law became my lover. I embraced every facet with all my heart, and I had no tolerance for anyone who did anything less. Complete obedience not only became my goal, but also my expectation. Not only was this true for me—but for everyone.

"Things I might have previously overlooked suddenly became cause for immediate confrontation. I saw myself as the defender of the law. In my mind at least, I was 'God's angel of justice.' Whenever I observed someone flagrantly ignoring the law, my response was swift and deliberate. I would call them out publicly and demand immediate full punishment for their crime. Ultimately, my zealousness earned me the nickname *Aleph Eben*, 'the first stone,' because, whenever the elders imposed the death penalty, I was the first one to pick up a rock.

"The older members of the Sanhedrin not only noticed, but also encouraged me. I reveled in their approval, which fueled my intolerance for anything short of perfect obedience to the law. There was one exception, however. He didn't voice his disapproval directly, but I could tell Gamaliel had reservations about my new-found zeal. I saw disapproval in his eyes and heard his condemnation in the tone of his words.

"He despised legalism. Instead, he would champion things like moderation and balance. 'The law of God and the love of God are like his heart and his soul,' Gamaliel would often say. 'They are two sides of the same coin, and we must never try to separate the two.'

"I, of course, took issue with that," Paul said.

"'There is no love in the law,' I said defiantly, 'only justice.' But instead of arguing with me, Gamaliel's face fell in disappointment.

"'My son,' he said. 'Do you not know the love of God is woven through every fiber of creation? His love gives us shelter and strength in troubled times. In fact, love is the strongest thing on earth—even stronger than death.'

"Under the weight of his rebuke, I found myself at a loss for words, and with nothing to say, I took a seat at my master's feet.

"His ways of toying with me were subtle, but effective. For example, he always referred to his students as his 'little puppies' because of the way we followed him around. Yet, he called me his 'little *Shu'al*,' his 'little fox'—a humorous bit of wordplay with my name, but still I felt the sting of it."

I knew from my language studies in seminary that ancient Hebrew originally contained no vowels, only consonants. The reader supplies the "intonations," or vowels, by context which sounds harder than the reality. For example, try reading the following sentence.

"Lv th Lrd yr Gd wth ll yr hrt."

"This is the first line of the forty-sixth Psalm and reads, 'Love the Lord your God with all your heart.'

"Gamaliel was doing this, but by transposing the supplied vowels in Paul's name, he changed the meaning.

"I'm not sure he meant his words as a compliment," Paul said. "The wild fox was intelligent and cunning, but also solitary, which described me quite well. Like the wolf, the fox is also fierce and dangerous, and that was also true of me. I ruthlessly lived up to the name as those who engaged me in debate would learn.

"One summer day, Gamaliel lectured us about the power of evil. As always, we sat bunched in a circle around the teacher. I took my normal spot at his feet. For some reason, I was in a particularly snarly mood that day, perhaps because of the heat, and I was tired. Anger coursed through my veins, strangling any love which might have been left in my heart. Without thinking, I interrupted him with a question which had been eating away at my soul.

"Why would a loving God even allow pain, heartache, and evil to exist?" My question implied God was not so loving after all. Suddenly the room was silent, and everyone's eyes turned from me to the teacher.

"I'm sure they wondered if he would scold me. Would he call me out? Or would he answer the question?

"In truth, I wondered the same things myself," Paul said. "But Gamaliel was a very wise and very compassionate man. He knew all too well the depth of my pain, so his answer was gentle.

"'My little fox,' he said. 'Humanity brought heartache into this world by their own evil disobedience. One day, God will remove evil, but until then, the only thing he has promised us is to get us through our heartache. That's enough. That's more than enough.'

"Gamaliel continued in a strong low deliberate voice. 'The Lord God brought Israel through the hardship of Egypt.'

"He then rose to his feet and began walking around the cluster of students, causing us to swivel our heads in unison as he spoke. 'He brought them through the depths of the Red Sea, through the wanderings in the wilderness, and through the waters of the Jordon River, all the way to the Promise Land. And one day, he will bring you through this as well. That's his promise. Not that we will escape pain, heartache, or evil, but with his help, we will get through it.'

"With that," Paul said, "the great teacher extended his hands toward me, he raised me to my feet, and wrapped his arms around me in a strong embrace. For a time, the two of us wept for the evil that has befallen this broken world, and for the hopelessness in my heart.

"Of course," Paul said, turning toward me and looking deep into my eyes. "You know all about the evil and hopelessness of our broken world. Don't you, Dr. DeVos?"

His observation was truer than I cared to admit. I'd often seen both in my personal life and in my practice. I was not ready to have this conversation, so I simply ignored his question.

"We'll pick this up again in our next session," I said.

He nodded in agreement and stood to leave. As he made his way toward the door, he stopped, raised one eyebrow, and spoke.

"Perhaps your pain and mine are not so different. I think we carry some of the same scars after all."

Then, realizing he might have gone too far, Paul tugged on his ear, smiled, and pointed toward mine.

In the summer of my sophomore year at Hope, my brother Seth and I were stumping in an old part of the east orchard. On average, sweet cherry trees have a life span of about twenty to thirty years. Sour cherry tree life spans are even less, so we were constantly replacing old trees with new. We had cut down these trees a few days before and now we were pulling the stumps. Seth rode the Kubota, a narrow tractor that can maneuver well in the tight spaces of an orchard. I wrapped a chain around the stump, hooked it on the Kubota's front bucket, and Seth hydraulically jerked the stump out of the sandy soil.

Three trees from the end of the last row, the chain snapped and flung back around toward my head. Fortunately, I ducked out of the way but one of the links clipped the top my ear tearing the cartilage and skin. Blood splattered everywhere. Seth quickly wrapped my head like a turban with his sweatshirt and drove me back to the house, then he and Sea drove me to the med center. Seventeen stiches later, I had a scar and a story to tell, and Seth became my guilt slave for quite a while.

I suspected Paul was not referring to the scars from the chain but from the scars on my soul from losing the woman I loved.

"If you would let me," he said, "maybe *I* could be the arms of God for *you*."

I stood with my arms up, intending to protest, but before I could say a word, I found myself engulfed in his embrace. A long time had passed since anyone except Lucy had held me in their arms, and his sudden act of affection caught me by surprise.

chapter 28

DRIFTING

God wants you to get where God wants you to go more than you want to get where God wants you to go.
—Mark Batterson, *In a Pit with a Lion on a Snowy Day*

After a long, strong embrace, Paul made his way toward the door, but I stopped him.

"Do you mind if I ask you a personal question, Paul?"

"No. I have no secrets from you. As I have told you repeatedly, God sent me here for your sake, not mine."

"I'm struggling with the whole God thing. I don't understand. After going through so much personal tragedy, how did you ever restore your faith in the goodness of God?"

"I will tell you my answer, but I will also tell you that you must find your own way down this dark path. I, and others, can walk with you for a while, but the direction you take is ultimately your decision. You must either take a leap of faith or a leap of denial. I must warn you the decision will not come easily. No perfect solutions exist in this imperfect world. Each of us must find our own way.

"You are not the first to shake an angry fist in God's face, and you will not be the last. The Evil One is good at what he does, and he'll do whatever he can to drive a wedge between us and God. Doubt, disappointment, disease, death, and deception are all at his disposal, and our only defense is the truth. The One who once called himself 'The Truth' calls us to remember his death every time we break bread together. Remember and hope. Remember and trust. Remember and wait. Remember him who promised to remember the thief on the cross, and finally, remember he has also promised to do the same for us.

"Sometimes the truth hardly seems like enough to combat all the lies, but truth is enough—more than enough. When Satan whispers anything else in your ear, remember who he is. He is a liar and the Father of Lies. Deception is his native tongue. He's always been that way, always."

Turning toward the front window, Paul continued his discourse.

"Satan's lies started in the Garden of Eden when he slithered up next to Eve and told her God cannot be trusted. I'll never know why she chose to believe him, but immediately the fear of being abandoned was born and has been part of the birth package ever since. We can't escape it. Insecurity is in our blood. Trusting comes hard for us. Faith and doubt do a dance in our heads and they spin us round and round. We're all natural-born doubters, and if we're not careful our doubts will separate us from God and the people we love.

"For example, whenever people we care about abandon us, or are taken from us, we search for a reason. Somehow, we hope having a reason will lessen the pain, which doesn't happen, of course, but we still search for an answer. Instinctively we know somebody is at fault. We blame ourselves when we can't find anybody else to blame. Like I said, self-blame is part of our primal nature and has something to do with our inherited guilt. You know the story.

"One day Adam did what he *shouldn't* do," Paul said, as if it were inevitable. "Then God did what he *had* to do. He distanced himself from humanity. He exiled Adam from his presence. No cool afternoon walks and fewer long late-night talks. After that, when they did talk, Adam always felt their conversation was one-sided, and the worst part was he knew he was at fault, bur he blamed Eve when he couldn't bear to take the responsibility alone. As soon as he did, there was a distance between the two of them as well. They still knew each other, and they still knew God too, but not like they used to know him.

"Now, rather than really knowing God, they and their descendants simply knew about him," Paul said with a sigh. "We've even made up words like immutable, incorruptible, and unknowable to describe him. Those words haven't helped much. When we find a word to describe who God is, we also describe who we're not, which only serves to highlight the insurmountable distance between us.

"From the moment humanity was shut out of Eden's gate," Paul said, turning and walking in my direction, "we've longed to claw our way back inside. Try as we might, the gate will not open. When the weather is dark or stormy or cold, our old insecurities return to haunt us. The distance between God and us seems to grow even greater and fear enters our hearts. You know what I'm talking about, right?"

I nodded, and he continued as if he were giving a lecture in theology.

"At some level, we're all afraid of the dark, but sometimes we're even more afraid of the light. We're afraid our deepest, darkest secrets will be exposed, and God will banish and abandon us forever. In one form or another, we've all inherited the fears of our forefathers. The only thing that could soothe our troubled hearts would be if God himself were to come down here and save us. That's why Jesus had to be born. Not only did Jesus's death appease God's wrath but also proved how much he loves us.

"But," Paul said, walking toward the door, "of course, you know the story as well as I do."

He walked out and left me alone with my thoughts.

chapter 29

Remembering

> What do we do in the dark night? We do nothing. We wait. We remember that we are not God. We hold on. We ask for help. We do less. We resign from things, we rest more, we stop going to church, we ask somebody else to pray because we can't. We let go of our need to hurry through it. You can't run in the dark.—John Ortberg, *Soul Keeping: Caring For the Most Important Part of You*

Like Paul, Death wouldn't leave me alone. The call came toward the end of the fall term.

"You better come home, Rocky," my brother Seth told me. "The Silver Fox died last night."

My grandfather Sea's funeral was set for Sunday afternoon. After my last class on Friday, Lucy and I made the drive to Sutton's Bay. The farther north we went the more vibrant the colors got. Fall is my favorite time of year. We had no need to rush because there was nothing to do when we got there except grieve, and I had had enough of grief. Instead of dwelling on Sea's death, I tried to remember the man and his life and his impact on my life.

Sea left this earth like he lived his life, with grace and without regrets. He died under a Harvest Moon in October after spending most of the day with my dad and my brothers pruning and shaping the young cherry trees.

"I don't believe God ever intended for anyone to retire," he'd say. "Retirement just isn't natural. I plan to work on these trees 'til the day I die. After that you can sprinkle my ashes on the hill in the honey crisps next to Hattie."

"For where your treasure is, there your heart will be also," Jesus said.

Most of the people Sea treasured were in heaven now.

Sea didn't know at the time, but God had a plan for his life.

He met and married Grandma Hattie in his senior year at Michigan State University School of Agriculture and Applied Science (now just called Michigan State).

Harriet Faye Lawrence—a feisty woman with curly blonde hair, ice blue eyes, freckles on her nose, and a touch of blush on her cheek—wore pants before they were fashionable. Everybody knew her as the girl with the floppy straw hats.

The story goes that, as a junior, Sea asked his friend Jack Jansma to introduce him to that *hatty* girl after biology class. He thought her name referred to her headgear. Sea later learned Hattie was short for Harriet. A year after they met, one of the college chaplains married them in the Horticulture Gardens.

After graduating, Sea and Hattie signed a land contract to purchase Bill Benson's farm north of Sutton's Bay. Our family has lived there ever since.

The Bensons wanted to continue living in the main farmhouse for five more years, so he and Grandpa Sea built the little cottage down by the bay. The house was small, only one bedroom and a loft, but comfortable. Over the years, several of us have lived there for short periods of time.

For the last fifteen years of Sea's life, he moved back to the bay cottage year-round. We always stayed there with him when we came up to visit the family. The loft had a queen-sized bed with a trundle that pulled out for Lucy. After Grandma Hattie died, Sea always seemed extra glad for the company. He said the cottage felt empty without her. Being there now without Rachel, I understand what he meant. As I sat there feeling sorry for myself, Laurie from Summerdike's office phoned.

"I'm sorry to bother you," she said, "but I finally heard back from the police in Dearborn. We can take Shalhoub off the list. He was never really missing. Whenever he'd disappear, he was just volunteering at the Burn Center at Children's Hospital in Detroit. He'd read to the kids who had no one else. I talked to Dr. Rohda Almasi, the head of surgery there."

"Dr. Almasi said even with the best medical care some will not survive. All he can do is provide a calm, comforting place for them to die. That's when he calls Gabriel. Most people do everything they can to avoid being around a dying child. He's the opposite. He comes, sits with them, and reads them stories. I suppose he does this because he could not be with his own daughter when she died some years ago. Maybe this is his way of making up for his absence, I don't know.

"Dr. Almasi told me about a little girl named Isabella who was in an automobile collision with a fuel tanker. Her parents died instantly. Isabella received severe burns. She also had inhaled the toxic gasses from the fire. She had two maybe three days to live. The doctors could do little but try to numb her pain. That's when Dr. Almasi called Gabriel.

"He came immediately. He knew what little girls liked. And he always brought his suitcase full of wonderful books. He had *Charlotte's Web*, *The Hobbit*, *Alice in Wonderland*, *The Lion, The Witch and the Wardrobe*, and, of course, *The Velveteen Rabbit*. Gabriel read each one with tenderness and care.

"He stayed by Isabella's bedside all that day and into the next, reading whenever she was awake enough to listen. About three o'clock the next morning, as he read her *The Hobbit*, Isabelle quietly joined her parents.

"An hour later, when Gabriel left the hospital, he was beaten and robbed in the parking lot. No one found him until about six o'clock. They did what they could to stop the bleeding, and then sent him to Detroit Medical Center for surgery. In all the commotion, his paperwork got lost. Weeks passed before his family learned his whereabouts. When they went there, they learned he was in a coma and might or might not ever awake. For months, they have prayed at his bedside, and only this week, they remembered to call the Dearborn Police and cancel the APB."

"That's some story," I said, trying to wrap my mind around it.

"Yes," Laurie said, "and get this. When Dr. Almasi apologized to Gabriel's family for the delay notifying them, they said there was no need. Gabriel would have felt the pain he had endured was worth it if he could bring a little comfort to Isabella in her last hours."

When we hung up, I went to the big house and had a long talk with Lucy. She really is a remarkable child, so much like her mother. I must start making time to be with her before she's grown up and gone.

"Tonight, when you're done playing up here with your cousins, I want to read to you, like I used to," I said. "You know like before you go to bed. Your mom used to love *The Lion, the Witch, and the Wardrobe*. How about we start reading that? I think Sea's got a copy down at the Bay Cottage."

"Sure," she said, "but can we start reading the book when we get home? Carry and Carla are having a sleepover with Grandma Frankie and we were going to bake oatmeal cookies."

"Sure," I said, "I guess that would be all right, as long as I get a couple of those cookies."

chapter 30

COMFORT

Behind all your stories is always your mother's story, because hers is where yours begins.—Mitch Albom, *For One More Day*

The next day, we went to the funeral at Orchard View Church, a two-story Greek-style structure with white clapboard siding and four fluted pillars supporting the front porch. The towering steeple has a twelve-foot-tall brass cross which turned green with age. With the folding chairs set up in the narthex, the little church holds just over two hundred and fifty people, and every seat would be filled for Sea.

My brother, Simon, drove Sea's '53 Chevy pickup to the church and parked out front. He and his wife Brenda stood on the front steps with their daughters, Carry and Carla, when we pulled up. I hugged him and held him in silence. Sometimes when there aren't really any words to say, words aren't necessary. Seth and I had lost our grandfather, but Simon had lost his best friend. His pain was beyond words, so for a while, I just held him in my arms and wept with him in silence.

After the rest of the family arrived, we went inside together. As we entered the sanctuary, a flood of childhood memories danced in my head. I grew up in this church, and not much had changed in the years since. The floor was fruitwood, the pews were white with pale green cushions, and the front wall had two towering ranks of organ pipes covered with delicate hand-painted cherry blossoms.

A large-framed picture of Sea and Hattie graced the stage. Normally, the picture hung in the front entrance of the winery. Hattie wore a big yellow, floppy straw hat with a blue and white polka dot ribbon. Grandpa had his arm around her shoulder. Sea and Hattie stood in front of the '53 pickup.

The communion table stood to the left with the baptism bowl and pitcher, which had a single yellow rose leaning from the spout. Yellow roses were Grandma Hattie's favorite. Next to the pitcher stood a cornucopia with apples, gourds, Indian corn, carrots, brussels sprouts, and beets poured out of the bell. I knew that was my mother's touch.

Mom is a hard worker. She sells her baked goods in the store in front of the winery. She always has a smile on her face and her joy is contagious. People couldn't help but smile when they were around her.

Mom gently put her right arm around Dad's shoulder when they slid into the pew. She kept her arm there the whole service. I watched as she blinked rapidly, trying to hold back her tears. She could not. Her tears slowly trickled down her cheeks, streaking her makeup. Seeing her cry made me cry. Lucy was sitting between us to her left. When she started to sniffle, Frankie reached out with her left arm and hugged her as well. Loving comes natural to Mom.

"As a mother comforts her child, so will I comfort you."

174

Isaiah could have been talking about Mom. Comfort is her role in life. Growing up, her smile always made things better. Watching her comfort Lucy comforted me.

Simon and his girls sat to my left, and Carry and Carla kept bending forward and looking around me to see if Lucy was okay. She's close to her cousins, and sometimes she'll ask me why we didn't move back home to the farm.

"I'm not a farmer," I'd say, and we'd drop it.

chapter 31

WAITING

Waiting is our destiny. As creatures who cannot by themselves bring about what they hope for, we wait in the darkness for a flame we cannot light. We wait in fear for a happy ending that we cannot write. We wait for a 'not yet' that feels like a 'not ever.'—Lewis B. Smedes, *Keeping Hope Alive*

The pulpit, a massive wooden structure, sat to the right of the stage. The organ sat below the pulpit. The service officially started when Martha Hayworth stopped playing the organ.

Pastor Vandyke had taken a call to a large church on the south side of Chicago three months before, so the church council recalled Reverend Jacob Lankheet into temporary service. He was an old man, retired now, and well into his eighties. He had been the pastor here all the years of my youth, and he was a close friend of Sea's. The elderly pastor slowly ascended the steps and took his place behind the pulpit.

His base voice was deep and clear. He spoke with authority. His massive head of silver hair hung past the collar of his crisp white shirt. He had on a blue pinstriped suit, polished brown wingtips, and a blue and orange striped tie that reminded those in the know he had graduated from Hope College.

"Our help," he said, "is in the name of the Lord for he is the creator, and the caretaker of life. We're here today in memory of my friend, Sebastian Peter DeVos. He was born into this world September 9, 1930 and born into eternal grace October 3, 2017. He has given up this old body now and taken on a new body—this one strong, straight, imperishable, eternal, indestructible."

He said the words slowly and deliberately, leaving no room for doubt.

"Don't grieve for Bass," he whispered, swallowing his own grief. "He is with the Lord and the people he loves. He's been wishing and waiting for this, and those of us who loved him would not wish him back."

You could tell from his tone that, over the years, the two men had grown as close as brothers. As he spoke, my heart swelled with an unexpected confidence, and my eyes welled with tears. Jake Lankheet, a man you could believe in, had no guile. When he entered the room, you could smell the faint cologne of integrity. When you're not sure you believe in God anymore, you will find help if you listen to someone who does.

I had been preached at a few times in the last years, but with Jake the sermon was different. To him, the message was personal, almost like he had been reading your mail. Charisma, personality, magnetism, the Spirit of God— whatever word you use, he had it. When Jake spoke, somehow you knew the words were from God's lips. I'd been waiting for this.

When Rachel died, anger bullied its way into my heart. I was mad at God for taking her. Hearing God's still small voice is hard when you're shouting at him. As Jake spoke, my troubled spirit slowly began to quiet. To my surprise, when I stilled the angry voices in my head, the still, small voice of God started whispering in my ear. Who knows, maybe he was whispering the whole time.

"Be still," he said through the psalmist, "and know that I am God."

For forty-five minutes, Jake talked intimately, eloquently, and personally about Sea, about God, and about the faith that bound them to each other. Through it all, no one ever looked at their watch. Sometimes we laughed, sometimes we cried, and sometimes we just let his words wash over our hearts. You could tell he knew God and Grandpa intimately—maybe better than any of us—so he deserved to have the last word.

When Pastor Lankheet finished, he asked us to all rise. Then he came out from behind the pulpit, descended the stairs, and stood on the floor in front of my family.

"I can see it," he said just above a whisper. "I can see my friend, Sea, walking strong and steady through the gates of heaven. The fragrance of cherry blossoms filled the air, and as he crossed the threshold, the love of his life leaped into the big man's arms. Dipping her back, he kissed her passionately. As he did, her floppy straw hat fell into the flowers at her feet. Too much time had passed since her lips last touched his. For several moments, the two old lovers refused to let go."

Jake had a way of describing things that put you in the story. You could see the action unfold in your mind's eye, and today he was at his best.

"There comes a time in your life," he said, "when you realize you've outlived the people you love the most. The great attraction of death is that suddenly you will find everyone you've ever lost. And for Sea, everyone included Louis.

"Lou quietly took his place toward the front of the crowd. The young man stood strong and straight in his dress whites and patiently waited for his father to notice him. When Sea saw him, he tearfully pulled his oldest son into the family embrace."

For a moment Jake turned in my direction and paused to catch his breath. He continued when he was sure that our eyes had locked.

"As the three of them celebrated their family reunion, Louis pulled away for a moment. He motioned for Rachel to come and join them, and she ran toward the love feast.

"Then it happened. Jesus stepped forward, slipped his arm around Sea's shoulder, and walked him into the throne room of God.

"This is the one I've been telling you about, Father," the Savior said. 'This is Sebastian Peter DeVos.'"

Again, Jake paused, letting us paint the picture in our minds. Then, lowering his deep base voice an octave, he spoke very slowly.

"'You don't have to introduce me to Sea,' the Father said. 'We've been close for a long, long time now.'"

"This is the gospel of God," Jake said with a confident nod. "Believe it and go in peace."

Then he raised his hands toward the heavens and gave his benediction.

Mary Hayworth started playing the postlude, and we did what Dutch people do. We went downstairs for coffee, ham buns, and potato salad. This was a time for people to see old friends, unpack their grief, and share their memories of Sea. At one point, Jake walked over, put his arm around my shoulder, and asked if we could meet for coffee.

"Sure," I said. "I'd like that. Lucy is going to spend tomorrow shopping in Traverse City with her cousins and Frankie, so I can meet any time you want."

We agreed to meet at eight-thirty at the 49th Parallel Café. The next morning when I arrived, Jake sat at a small table by the fireplace. Both were warm and inviting.

chapter 32

LISTENING

We see a hearse; we think sorrow. We see a grave; we think despair. We hear of a death; we think of a loss. Not so in heaven. When heaven sees a breathless body, it sees the vacated cocoon & the liberated butterfly.
—Max Lucado, *Max on Life*

As I walked into the café, I saw Jake's faded navy pea coat and gray, wool Tigers cap hanging on the hook by the front door. He was sipping a cup of coffee at a small table by the fireplace, and I slid into the chair across from him. We made the usual small talk, ordered the bunkhouse breakfast, and reminisced about Sea for a while.

"What's with the Tigers cap?" I asked.

"Always been a fan," he said. "If I'm not mistaken, you, me, and Sea took in a game or two in Detroit."

When he said it, I half remembered so I decided to let his comment slide—too much to explain. After pancakes, bacon, and scrambled eggs with sausage gravy, our conversation took a more serious turn.

"I can't imagine how much you must be hurting, Rock, losing your beloved grandfather while you're still grieving for your wife," Jake said, getting right to the point. "I also know there's nothing I can say to make you feel better. However, I wanted you to know you've been in my thoughts and prayers a lot lately."

"Thanks," I said, knowing he wouldn't make that kind of statement lightly. I tried to hold back my emotions, but there's something about Jake Lankheet that strips away all pretense. As my eyes leaked a few tears, he put his hand on mine and spoke in a low, compassionate voice.

"People sometimes say 'God won't give you more than you can handle,' but that's just not true. When Alice died, I was wrecked for quite a while. Losing her really shook my faith in the fairness of God."

Until that moment, I'd forgotten Jake's first wife, Alice, died when he was a young pastor in a small church outside of Detroit. After a drunk driver killed her, Jake had three girls to raise on his own. Five years later, he married LuAnn and three years later, they moved to Sutton's Bay. Life has a way of blunting the stabbing pain of death, but loving someone changes us. We give them a piece of who we are, and we take on a piece of who they are, so after they're gone, we can't go back to who we were. This reality was true for Jake. He was different now. Each passing year absorbed some of his grief, but Alice would be a part of him for the rest of his life.

"For almost a year," Jake said, "I was so mad at God I could hardly get through the day. I was mad at Alice too. Oh, I knew she didn't mean to die, but that didn't stop me from questioning how she could leave me. I had some awful thoughts in those days. I look back now and wonder how those people at Grace Church sat through so many angry sermons without complaining. I just about put my fist through that pulpit every Sunday. Thankfully, the congregation lived up to their name. Little by little, Grace Church and God's grace had their way with my hardened heart, and I let go of some of the anger. Tell me, son, how are you doing?"

"The truth is, I'm a little mad at God right now too."

"I know you are. I can see your anger on you, and I don't blame you, but I also know pain never leaves us where it finds us. Pain makes us either bitter or better. We get to choose which. I made my choice a long time ago. Now for Lucy's sake, and for your own sake, you must make the choice. I hope you choose wisely."

After a couple minutes, Jake broke the silence.

"When we lose someone we love, we start to question the fairness of God. We ask things like 'why me,' 'why now,' and 'why her?' A herd of unanswerable questions start to trample our faith. We begin to hurl them toward heaven, and how they get answered will either draw us closer to God or push us farther away.

"I'm not sure why," he said, without looking up, "but when our hearts break, we try to bargain with God. 'I promise,' we say. 'If you do this for me, I'll do that for you.' God never takes the bait."

"You're right," I said, "I did some of that—didn't help. For Lucy's sake, I went through the motions of faith at Rachel's funeral. Eventually, though, the anger and the grief caught up with me. My world was falling apart and so was I. In fact, I still am.

"Before Rachel's death, I was confident of myself and my faith. After she died, I didn't know who I was any more. I didn't know who God was either. Like Job, I found myself in the pinch between God and Satan, and I darn well didn't like it.

"My mom used to say, 'wouldn't it be awful if we gave up on God when we were one prayer away from a miracle?' But when Rachel died, my miracle died with her. I felt like God had given up on us. So, for a while I just stopped praying. Do you know what I mean?"

"I do," Jake said. "Death is Satan's best work—the crowning achievement of what he initiated in Eden. Perhaps the only thing worse than watching someone you love die is watching them suffer, and we've both done that. Day after day, I watched Alice twist in agony until finally I pleaded with God to take her. Then as soon as he did, I started wishing her back. I felt guilty about her death for quite a while too, like her death was my fault for praying what I did.

"I was inconsolable for quite a while," Jake said with a sigh. "In the end, I found the old Dutch catechism is right. 'Our only comfort in life and in death is that we belong, body and soul, to our faithful savior Jesus Christ.' That means death doesn't get the last word. In Christ, love is stronger than death. I knew Alice was where she needed to be, and I'm where I need to be, at least for now, and somehow, I needed to learn to make the best of that, to find comfort in the knowledge. That's our only comfort, son."

"I know I shouldn't," I said, "but to be honest with you, I feel more abandoned by God than comforted by him right now. In some ways, I'm okay with that."

"Explain what you mean."

"I don't know," I said. "I guess I'm just so angry at God right now I don't want to talk to him. I don't want to listen to him either."

"So, you're kind of taking a break from God?"

"I suppose that's as good a way as any to say what I mean."

Jake nodded. "Like I said, at one time in my life I kind of took a break from God too. The problem is not believing in God didn't really help me make sense of the world either. If there is no God, or if God doesn't care, if everything is just random chance, then life is nothing but a cruel joke. Without hope in God, there is no hope at all. That's what always drives me back to the Book. The Bible doesn't answer all my questions but does answer some of them. Over the years, I've learned to trust God with the rest. Does that make sense to you?"

"I guess so. Maybe. I don't know."

"Let me see if I can explain this a little better for you," Jake said. "The writer of the book of Hebrews says 'Faith is confidence in what we hope for, and assurance about what we do not see.'

"In other words, faith is not about facts. Faith is the reasoned result of sure hopes and unverifiable certainties. Like you, I wish this weren't so, but it is. The skeptics are right when they say we follow a God we can't see, for reasons we can't explain, hoping to join him for an eternity we can't fathom. But we do because somewhere deep in our hearts we know our faith is valid."

"I guess I know that too," I said. "I just wish faith didn't always have to come down to blind trust."

"Life is all about trust," Jake said. "Every day we put our trust in the government, the banks, the medical profession, the clock, and the people around us. At some point, each one of them has let us down, yet for some reason, we seem to trust them more than God. In almost every aspect of life, we accept there are certain things we may never totally understand, but with God, we want answers, bullet points, three simple steps. We threaten to walk away when we don't get them. The problem is there's no place else to go. Like I said, 'if there is no hope in God, then there is no hope at all.' Think about it. I'm serious, Rocky. This is critical. I don't blame you for being angry, but you must get this one right, because forever is a long time to be wrong."

For several minutes, the two of us sat there nodding silently like a couple of bobblehead dolls. My mind drifted back to something Paul said in one of our sessions. "Sooner or later, grief comes knocking on everyone's door."

Jake broke our silence. "Sometimes people die, sometimes dreams die, sometimes innocence dies, and sometimes hope dies too. A little piece of us is gone forever because grief knocks the wind out of our souls and leaves us breathless and wheezing spiritually. Satan knows this is his time to pounce. He sends the demons of doubt and despair to haunt our thoughts.

"But we need to guard against letting such thoughts linger too long. Staying too long in the dark shadows of grief will alter our life. We won't walk away unchanged. Grief always leaves us scarred. We're different. We're damaged goods. We will forever walk through life with a limp.

"Not that being damaged is all bad. Sometimes the mosaic of broken pieces is more beautiful than the whole. We may be hobbled and humbled, but we are also often deeper and more deliberate. We know things we didn't know before—things we can only share with those who've also walked the dark path."

I knew Jake had walked this path.

"I believe in God," he said, "and I believe in you. Even more important, God believes in you, so I know you're going to get through this. I promise. Nothing in this world lasts forever, not even a broken heart."

I knew he had no way of knowing that for sure, but hearing his assurance made me feel better.

Later that night, after dinner, Lucy and I gathered our stuff together and left for home. A cold rain fell gently. The darkness and the monotonous swish of the wiper blades soon lulled Lucy to sleep. As I drove along the dark winding highway, I knew what Paul meant when he said, "grief has a way of piling up on you." Still, I also knew, somehow, I was going to be all right. I'd made what some call "a leap of faith." The eternal flame of hope began to flicker once again in the dark corners of my heart.

We say our best prayers when we're on the edge of emptiness. That night, I prayed like I hadn't prayed in a long time.

I believe in you, Father. I believe in your goodness. At least I'm trying to. I believe in Jesus, and I believe in the resurrection too. Somewhere deep in my broken heart, I know you have a plan and a purpose for all of this, but you don't make believing easy. Sometimes doubt and uncertainty have their way with my heart. I want to trust you, Lord, but trusting is hard—really hard. I wish acceptance wasn't so darn hard.

Not a great prayer, I admit, but at least I was praying again.

chapter 33

CONFRONTATION

They found him in the temple courts, sitting among the
teachers, listening to them and asking them questions.
Everyone who heard him was amazed.
—Luke the Physician *The Gospel of Luke 2:46*

I looked forward to resuming my talks with Paul. We
missed a session while I was gone, so a couple of months had
passed since I'd seen him. In many ways, Paul reminded me
of Jake—easy to listen to. There was something delightfully
disarming about the man. His accent was engaging. He
had a way of drawing me into his stories, and in his words
contained wisdom. The more I talked with him, the more
I realized he'd spent considerable time studying the New
Testament—the writings of the apostle Paul in particular.
I also realized, despite his psychosis, he was a holy man. I
envied his faith. In many ways, his version of Christianity
was more real, more genuine, than mine.

The way Paul would weave bits and pieces of biblical
history into his story set him apart from most of the patients
who had grandiose delusions. If, as I now suspected, Paul
was in fact Laubstein, he'd done his homework. Not only

was he an archeologist, but also a student of the apostle and his world. So today I decided to put his knowledge to the test. I knew this was risky. He was still fragile emotionally. However, if I could get him to talk about the defining moment in the apostle Paul's life, his words might trigger something inside him. If so, this might also help us figure out what prompted him to take on the apostle's persona.

"Tell me about the first time you encountered Jesus," I said. "Describe what it was like that day on the road to Damascus."

"Which question would you like me to answer first?" he said.

"What do you mean by that?"

"Well," he said, "I was just a boy the first time I encountered Jesus. Then, twenty years later, we came face to face again on the road to Damascus."

Paul's response took me by surprise. I had not expected the early encounter, so I paused briefly before proceeding.

"Okay," I said. "Take me to school. Tell me about your first encounter with Jesus."

"I was in Torah school in Jerusalem," Paul said, standing and gesturing as he spoke. "In those days, Gamaliel set the seating. As his student, we were each assigned a place that reflected our academic prowess. In the first row, front and center, on the carpet at the Rabbi's feet, sat the best and the brightest. We were the ones with the most promise. Behind us, the less accomplished sat on mats. We did most of the talking. They mostly listened to the discussion. Together we met for instruction each morning.

"Life is made up of a myriad of moments," Paul said. "Most of them are pretty ordinary, but a handful of them will stick with us for the rest of our lives. They haunt us or inspire us or become life-altering in ways we couldn't possibly imagine at the time. The moment might be one of decision, clarity, crisis, opportunity, or failure. Regardless, this defining moment remains with us throughout our life. I've had several of those sticky moments in my life, but perhaps the most poignant one happened that day at the Temple in Jerusalem.

"Sometimes, God calls to us like a rooster at sunrise. When he does, our first inclination is to ignore the call. We want to roll over and go back to sleep. That happened with me. Years later, I would look back on that moment and wonder how I could have missed the significance, but I scarcely gave the encounter a thought at the time.

"Avraham of Syria sat two seats to my left. He was an Iscariot, a Zealot who would slit a Roman's neck in the night if he were given half a chance. Almost taunting the teacher, he asked about Judas of Galilee, the one who had led the revolt against the tax of Quirinius a decade earlier.

"'Many of our people,' said Avraham, 'believed Judas the Galilean was the messiah. They willingly followed him to their death. But you did not, Rabin Gamaliel. You refused to take up the *sica*, the Zealot's sword, and fight for our people. Had you joined, many more would have followed. Perhaps the outcome might have been different. But you chose not to, so tell us, please, how did you know he was not the chosen one?'

"'Truth requires patience,' Gamaliel replied calmly. 'If a man or an idea is of human origins, you will know because, eventually, they will die out. They will never die if they are from God.'

"We all silently nodded in agreement," Paul said. "But truthfully, as young men we had little patience in our hearts. Then it happened. From behind me a voice challenged the teacher.

"'Despite what the Sadducees say,' said a young Galilean who stepped out of the shadows. 'The prophet Ezekiel reminds us death does not always have the last word, and unless I'm mistaken, you Pharisees agree. Like him, you also claim our Father in heaven is the giver of life and love, so if he chooses, his breath can bring even the dry bones of death back to life.'

"Immediately I shot to my feet," Paul said, still feeling the emotion of the moment.

"'Who is this ill-mannered Philistine who dares to challenge the words of Gamaliel? Do you not know you address the grandson of Hillel, the Nisi of the Sanhedrin?'

"'For two days, I've sat here listening to Rabin Gamaliel,' the ruddy-cheeked boy replied with a smile. 'So yes, I know exactly who I address. As for me, I am simply a son who is busy about his Father's business.'

"'Who is your father?' Paul demanded.

"'Sha'ul, Sha'ul,' chided Gamaliel. 'Let him answer the first question before you ask him a second. Besides, I am intrigued by this young one's thoughts. Please, go on, young scholar. Tell us what you think the prophet's words mean."

"'Ezekiel spoke of the rebirth of Israel,' said the boy, slowly pacing in the back of the great stone hall. 'In the harsh oppression of the moment, and against impossible odds, the Father of life wanted his people to know he was not done with them yet. Israel would one day be restored. Even then, the Lord was preparing the way for the appointed one. He knew his servant David would reestablish his kingdom soon. And perhaps, perhaps the Father is not done with us yet either. Has he not given us the sacred scriptures as a window into his heart and as mirror to see ourselves in their pages?'

"The Galilean paused as if his mind went somewhere else for a moment, and then he continued."

"'At the time, the nation of Israel was scattered like dry bones upon the desert sand. Her people believed there was no hope of resurrection from the dead, but as we know, with Elohim all things are possible.'"

Paul continued. "Many marveled at his knowledge; even the teachers of the law wanted to hear more from him, so Gamaliel invited him to come forward."

"'We would all be pleased if you would join us. Come, sit beside me and identify yourself.'

"I was not pleased to have his company," said Paul, somewhat ashamed at his actions. "As he sat beside me at Gamaliel's feet, I could not help but notice he had the calloused hands of a commoner. His cloak was foul-smelling and stained with sweat, and he wore the apron of an artisan or craftsman of some kind.

"He said his name was Yashua, but before he could say anything else, I jumped back into our argument.

"'Ezekiel was speaking of the land of Israel, of the nation, not of a man,' I said angrily, still trying to defend my rabbi. 'Would you have us believe the Lord intends to breathe life into the bone boxes of the dead?'

"He turned to me, looked into my eyes, and gently rested his hands on my shoulders.

"'Sha'ul,' he said softly, 'Sha'ul, why do you persecute me? Do you not know that the people are from the land?'

"'From the dust the LORD God formed *ha a-dam*, the man, Adam,' the sacred writer said. And he breathed life into his nostrils.'

"'So, you think he will bring about the restoration of all things,' I said, 'even the resurrection of the dead?'

"'His love for his people is never ending,' said the Galilean. 'And he is the same yesterday, today, and forever, is he not? If that is true, then surely what he has done he will do again.'

"'Next I suppose you'll tell me his love extends to the Goyim as well."

"'He does love them,' the boy said.

"'He loves Israel,' I said, shooting to my feet. 'You speak blasphemy. We alone are his chosen people.'

"The young Galilean said, 'In the second book of the law, we read, 'For you are a people holy to the LORD your God. The LORD your God has chosen you out of all the peoples on the face of the earth to be his people, his treasured possession.'"

"'Treasured,' I said boldly. 'Unique, peculiar, special.'

"Then I sat down next to Gamaliel, feeling confident that, by quoting Torah, I would have the last word. I was wrong.

"'You speak the truth,' said the boy. 'You are correct. Israel has a unique place in God's heart. But as the Creator and caretaker of all living things he cannot help but love the Goyim as well. Let me tell the son of the goat herder a story that might help him understand.'"

"His words enflamed my soul. I wanted to rise and strike him on the cheek, but Gamaliel put his hand on my shoulder."

"'Let him speak, my son,' he said softly. 'His own words will expose either his irreverence or his insight. Either way, we will know who he is, so let us see which he will expose.'

"'Suppose a man had twelve sheep,' the boy said. 'And imagine he loved them all equally. In fact, imagine he loved them so much he gave them names like Ruben, Simon, Levi, Judah, and Dan. To each one he gave a name. Imagine also he had in his possession a goat, an ill-tempered, unruly goat that irritated the sheep. But, because it was his, the man loved the goat as well.

"'Now, just for a moment,' the boy said, pausing slightly. 'Imagine what would happen if the goat were to get lost. Would the man not secure the twelve safely behind the sheep gate, and then go out looking for the one that was lost? And when he found the goat bleating and bleeding, tangled in the thorns of this twisted world, would he not return to the twelve, rejoicing with the goat on his shoulders?

"'And finally, if he brought this pathetic, ill-tempered, unruly goat back into the fold, would his action diminish his love for the sheep? Of course not.'

"The boy had hardly finished his story when a woman's voice screamed his name from the court of the women. 'Yashua,' she said, 'Yashua, your father and I have been looking for you. We were worried you were lost.'

"'There was no need to worry,' he said, walking toward her. Then he put his arm around her, and together they walked out of the Temple courts.

"'Mother," he said as they left, 'did you not know I would be in my Father's house doing my Father's business?'

"'The unruly little lost goat has finally been found,' I said smugly as he left.

"My comment caused much laughter in the assembly," Paul said with a slight grin. "With that, the boy from Galilee was soon forgotten by most, but I could not forget him. He embarrassed me in front of the whole assembly. Given the chance, someday I would return the favor. Of course, at the time I had no idea what any of this would mean for me or for him. Looking back now, this meeting was clearly a foreshadowing of the future.

"Like me," Paul said with a determined look on his face, "Yashua was living with a growing awareness God had gifted him to do something special with his life. I would later see our time together at the Temple as a defining moment in his life and mine."

Paul paused for a moment as if he were just realizing the ramifications of what he'd said. Then he leapfrogged over two decades and picked up the story of his encounter with Jesus.

"Twenty years later on a beautiful spring day," Paul said, "I watched as he continued what he started. The air in Jerusalem smelled of olives and evergreens. That day, like every day in the city of David, the past and the future walked hand in hand down the streets.

"I stood in the outer court talking with my friend Moshe as the merchants and moneychangers did their business. Suddenly, we were interrupted by the sound of men shouting and coins clinking against the marble floors. Looking up, I could see the precocious young Galilean had now become a man. He was tall and muscular, determination etched on his face. I watched in horror as this same Yashua turned over the tables of the moneychangers. Once again, he insisted he was doing his Father's business.

"A week later," Paul said in a more somber tone, "at both his trial and his execution, he again called God his Father. I was enraged each time he did."

Paul sat back down in the chair, looked at the floor, and shook his head slowly from side to side and whispered apologetically.

"I felt my mission was to eradicate any remnant of faith in this false messiah. But then, as you know, he spoke to me once again on the road to Damascus. 'Sha'ul, Sha'ul, why do you persecute me?' In anger and resentment, I had wanted to expose him for who he was, but instead with love and forgiveness, he exposed me for who I was. Suddenly, in that moment, I saw one thing clearly—I was the chief of sinners."

At this, Paul became quite emotional, and wanting to help him compose himself, I broke all the rules and entered his fantasy.

"You may have played a part in all this," I said, "but certainly Jesus's death on the cross was not all your fault. I think you're being too hard on yourself."

"I think we dismiss our guilt too easily," Paul said softly, shaking his head ever so slowly. "The snowflake doesn't feel responsible for the avalanche. The raindrop never thinks he's the reason for the flood. However, things accumulate in life. Snowflakes, raindrops, anger, jealousy, cruelty, and injustice pile up. When something happens, they each have a piece of the tragedy. So yes, Dr. DeVos, I am the chief of sinners. Thankfully, the only thing greater than my guilt is God's grace."

Once again, the chime on my iPhone reminded us both our time was up. I reached into my pocket hoping to muffle the sound. I was engrossed in his story and wanted him to keep talking. Unfortunately, he didn't. He stood up, sighed, and without saying a word slowly walked out of my office.

Paul may not have worn a watch, but he understood our limited time. Like the man whose persona he'd assumed, if he was anything, he was a legalist. The rules were the rules, and he would abide by them.

chapter 34

Peripeteia

> What if you knew there was a moment coming, one where God would meet you in such a way that nothing would be the same again?—Erwin Raphael McManus, *Seizing Your Divine Moment*

When Paul left my office, his story lingered. Instead of me getting into his head, he got into mine. The more I thought about the story of the apostle's encounter with Jesus that day in the Temple, the more I realized the significance. Their meeting was the hinge of history. Everything turns on what was then a precocious boy's words. The meeting was not only a defining moment for Jesus and Paul but a defining moment for anyone who calls himself or herself a Christian.

The Greeks have a word for such rare pivotal moments—*peripeteia*, the turning point when the plot of a story, or of someone's life, takes a decidedly different shift. Sometimes, the turning point is an ironic twist, which takes the tale in a dark direction. Other times, the defining moment is when the hero finally gets his due. Either way, the moment of truth is usually the time when all the pieces of the puzzle start to fall into place.

The turning point is the stuff of the Bible—the dove returns to Noah's ark with an olive branch in its beak. Ancient and barren Sarah miraculously gives birth to Isaac. The raging waters of the Red Sea split in two. Little David defeats the giant Goliath. Again and again, in the pages of the Bible, we're told God steps in and does what only God can do. His intervention happened so often we start to expect the same kind of response from him in our everyday lives.

In the New Testament, Jesus's miracles abound. They're so commonplace we start to think this kind of thing happens all the time. The problem is such moments are too infrequent. Maybe they always have been. When we read the Bible, we can easily forget we're really getting the highlight reels of history. There are miracles here and there but a lot of living goes on between them. The bulk of their lives are like ours, very ordinary and anything but miraculous. Somewhere inside, we all know that's true, so we pray for miracles. However, we also know those kinds of prayers are rarely answered. Still, for people of faith, the carrot of hope always dangles in front of us. If God is who he says he is, then the possibility of peripeteia exists.

Like I said, miracles rarely happen, but they do happen. Once in a blue moon, God surprises us. He bends his will to ours. The veil is pulled back and the thin space between heaven and earth is momentarily spanned. A lost coin or a lost sheep or a lost son or a lost opportunity is found. There is only one response when this happens. We call our friends and family together and we celebrate. We promise ourselves we'll never forget what happened, but in time we do forget. Forgetting is human nature.

The apostle Paul was the rare exception. He never forgot. His peripeteia moment came one day on the road to Damascus. After his radical conversion, he put his life in

God's hands and never looked back. That was his moment of clarity. Suddenly, he understood God and his mission. That meeting shaped every step of his life thereafter. That day on the road to Damascus, the chief persecutor of the faith became its chief preacher.

For over a year now, I've thought that my peripeteia moment was Rachel's death. Certainly, everything changed after that. Yet, now I'm beginning to wonder if the turning point in my faith was my first encounter with Paul. Since meeting him, little by little, hope began to have its way with my troubled heart.

chapter 35

RUNNING AWAY

After all, it's one thing to run away when someone's chasing you. It's entirely another to be running all alone.—Jennifer E. Smith, *The Statistical Probability of Love at First Sight*

On Wednesday, Lucy and I went up north for Thanksgiving. We planned to return home on Friday, but Lucy asked if she could stay with her cousins for a couple of days. She always enjoys spending time with them. I wanted to say yes, but I also had a lot of papers to correct. My Developmental Psych essays still sat on my desk. I'd intentionally left them home so I wouldn't be tempted to work on them.

My brother Seth provided a solution. Lucy could catch a ride back to Holland on Sunday with him. Seth and his wife planned to spend Sunday night at our house, then they were going to do some Christmas shopping in Grand Rapids on Monday. With arrangements for Lucy made, I went back to Holland alone on Friday afternoon.

As I drove, my mind wandered randomly. I thought about the grading which waited for me. I hoped I'd have time to watch some of the MSU game. I thought about going to church alone and decided against it. Then I remembered Paul was going to speak at the eleven o'clock service at the mission on Sunday. In our last session, he invited me to come and hear him, and I said I'd think about it. I decided, if I could get my grading done, I'd take him up on the offer. The service might be a good way to observe him interacting with his peers. I was also a little curious about what he'd say.

I spent Friday night and much of Saturday grading essays. Thankfully, I finished in time to catch the end of the MSU game on TV. They won by a field goal. I went to bed early and slept better than I had in months. The next morning was sunny and clear, a crisp November morning. All the leaves were off the trees in Holland. The snow that had fallen during the night was mostly melted now. Winter was in the air. I turned down River Avenue, parked in the lot next door to the administrative office, and walked across the street.

A hand-painted mural with a picture of the Big Red lighthouse hung above the front door and a small sign with the words Men's Ministry Center glowed in green neon. That was the official name of the ministry, but everyone called it the Lighthouse Mission. Three weathered-looking men were passing a cigarette among themselves in the dim light of the neon sign. I could see their breath. Smoke hung in the air like a cloud. A slightly built boy in a hoody and a larger Hispanic man stood leaning against the wall with their arms folded. Another man sat hunched over in his wheelchair. As I approached, one by one they sheepishly glanced up at me, then quickly looked away.

I had taken Paul's advice and dressed casually for the occasion. I had on blue jeans, brown Keen hiking boots, and an old black sweatshirt with Rutgers written in red letters across the front. In their company, I felt overdressed.

"Good morning," I said, to which they all barely responded with a silent nod.

The man in the wheelchair wore an army jacket with the name O'Malley above the pocket. The name triggered a memory for me. He had been a patient of Rachel's. I was about to say something to him when I suddenly realized the young one peeking out from the hoody was Stewie Overbrook, a young man Rachel tried to help when he first came to Holland.

"Hey, Stewie," I said, "it's me, Doctor DeVos ... Doctor Rocky."

"I know," he said, looking down with a panicked look on his face. His reaction puzzled me for a moment.

Why didn't Stewie say hi to me? Was he embarrassed? Was he afraid? Did I offend him in some way? Then I realized the problem.

In a poem entitled "The Night Torn Mad with Footsteps," Charles Bukoeski wrote "like the fox I run with the hunted." He meant we live in a world divided. There are insiders and outsiders, those who conform to the rules of society and those who don't—the hunters and the hunted. Like Bukoeski, Stewie was in the latter camp. He felt out of place in our world, and he'd found his place in theirs. Sooner or later, we all find our band of brothers, and for Stewie this was the men at the Lighthouse Mission.

One of these guys probably put him up to stealing the cigarettes a couple of years earlier. Rachel asked about the theft when they met, but he wouldn't talk about it.

"I'm no rat," Stewie said, refusing to give up his partners in crime.

Now Stewie was probably afraid talking to me might cause them to wonder if he'd given them up.

As the saying goes, "there is honor among thieves." Not wanting to make Stewie feel any more uncomfortable than he already was, I made my way past the three of them without saying another word.

I would later learn from Dwight McKay that the large man was Leo Rodriguez, a petty thief and embezzler, and as I suspected, the one in a wheelchair was Atticus O'Malley. When I went back to the office the next day, I read Rachel's notes in O'Malley's file, and things started to come into focus. Like Stewie, he and Rodriguez were also running away from the demons of the past.

O'Malley mostly kept to himself. He was a mumbler, who rarely looked you in the eye. Clean-shaven, he had skin like peach fuzz and a milky little mustache. His long, caramel blond hair hung past his shoulders and lay on the khaki-colored camouflage shirt.

O'Malley took a bullet in the spine—between the T10 and T11 vertebrae—during the second Gulf War, and he's ridden a wheelchair ever since. After the field surgeon removed the bullet, Atticus was partially paralyzed from the waist down. Before the war, he'd competed in several marathons. Right before he went into the army, he took third place in the Grand Rapids Riverbank Run. He told Rachel he never felt more alive, or closer to God, than when he was running.

O'Malley still had some feeling in his legs. Pain mostly. The doctor said the pain was his nerves firing—trying to regenerate. Nerves regenerate at a millimeter a month, and his were damaged severely. For a few months, he held on to the hope of recovery. Eventually, he left the rehab facility in Virginia and moved back home to South Haven.

Atticus was always kind of an introvert. The wheelchair added to his lack of self-confidence. The only girl he ever dated was his high school sweetheart Bonnie Jean. The two of them got engaged before he left for Iraq and planned to get married when he came home. The injury changed all that. O'Malley refused to get married in a wheelchair.

"This isn't what you signed up for," he said to Bonnie. "You fell in love with a whole man, not a cripple."

She tried to tell him that his physical condition didn't matter, but he wouldn't listen. Over time, alcohol turned to cocaine and, ultimately, got the better of him. A couple times a month Bonnie would call, and sometimes they talked on the phone for hours. He'd promise to get sober, but he didn't. A couple of months later, when his dad found him passed out on the floor of his bedroom, they rushed him to the ER. He was in a coma for three days.

They had to kick start his heart a couple times with the paddles. That put the fear of God into everyone about how bad things had gotten and so, after he got out of the hospital, Bonnie and his dad checked him into the West Michigan Recovery Center. When his insurance ran out, they brought him to the mission. That was seventeen months ago. He found Jesus there, or at least he found the stern, sober, scare-the-hell-out-of-you Jesus. Since then, he's been sober in every sense of the word. He doesn't use drugs, he doesn't drink, and he doesn't laugh anymore. The only time he ever smiles is when Bonnie calls, and even then, smiles are rare.

The lady from the VA arranged for him to see Rachel a few times when he first came home from Iraq. She was making some progress with him, but when she died that ended. Like a lot of people in the system, Atticus fell through the cracks. Seeing him sitting there made me feel a little guilty.

"I should have tried to connect with him," I thought. "Rachel would have tried. Maybe things would have been different for him if I had."

I pushed open the door, and the three men took their last drags from their cigarette and silently followed me inside. The outer corridor was full of people—some sitting, some standing—talking in clusters of three or four. One by one their eyes fell on me, and I felt out of place. Then I made eye contact with Paul. Thankfully, he immediately interrupted his conversation with someone and called out my name.

"Dr. DeVos," he said, "I'm so glad you decided to come."

Paul wore a pair of faded jeans and a heavy black wool sweater with the red, white, and black Canadian Hockey team logo on the sleeve.

"Got the sweater at the mission store," he said before I could ask. "Do you like it?"

"Looks nice," I said. "Perfect for this cold weather."

I wasn't sure if he was messing with me or if maybe he was unknowingly trying to tell me he was the priest, that Father Aboud was hidden somewhere in the basement of his mind just waiting to be found. Either way, as we talked, the room seemed to warm to me. If Paul accepted me, so did they. Together, the two of us walked down the hall and went into a larger room with several multicolored fiberglass chairs lined up in rows. A red haired-woman named Sue-Ellen—the only woman in the room—quietly played a keyboard in the corner. Some men were already sitting in the chairs. Others milled around drinking coffee and talking in groups of two or three.

From what I could hear, the conversation was typical. They discussed the weather, the Lions' loss to the Packers, and the general unfairness of life. From behind me, I overheard one of the men talking to one of the three smokers I'd seen outside.

"You know how this works, Leo," he said. "The sooner someone gets saved, the sooner we get to eat. Today is your turn."

Leo Rodriguez was a gray-haired man in his sixties. He had three days of stubble on his face and wore bib overalls, a tattered green-plaid wool shirt, and a black-and-yellow-striped stocking cap. Leo said nothing but nodded his head in agreement. A few minutes later, a worship leader started the singing. Some people continued to stand in the back, but most of the men took a seat. There was a prayer, several hymns, and some talk about mission protocol. Then the song leader, a man who introduced himself as Brother Michael, stepped to the front of the stage.

"Today," said Michael as if he was excited about it, "one of our own will share the lesson. At this time, I'd like to invite Brother Paul to come forward. I want you to give him a warm welcome."

Several men clapped, some stomped their feet, and a guy in the back yelled.

"Short and sweet, Pauly," he said. "Short and sweet."

chapter 36

MIRACLES

The logical man must either deny all miracles or none.—Charles Alexander Eastman, *The Soul of the Indian*

Paul slowly made his way to the front of the auditorium, greeting several people along the way. As he climbed the steps to the stage, Brother Michael handed him a huge, red leather Bible. Paul held the Book tightly with both hands and nodded slightly. As he did, Brother Michael sat down in a chair behind him. Paul walked slowly to the front of the stage and looked around the room.

"I want you all to take a minute and look around the room."

People turned slightly and read the faces of those seated around them. Then Paul continued in a Middle Eastern accent, lending a certain credence and credibility to his words.

"If Yashua, if Jesus as you call him, if he were here today in this room, I do not believe many of us would recognize him. No, no, we would not."

After setting the Bible down on the lectern, he raised his hands. Closing his eyes and nodding his head ever so slightly, and in a very quiet, deliberate voice, forcing us to strain to hear him, he slowly began to share from the book of Isaiah.

"He had no beauty or majesty to attract us to him," Paul said in a very quiet, deliberate voice, forcing us to strain to hear him. "Nothing in his appearance would draw us to him. Like so many of you in this room, he was despised and rejected by men, a man of suffering, all too familiar with pain."

For a moment, Paul paused, sighed, took a deep breath, and slowly continued.

"Surely, he took up our pain and bore our suffering, yet we considered him punished by God, stricken by him, and afflicted. He was pierced for our transgressions. He was crushed for our iniquities. The punishment that brought us peace was on him, and by his wounds, we are healed. We all, like sheep, have gone astray, each of us has turned to our own way; and the Lord has laid on him the iniquity of us all.

"This is the word of the Lord for us today," Paul said.

Then, gracefully, he sat down on the front of the stage. For a moment, I wasn't sure if he had finished his message, but then, I realized he was simply staying in character. In first century Israel, they stood to read Scripture and sat to deliver the *derasha*, the inspirational part of the message.

"Lukas the physician tells the story," Paul continued, "in what you call the book of Acts. I remember this as if it were yesterday. Barnabas and I traveled south from Iconium to the city of Lystra. An impressive two-story, sixty-foot-long archway held up by exquisitely carved alabaster Roman columns stood at the entrance to the city. Inside, magnificently colored frescos and marble statues of the twelve Roman gods and goddesses lined the walls. The arch was as good a place as any for me to talk about the power of the one true God."

As he talked, I made a mental note. An archeologist like Laubstein would know this kind of architectural detail.

"A man crippled from birth lay on a mat near the entrance to the massive arch. His clothing and appearance confirmed he was Greek, a native of this land. He was in his early twenties, and he had strong arms and a handsome face, but his feet were twisted inward, crippled, and deformed. He watched intently as if his ears were hungry for my words.

"The wind blew in from the sea that cool day. The Spirit was on the loose—the smell of miracles were in the air. I believed the crippled man's faith might be strong enough to heal him, so I knelt and looked into his eyes.

"'You can do this,' I said in a very soft, very deliberate voice. 'You can walk. But if you would do the impossible, your faith needs to be stronger than your excuses.'

"With his eyes fixed on mine, tentatively he began to try to push himself up from his mat with his arms. He began to shake, and two men stepped forward to help. An older man, who looked to be his father, grabbed one of his arms. Then a young boy grabbed the other, and together they lifted him to his feet.

"Then the miracle happened," Paul said. "Slowly, but deliberately, the crippled man took a stumbling step. The crowd gasped as he started to limp around on those spindly legs of his. Someone behind him started yelling out in a loud voice.

"'Artus is walking,' he said. 'The cripple is walking.'"

The whole crowd began to cheer. The three men then started laughing and limping around the plaza. Artus twisted and shuffled his way between the two in a jerking motion. He had the look of a toddler learning to walk."

As Paul continued to speak, I noticed Atticus O'Malley was fidgeting in his chair. He turned to the side, dropped his head in his hand, and looked down at the floor. I could feel the pain and disappointment swelling up inside him. In fact, I half expected him to wheel himself out of the room in disgust. Surely, to hear about someone getting the miracle you've been denied must be painful. Honestly, I was disappointed Paul would choose to tell this particular story in his presence. A true saint would not. How calloused, how inconsiderate.

But as I chastised him in my mind, I realized I'd done the same thing. Many times in my life, I've assured people that for a Christian, death is simply the doorway to eternal life. That's what preachers do.

"Heaven is a better life by far," I would say with a confidence that bordered on arrogance. "A life beyond our asking or imagining. In fact, death is Jesus's greatest miracle."

But look where I am now. I wake up most nights hearing the echo of Rachel's voice in the dark. Then, I realize I heard her voice in a dream, and I'm reduced to a whimpering child. I could only imagine how many times Atticus had done the same thing. But in his case, when he wakes up, he realizes he has been dreaming about running. My heart broke for this broken man.

Paul, on the other hand, seemed oblivious to his pain. He went on telling his story as if Atticus wasn't there. Whoever he was, he could preach—that was for sure. Clearly, this man had training in homiletics. More and more, I started to believe Paul found his way to Holland after leaving Canada.

"A priest from the temple of Zeus stepped out from the crowd shouting in a loud voice," Paul said, waving his arms in a dramatic flair.

"'Zeus and Hermes have come down to walk among us,' the old priest said.

"Before Barnabas and I realized what was happening, the old cleric brought an ox laden in garland and announced he would sacrifice the beast in our honor.

"Wait," I shouted, "you misunderstood. We did not bring about the miracle. We are but messengers of the God we serve. This man was healed by God and by the grace of his son Yashua, the Christ."

"But," Paul said in a disappointed voice. "As is so often the case, their ears didn't want to hear the truth. I knew even then we were standing in the shadow of death."

chapter 37

Stoned

In a futile attempt to erase our past, we deprive the
community of our healing gift. If we conceal our wounds
out of fear and shame, our inner darkness can neither be
illuminated nor become a light for others.
　　　　　　　　—Brennan Manning, *Abba's Child*

Paul's words 'in the shadow of death' caught me by
surprise. I knew this story, but I'd forgotten what happened
next. Almost as if he wanted me to catch up, Paul sighed and
then took a moment to collect his thoughts.

"The next day," he said, continuing his story, "an alliance
of Jews from Antioch and Iconium arrived in Lystra. Together
with some men from the local synagogue, they accused me
of healing in the name of Hermes. I denied their accusation,
but, of course, they didn't listen.'

"'Blasphemy,' shouted one of their number. I'd come to
know that word as a precursor to trouble.

"'Stone him,' said another.

"With that, a mob of angry voices picked up the chant.
They pounced on me like a fox on a rabbit. I had no chance
of escape. They stripped off my tunic and dragged me outside

the city gates. The cacophony of noise was deafening. One of the men from Antioch slapped me across the face while others spit curses in my direction. My situation humiliated me. Finally, someone shoved me, and I fell down a steep rocky embankment. Bruised and bleeding, I tried to get back on my feet, but the mob began pelting me with rocks.

"I should have been frightened," Paul said with a strange smile. "But I was not. I could only think of Stephen's stoning fifteen years earlier. The irony struck me—I was getting what I'd given.

"On that day like this one," Paul said, "the elbows of an angry mob crushed and carried me along. There was only one difference—I was one of the accusers then. Together we had pushed our way out through the Lion's gate of Jerusalem's east wall. We turned north and stopped at a place that drops off rather precariously to the jagged rocks of the Kidron valley below.

"I remember thinking, 'This is a beautiful day for a stoning.'

"I stood with my arms folded and my back against the wall as one by one the would-be executioners laid their coats at my feet and picked up their projectiles. I had looked at Stephen with the same cold, calloused look of self-righteousness my accusers were looking at me now. I was about to get what I'd long deserved. Stephen's pain would soon be mine. Justice would be meted out by the mob.

"At the time," Paul said in a soft and eerily calm voice, "I couldn't understand how Stephen could be so calm. He just stood there as rocks rained down on him. He appeared oblivious to the stones. With his arms raised toward the clouds, he looked like a prophet about to make a pronouncement. Then he cried out in a loud voice.

"'I see the heavens opening up, and the Son of Man is standing at the right hand of God.'

"I didn't realize at the time," Paul said apologetically, "but death was not Stephen's enemy nor mine. Satan wants us to believe death is the end, the destroyer of life, but death is merely the doorway to eternal life.

"As I have said many times before, 'For to me, to live is Christ and to die is gain.'

After a pause, Paul continued. "This thought brought me great comfort on the day of my stoning. I looked toward the clouds hoping to see the Lord. Instead, I saw a huge stone tumbling toward my head. I leaned to one side, hoping to avoid being hit, but the rock landed with a thud. My knees buckled beneath me. As I knelt in the sand, a jagged rock struck my forehead and gashed it open. Blood splattered everywhere. I must have passed out, because the next thing I remember was Barnabas and the others standing around me, mourning my death."

"To their great surprise, I opened one eye and coughed slightly. I had the taste of blood in my mouth. Truthfully, my survival surprised me as much as them. I said it would take more than a few rocks to kill me. There is a time appointed for each of us to die, and my time had not come.

"Barnabas chuckled with a nervous laugh and helped me to my feet. He and the others brought me to the house of Timothy's grandmother, Lois. She cooked some lentils for us while Eunice nursed my wounds. Together, Barnabas and I took some nourishment and slept on the floor in front of the fire. I slept like a stone. The next day, we set out for Derbe, some sixty miles to the south.

"I tell you the story of my pain," Paul said, "because every person in this room has experienced pain. We've all had our share of physical pains and emotional pains and hunger pains. We also know the pain of being turned on or rejected or knocked down by people we thought we could trust. This room is full of pain."

"You've got that right," said a man to my left, and others were *amening* him and nodding in agreement. In the low rumble, I noticed Atticus had lifted his head and looked up at Paul once again.

"Preach it, brother," I whispered under my breath, and he did.

"I came today to tell you that Yashua knows your pain. He knows your pain so well he took it with him to the cross. He gave his life that we might have life. So, in his name I say to you, 'rise up and walk.' Walk away from your past. Walk away from your pain. Walk away from your addictions and your fears. Just as Christ has forgiven and forgotten our sins, so too we must forgive and forget the sins of our past. When we stop remembering the hurt, we can finally begin to heal. May God's grace give you the courage to walk away from those memories, and may you walk in the footsteps of the Savior for the rest of your life."

For a moment, I thought I was about to witness a miracle. Atticus looked like he was going to get right up out of his chair. Then red-haired Sue-Ellen began to play "Just As I Am" on the keyboard. Brother Michael quickly rose to give the invitation, and the moment was lost.

"If Brother Paul has stirred your heart this morning with his fine message," Michael said, "then just walk forward and give your life to the Lord."

Michael was smiling like a kid with his grandma in a candy store. He knew he'd soon get what he wanted.

"There's no rush," Michael said. "We have all day. That fine meal the widow ladies from the Wesleyan church made for us will be ready whenever we are. If you feel the Lord tugging at your soul, just get up and come forward."

Once again, I noticed Atticus stirring in his chair. Then several of the men sitting around him looked down the row and whispered at Leo.

"Like Jesus," the man to my left said softly, "sometimes we need to be willing to sacrifice ourselves for the sake of others."

Leo shifted in his chair. Clearly, he was uncomfortable with the idea, but he was a man of his word.

"Oh, all right," he said, clearly annoyed by the notion of what he was about to do. With that he got up and walked to the front of the room.

"I am a sinful man," Leo said. "Lord only knows the things I've done. Only a miracle could save a wretch like me."

Michael beamed like a used car salesman.

"Brother Leo and I have some urgent business with Jesus," he said. "I'm going to give the blessing, and then the rest of you are dismissed."

As the others moved quickly toward the door of the cafeteria, Michael led Leo through a door labeled 'Prayer Room.' Leo had the look of a lamb being led to the slaughter. But like they said, today was his turn.

chapter 38

COMMUNION

> We don't come to the table to fight or to defend. We
> don't come to prove or to conquer, to draw lines in the
> sand, or to stir up trouble. We come to the table because
> our hunger brings us there. We come with a need, with
> fragility, with an admission of our humanity. The table
> is the great equalizer.—Shauna Niequist, *Bread and Wine*

We were about to sit down to a feast. Our dinner would
include roast pork, mashed potatoes, crescent rolls, green
beans, and grape Kool-Aid. Like everyone else, I was hungry.
I wanted to sit by Atticus O'Malley and try to reconnect.
Unfortunately, by the time I made it into the dining hall,
his table was full. Each table sat twelve. I took my place with
Paul at a table on the far side of the room. Across from us sat
a foul man by the name of Scratch Weinstein.

I did not want to break bread with him. Unkept and
unclean, his smell entered the room before he did. His
clothes were wrinkled. His teeth were yellow. His mahogany
brown beard and hair were greasy. He also had a bad case
of psoriasis or something similar. A scaly rash covered his
arms, his neck, and part of his face. Weinstein couldn't seem

to leave the rash alone. He would scratch or dig at an itchy spot or rub against something all the time.

Most people kept their distance from his kind of guy and for good reason. He was itching for a fight when he wasn't itching somewhere on his body. He was angry and insecure, and he'd argue about anything from politics to the weather to the way you combed your hair. Like I said, most people avoided him, but not Paul. Before we sat down, he called Weinstein over and invited him to join us.

"Did you enjoy the service?" Paul asked.

"Not my kind of music," Weinstein said, scratching himself profusely.

"What kind of music do you like?"

"Who said I like music?"

"I believe we're going to get a pretty great meal for lunch," Paul said, hoping to find some common ground with the man.

"Pork, ain't it?" Scratch said. "I don't eat pork. I'm Jewish."

"Me too," Paul said. "I don't think God cares near as much about what we put in our mouths as he does about what comes out of them."

"What are you insinuating?" snapped Weinstein.

"I'm not insinuating anything," Paul said, putting his hand firmly on Weinstein's shoulder. "I'm just saying a good meal can be hard to come by for men like us. So, personally, I think God would want us to enjoy it."

With that, Weinstein slumped down into his chair with a frown, and Paul pulled up a chair next to him. When the church ladies brought the platters of food, Paul dished up a healthy portion to all. Then, taking a fork full of pork, Paul turned to Weinstein.

"In the *Sefer Shmuel* scroll," Paul said with a grin, "we're told that David was lacking provisions and hungry. He was so hungry, in fact, he went to Ahimelech, the priest of Nob, and asked him for the showbread. Only the priests could eat the sacred bread, but David believed God was sometimes willing to suspend the law in a moment of great need, and so do I."

With that, Paul put the fork full of pork in his mouth and smiled broadly.

Weinstein watched him for a moment in disbelief. Then hesitantly he put a little pork on his fork, and with a pained look on his face, he slid it between his lips.

"Who knew pig could taste so good?" he said, raising his eyebrows ever so slightly.

Everyone at our table laughed.

Maybe it was because he was preoccupied with the pork, I don't know, but he stopped itching. As we ate our meal, the redness slowly seemed to fade away.

About the time we finished, Leo walked in and sat down across from us at our table.

"I'm starved," he said in a gruff voice. "Nothing works up an appetite like getting saved."

"Have you done this before?" I asked.

"About once a year," he said. "We take turns—no big deal."

"So getting saved doesn't really mean anything to you?" I said.

"Oh, no," he said, "salvation means everything to me. Jesus is about all I've got left in this world. I've had him for a long time, or maybe better, he's had me."

As Leo devoured his pork and potatoes, I learned he had been a tax accountant for the state of Illinois earlier in his life. He grew up in New Jersey, not far from Rutgers. After getting an associate degree in accounting at Essex County College in Newark, he and his family moved to Cicero because he'd been offered a job with the state of Illinois.

"I was living the good life," he said. "I had a wife and two boys, and I was an elder in a Baptist church on the west side of Chicago. Then life came crashing down around me. I got caught embezzling, and I spent ten months in Cook County. By the time I got out, Alice had moved back home to Kansas and filed for divorce."

He said he called her a few times and tried to get her to reconsider, but she wanted nothing to do with him. Eventually she got married again, and her new husband Thomas adopted the boys. That's when Leo started drinking heavily.

"Do you ever see your sons?" I asked.

"No," he said, shaking his head. "Thomas is their daddy now. Besides, they're grown men with families of their own to worry about. Nowadays my family is just me and Jesus."

"How about Michael?" I asked, turning the conversation back to Leo's conversion experience. "Do you mind that he uses food to manipulate you?"

"No," said Leo. "Michael's a good man. He looks out for us, and he's just following his heart. You can't blame somebody for doing that. Besides, once in a while, somebody gets saved for real."

I began to see them in a different light as I sat and talked with Paul, Leo, Weinstein, and the rest of the men at our table. They were a community, a church unto themselves, and in a way, the Kool-Aid and crescent rolls were their communion. They shared what they had, and they looked out for each other in a way that was more Christian than most. On my way home, I asked God to forgive me for being such a cynic. Later that night, I wrote a check to the Lighthouse Mission. I learned that day miracles come in all different shapes and sizes.

chapter 39

Selah

'Wait on the Lord' is a constant refrain in the Psalms, and it is a necessary word, for God often keeps us waiting. He is not in such a hurry as we are.—J. I. Packer, *Knowing God*

Christmas was knocking on the door and I had a lot to do to get ready. Rachel always bought the gifts, did all the decorating, and wrote our family Christmas letter. She would hand sign and address each envelope. She loved that sort of thing. She was good at writing letters, and I was good at letting her write them, but they became my job at her death. The unfairness caused me to be a bit sullen and melancholy.

Like I'd promised, I started reading, *The Lion, the Witch and the Wardrobe* every night before Lucy went to bed. In the chapter we read that night, Father Christmas arrives on his sleigh and explains 'the long season of sadness was coming to an end and Christmas has finally arrived.' Maybe he was right. Right or wrong, I sat down that night and tried to write our Christmas letter.

Unlike many people, we don't brag about the successes of the year or complain about the defeats. Our family tradition is different. Rachel would retell the Christmas story as honestly and accurately as she could. She was a gifted writer, and Christmas always brought out the best in her. I had my work cut out for me. I would have preferred using my laptop, but that's not the way she did the letters. I was doing this to honor her. So, I sat down at the desk, picked up her rosewood fountain pen, and set a clean, unlined sheet of white paper in front of me. Our logo at the top depicts the silhouette of a leaping fox—the symbol of the DeVos family.

Writing this would be a leap of faith for me. I wasn't exactly sure where to begin. Finally, I started with a little Dickens, knowing you can never go wrong quoting the classics.

Charles Dickens once wrote "It was the best of times, it was the worst of times." I think Christmas can be a lot like that. At least that's the way the first Christmas was.

The people of Israel were under the boot of Roman occupation and oppression. They began to wonder if the God of their fathers had abandoned them. Many gave up on their faith, many more wrestled with doubt. Hope flickered like a candle in the wind. In the long pause between the Old Testament and the New, the voice of God had gone strangely silent. They were living in the "selah," a word from the book of Psalms, which means "wait." Sit quietly and listen. Pause and reflect on what happened yesterday, and trust God with tomorrow.

Personally, I'm still working on that one. But I'm also encouraged by the fact that, biblically speaking, selah is never the last word. Linguistically, selah is an intermission which says there will be a pause in the action, but God is not finished yet. There is still more to come. In that sense, selah is a word of great hope because life is full of gaps—at least I know mine is. There are times when we feel our prayers go unanswered or fall on deaf ears. When that happens, old doubts return like a dormant virus.

Doubt is the traveling companion of some of us all the time, and all of us some of the time. We can't escape—we're human. There's more mystery to life than we care to admit. We don't know things. We pretend we do, but we don't. Most of the time, we hide our doubts away where no one else can see them. However, tragedy has a way of revealing our doubts, and death is the biggest tragedy of all.

Jesus's brother Judas once wrote "be merciful to those who doubt." I find his words comforting. Not that I don't have faith. I do. Still, sometimes I'm also plagued by these creeping doubts. I believe, and then I question. I pray, and I curse. I shake my angry fist at heaven, and then my knees tremble in fear.

Like a rabbit calling out the hawk, I demand that God show himself.

"Ollie, ollie, oxen free, come out, come out, wherever you be!"

So far at least, he hasn't come out. He just sits silently somewhere in the darkness. So, I'm forced to live in the Selah, the void, the long dramatic pause.

I take some solace in the fact that's exactly what happened at the end of the Old Testament when the prophet Malachi put down his pen. For a time, God pursed his lips.

"Shhhh," said the eternal Logos, "rest your ears. This is a time for silent meditation, trust, and prayer." The people of Israel did as they were told. They trusted, meditated, and prayed. They prayed good prayers. As good as any we've ever prayed. But for a time at least, their prayers went unanswered. God and his prophets were mute for four centuries. Not a peep, not a sound, not one word was uttered.

And like us, when that happened, little by little, the demons of doubt began to have their way with their hearts. They tried to resist but resistance was hard—truly hard. Many people simply gave up. Their faith faltered and fear invaded their hearts. The gap of silence was too long. But then, just before the last candle of hope was snuffed out, God finally broke his silence.

"And there were shepherds living out in the fields nearby, keeping watch over their flocks at night. An angel of the Lord appeared to them, and the glory of the Lord shone around them, and they were terrified. But the angel said to them, 'Do not be afraid. I bring you good news that will cause great joy that will be for all people. Today in the city of David a Savior has been born to you; He is the Messiah, the Lord.'

And then, once again, it was the best of times.

So, this Christmas, we wait, hoping the Lord will speak into our lives.

I signed it "In his grip, Rocky & Lucy."

But to be honest, I felt more like we'd slipped through his fingers this year.

The next day I gave the letter and Rachel's old address book to my secretary Margret. "Make me twenty-five copies of this," I said. "And hand-address the envelopes."

"I could easily run a set of labels for you," she replied.

"No," I said with a smile, "they have to be hand-addressed. Take your time. I want them to be neat. Act like your Christmas bonus depends on neatness."

Margret did a beautiful job with them. Rachel would have been proud. I made myself a mental note to get Margret and her husband, Dave, a gift certificate for dinner at Alpenrose as a thank you. The next night, I folded the letters, tucked them inside the envelopes, and sealed them. Lucy put a stamp on each one, and in my mind, I crossed that job off my to-do list.

chapter 40

LOVE

There's nothing more intimate in life than simply being understood and understanding someone else.
—Brad Meltzer, *The Inner Circle*

I was feeling conflicted. It had been over a year since Rachel died and occasionally friends wanted to set me up on a blind date. There was a part of me that wanted to go. I longed to be in a relationship again. But the thought of being with another woman, even as friends, made me feel like I was cheating on Rachel. So for now at least, like Paul, I decided to live a single, celibate life. But sometimes I had second thoughts.

"Tell me, Paul," I said, midway through our next session, "Did you ever love again?"

"Of course," he said, "life without love is hardly worth living. It is a sacred gift from the creator. He planted the desire to love and be loved deep in our souls. For this reason, the Torah teaches us to love God as he loves us. But what so many fail to see is that the best way to love God is not by scrupulously observing his laws but by loving those he loves. And of course, God loves all people. If only we could do that, the world would be a better place.

"When you ask, 'did I ever love again?' I wonder what you mean. Did I love the Torah? Did I love the children of Israel? Did I love my friends and family? You see, there are degrees to love, nuances, different ways to express it. The problem is that too often we reduce love to nothing more than passion. The romantic love between a man and a woman. The kind of love that makes your heart flutter. I suspect that's what you meant.

"Such love is addictive. We all long for it. We never get enough. Even in those fleeting moments when we find this kind of love, it only leaves us wanting more. The thirst for passion is never really satisfied, is it?"

I wasn't sure if Paul was making a statement or if he wanted me to answer so I said nothing.

He tilted his head, glanced my way, smiled ever so slightly and then continued.

"But there is also a more mature love, a love that surpasses romance, and it is the selfless, sacrificial love that is so rare. This, I think, is the love that is closest to the creator's love for us.

"In my travels to Corinth," he said, settling in to tell another one of his stories, "I met a man named Aquila from Pontus on the edge of the Black Sea. He came to Corinth when Claudius ordered all the Jews to leave Rome. He set up shop on the northwest corner of the market. The market of Corinth was laid out like a square, open at all corners with ten small shops built into each wall.

"Aquila had already rented a space in the market. With only forty shops in all, space was limited and expensive. Both of us being Jews, and both crafters of leather, Aquila invited me to set up my worktable in his booth, and we could share the rent. This meant we lived and worked in very close quarters. I found the proximity quite enjoyable. He and his wife Priscilla slept in the loft above the shop while I slept on a cot in the space below."

Once again, I thought this was the kind of architectural detail an archeologist like Laubstein would know about a place like Corinth. Every time I met with Paul, my mind would teeter-totter back and forth between Laubstein and Father Aboud. One minute, I believed Paul was the one and then the next minute, I'd be just as sure he was the other. And as much as I tried to suppress the thought, there were times I thought he was exactly who he said he was. Of course, I knew the apostle's reincarnation couldn't really be possible. Still, the man told a convincing story. Sometimes, we want to believe something so badly we make a little room in our minds for possibility.

"In time, the three of us became like family," Paul said. "Priscilla was a woman of substance and beautiful. Silver streaked her long black hair and reminded me of shooting stars on an autumn night. Her eyes were like that of a young calf, large, deep, and dark, and they flashed with a glint of fire whenever she got excited. When she brushed close by me, I would catch the faint smell of lilies after a spring rain. More than once, I told Aquilla that he was a lucky man. Each time he would nod and smile, but he said nothing.

"Aquila spoke when spoken to, but otherwise he was a man of few words. Priscilla, on the other hand, loved to probe the deep thoughts of life as we worked. Most afternoons, Aquila would sit quietly working at his bench, while Priscilla and I would engage in intense and challenging verbal banter. I was friends with them both, but like me, she was a lover of words. It intensified our relationship. In time, I grew closer to her than him. You could say there was a sacred love between us. Later, I would write to them, and about them and it was always 'Priscilla' and 'Aquila.' Her name first, then his.

"Honestly," Paul said with a blush in his cheek, "she is the only woman I've ever known, besides my Shamir, who could delight or frustrate me with the turn of a phrase."

This is definitely a man who has loved a woman. A priest, a man who has lived a life outside the company of women would not know of such things. He must be Laubstein. The architectural details, the passion—all point to Paul being Laubstein.

As the session ended, Paul got up to leave, but he paused at the door.

"God calls most of us to share our lives with others. But he calls some to more. He wants us to share our lives exclusively with him. Each of us must decide what is right for us on our own. There is no wrong answer."

chapter 41

DARKNESS

> Darkness cannot drive out darkness: only light can
> do that. Hate cannot drive out hate: only love can do
> that.— Martin Luther King Jr., *A Testament of Hope: The
> Essential Writings and Speeches*

Darkness comes early this time of year in Michigan. I
drove to and from work under an inky sky. I really didn't
mind because the streets of downtown Holland were lit up
like a Christmas card. Little white lights were woven through
the naked trees that lined Eighth Street, and the antique gas
streetlamps were each meticulously decorated with well-lit
evergreen wreaths.

On my way home, I picked up a pizza at Fricanos for
dinner. Lucy loves the way the cheese crisps up as it bubbles
over the wafer-thin crust on the edge of the pie. That and
some cookies made for an easy dinner. Later she did some
homework and went to bed.

Lucy finally fell asleep but only after I read a little more
of *The Lion, the Witch and the Wardrobe* and listened to
her prayers. I went back to the living room, lit a fire in the
fireplace, and sat down to wrap some Christmas presents. A

soft snow fell outside the window. As I looked out, I wondered if God was hiding out there somewhere in the darkness.

Still searching for answers, I pulled Rachel's Bible from the bookcase. Then I began to read Luke's account of Jesus's birth. She had highlighted the words "great with child," and "the days were accomplished," and "there was no room for them," and "the angel of the Lord," and "do not be afraid." I'd read the story many times before, but the words were surprisingly comforting. Some things need to be read in the old King James version. At least that's how I felt that night. Reading the words was like being swaddled in a warm familiar blanket.

I must have fallen asleep in the chair because, around midnight, I woke up frightened and confused. My heart was pounding like a hammer in my chest. My mind rapidly flashed back through scenes of the nightmare. For a few minutes, I found myself in the thin space that exists between dreams and reality. I tried to adjust my eyes to the dim light as I sat in the dark in front of the flickering fire. Then I slowly picked my way through my thoughts and fears, hoping to sort out the real from the unreal.

There's something about the unknown that frightens us. We want to explain away fear. Unfortunately, some things defy explanation—we must take them on faith. This was one of those things.

The dream was about Christmas, the first Christmas to be exact, and I watched it unfold in front of me. The birth was messy and difficult. When the child finally arrived, they placed the new born king in the manger. Then exhausted, Mary and Joseph fell asleep in each other's arms. Suddenly, there was this sense that they were not alone, that we were not alone. Something or someone lingered in the darkness. Suddenly the whole earth went silent and a deep, strong voice whispered ever so softly. I could barely hear it.

"You're in my domain now," the voice said. "From the pinnacle of the temple, as far as you can see everything here is mine. And from the first breath that filled those little human lungs of yours you knew it. You sensed the trembling frailties of human flesh. So, tell me, my little prince, how does it feel for the Lion of Judah to be born into the body of the sacrificial lamb?" And then there was this laugh, this sinister laugh. That's when I woke up.

"A dream," I said to myself. "That's all, just a dream." But the weight of the images and the hungering darkness pressed in on me.

In that moment, my loss and my pain seemed somehow less significant. Both paled in comparison to what waited for him.

The next morning, when I turned on my phone, I found a text message from Laurie at Sommerdyke's office. The message was short and to the point.

"Gabriel Shalhoob has risen from the dead. Last night, sometime after midnight, he awoke from his coma. His family got a little Easter for Christmas."

chapter 42

CHRISTMAS

For it is good to be children sometimes, and never better than at Christmas, when its mighty Founder was a child Himself.—Charles Dickens, *A Christmas Carol*

I had a couple of afternoon appointments at the downtown office, so I left Hope's campus early on Friday. The following Monday when I came in, there was a note on my desk from Margret, the psych department secretary.

"Gunny is coming for Christmas on the twenty first. Two days, don't fuss."

Gunnery Sargent Jack Rademacher was Rachel's father. He had been a Marine for most of his life, and he looked the part—built like a fireplug, short and sturdy with arms like tree trunks. His freckled face was leathered and ruddy. His hair was cut high and tight, shaved close on the sides with a crown of longer reddish-brown bristles on top. Ordinarily Gunny was a man of few words, so I could almost hear the conversation.

"Is Rocky there?" he'd ask.

"No, I'm sorry," Margret would reply in a cheery tone. *"He's gone for the day. Can I put you through to his voice mail?"*

Gunny would have responded with a long, silent pause, and some grunting. Then he would bark an order.

"No, just take a message. Tell him Gunny is coming for Christmas on the twenty-first. I'm hitching a ride on a cargo plane going from Twentynine Palms to Battle Creek. I'll rent a car there and be in about oh six hundred hours. Tell him not to fuss—I'll only be there a couple days."

Rachel and her mom, Tika, followed Gunny halfway around the world and back during his military career. Growing up, Rachel's home was always the Marine Corps Air Ground Combat Center (MCAGCC), also known as Twentynine Palms, outside San Bernardino, California.

As a child, Tika's family came up from Mexico each spring to pick fruit and vegetables. Eventually her father got a green card. After that, they lived year-round with a cousin, who had a house outside San Bernardino. While Tika went to high school and college, she worked part-time at McDonalds where she met Jack.

From the old pictures Rachel had, I could see Tika was a beautiful woman. Her mocha-colored skin, strong cheekbones, and silver streaked black hair revealed her Latin roots. The lines around her dark eyes also told the story of life-long hard work.

Unfortunately, I never met Tika. She died of cancer three days after Gunny got home from Desert Storm. She was sick when he left, but Rachel said she refused to die until she could say goodbye. From what I know of the woman, that would have been just like her. Like her daughter, Tika always put everyone else's needs ahead of her own.

Gunny lived about two miles off the base in a small, neatly kept two-bedroom craftsman style bungalow, which he and Tika bought a few years after they got married. Rachel grew up there.

At forty-eight, Gunny was forced to retire after putting in thirty years of service. Twelve years later, he looked like he was still in drill-ready shape. He worked in construction after leaving the Corps, and he occupied his free time hiking in Joshua Tree National Park and doing some volunteer work at Desert Palms Community Church.

About three-thirty in the afternoon, a blue Ford Fiesta with a Budget Rent-a-Car sticker pulled into the driveway. Gunny rolled out of the driver's door with a marine duffle bag in his hand and a smile on his face.

Lucy ran out to meet him and threw her arms around his neck.

"Grandpa Gunny," she squealed, "we miss you."

"I miss you too, Lucy," Gunny said.

Once inside, the old marine sat down on one of the bar stools that faced our kitchen. Then he lifted Lucy onto his lap. As he did, I opened a can of corn and poured it into a bowl with some butter.

"I thought I said not to fuss," Gunny snarled.

"No fuss. Just meatloaf and mashed potatoes—Lucy's favorite—and I know you like corn."

After dinner we sat in the living room, and Gunny played some board games with Lucy. Then finally, he opened his duffle bag and pulled out a stack of packages. They were wrapped in the Sunday comics.

"No use wasting money on paper," Gunny would say.

The truth is, he said the same every year. As always, he spoiled Lucy with gifts of games and electronics and clothes I'm sure he had some help choosing. I'm not sure who most enjoyed her opening them—Gunny or her. Like his daughter, the man was clearly a giver. Later, after Lucy and I had our nightly reading of *The Lion, the Witch and the Wardrobe*, she went to bed, and the adult conversation got more serious.

"How you doing, Rock?" he said. "And don't tell me you're fine. I know better. You look tired and skinny."

"Okay," I said. "I'm not fine, but I'm functioning. I'm teaching, and I'm still seeing clients. I'm trying to make things as normal as I can for Lucy, but she misses her mother."

"We all miss her," he said. "We'll always miss her, but we've also got to keep going somehow."

"I'm struggling with that, I guess," I said. "What breaks my heart is I know Lucy is too. I want to be there for her, and I try, but sometimes I've got all I can do to just get through the day. If I'm honest about it, I've lost touch with God in all this too. I kind of feel like he's abandoned us."

"Don't mistake God's silence for his absence," Gunny said, leaning in and talking so low I could hardly hear him. "He's just giving you a little space. He knows what you need. But trust me, boy, he still loves you. He can't help but love you. That's who he is.

I nodded like I agreed, but mostly I just didn't feel like arguing. I'd heard all the words before and knew them as well as he does. "God is love." At least that's what his Book says. But right now, I didn't feel very loved.

"I felt the same way you feel when I lost Tika. For a while, God and I drifted apart. I finally figured out the one who had moved was me. After that, I found God right where I had left him, in the pages of his Book. He spoke to me there. He still does. His words get me through everything."

"I feel strange telling a preacher he's got to read the Bible more," Gunny said, shaking his head and giving me a little grin. "But that's my advice, Rocky. If you ask me, the Book is a love story for the broken-hearted—a romance novel with a weird twist. Much to our surprise, the main character falls madly in love with the reader."

Like Rachel, his hazel eyes grew in intensity as he talked. For a moment, I felt like he was staring into my soul. Then he looked away, shrugged, and began to speak again.

"What do I know?" said Gunny. "You're the theologian, but I think that's what Christmas is all about. You know, 'for God so loved the world that he gave his only son ...'"

Once again, I nodded, but this time I really was agreeing with him.

"And as for Lucy," Gunny said, leaning back in his chair and smiling like the Cheshire cat, "I want to help you with that too. There's a new pilot program at Camp Grayling called M-LET (Michigan Law Enforcement Training). The purpose is to help twenty-five to thirty MPs a year transition into civilian law enforcement after their tour is up.

"Northwestern Michigan College and the Michigan State Police are partnering to provide the classroom instruction in civilian law. They're also hiring some ex-military guys to certify the recruits in weapons and explosives.

"Tom Reeves, an old friend from Marine Corps Logistics, heads that end of the program, and he's asked me to come and help him. The plan is to have two eighteen-week semesters, one in the fall and another one in the spring. I'd be a civilian contractor working on site during the training sessions and for a week before and after each of them. That means I'd work forty weeks and be off twelve.

"You thinking about taking the job?" I asked.

"The truth is, I already told him I would," Gunny said. "The spring semester starts in the middle of March. Since I'll be a lot closer to you and Lucy, I hope I can see her more often, especially in the summer and around Christmas. I'm not much of a cook, and I'm not sure what little girls like to do, but I'll do whatever she wants. I know at her age, Rachel liked to go fishing, so maybe Lucy will too. And if she wants, I could tell her stories about her mom."

"She'd like that, Gunny," I said. "I'd like that too. You would be a big help."

Our conversation ended a few minutes later when he yawned, said he was tired, and went to bed. I sat up for a little while. Rachel's Bible sat on the little triangle table next to her chair. Truthfully, I wanted to connect with her more than with God. But about then either one would do, so I picked up her Bible and started thumbing through it.

chapter 43

Released

It's hard to let go. Even when what you're holding onto is full of thorns, it's hard to let go. Maybe especially then.
—Stephen King, *Joyland*

I slowly looked through the pages of Rachel's dog-eared old Bible, searching for God knows what. Again and again, I paused to read her notes on the pages she'd highlighted. You can tell a lot about a person's relationship with God by the condition of their Bible. Someone once said, "a person whose Bible is well worn and tattered usually isn't." That was true of Rachel. She held up through all this better than I did. Like I said before, the cancer only seemed to drive her closer to God. Her Bible was a rainbow of colors with all the highlighting and notes in the margin.

I used to tease her about it. "Your Bible looks like a kid's coloring book. I don't know how you can even read something like that."

"The colors are my way of remembering my conversations with God."

From the look of her Bible, the two of them did a lot of talking.

In John's gospel, she had circled some of Jesus's words with a pink highlighter.

> Do not let your hearts be troubled. You believe in God, believe also in me. My Father's house has many rooms; if that were not so, would I have told you that I am going there to prepare a place for you? And if I go and prepare a place for you, I will come back and take you to be with me that you also may be where I am.

For a moment, I thought that's so Rachel. She knew one day when my heart was wrenching, I would reach for her Bible and hear her voice. So often I'd sat in Christ the Redeemer Church and heard her read the morning's Scripture lesson. She was always so confident, so sure God was speaking through her. I hoped she was right.

In 1Thessalonians she marked Paul's words in yellow.

> Brothers and sisters, we do not want you to be uninformed about those who sleep in death, so that you do not grieve like the rest of mankind, who have no hope. For we believe that Jesus died and rose again, and so we believe that God will bring with Jesus those who have fallen asleep in him.

She had underlined the words 'do not grieve,' with a blue felt tip pen.

That's not fair. You get heaven, and we get to deal with the hell of you dying. Grief is a part of that, whether you like it or not. In fact, since you've been gone, my dear, I've become fluent in the language of grief.

In 2 Corinthians she marked a section in orange.

> For we know that if the earthly tent we live in is destroyed, we have a building from God, an eternal house in heaven, not made with human hands. Meanwhile we groan, longing to be clothed instead with our heavenly dwelling.

And then off in the margin, behind the word "groan," she made a note in her own hand. She wrote, "some of us are groaning now, but our suffering connects us with God. He is no stranger to the anguish of death. Remember, death claimed his one and only son."

Then, just a verse later, she highlighted Paul's explanation for why all this has to happen. We have to die to this world, "so that what is mortal may be swallowed up by life."

She underlined the word "life" twice, and followed by her handwritten commentary, "LIFE, not Death. If you're reading this, Rocky, then I'm where I need to be, and you're where you need to be, at least for now, but not forever. God has promised us we will spend eternity together with Christ."

A little farther down the page, in a multitude of colors, she marked a sentence that spoke to her. "Now the one who has fashioned us for this very purpose is God, who has given us the Spirit as a deposit, guaranteeing what is to come."

Again, there was a note in her elegant handwriting.

"We were created to be eternal, but sin spoiled all that. Through his sacrifice, Jesus returned humanity to their default setting, and his Spirit guarantees we will stand guiltless before God."

Following that, in verse six, she had circled the word "therefore" with a green felt-tip pen. Then, next to it, she wrote a second note. As I read it, I remembered she had a way of explaining the deepest theological thoughts with the simplest words. This was one of those times. "This is Paul's hinge word. Everything turns on it. The two thoughts are permanently bridged with this one word, like he is saying because all that happened, then this must happen next. His thought is completed in verse seven.

"For we live by faith, not by sight. We are confident, I say, and would prefer to be away from the body and at home with the Lord."

The words "away from the body" and "at home with the Lord" were underlined in green.

Her words caught me by surprise. They reminded me of her pain. That only hurt me all the more.

In the back, in the last book of the Bible, Rachel highlighted one more section.

"He will wipe away every tear from their eyes." Rachel had underlined "every" in red. "There will be no more death or mourning or crying or pain, for the old order of things has passed away."

In the margin, Rachel had written her own three-word commentary on the verse.

In capital letters, she wrote "the biblical *pangram*."

Pangram is a Greek word that means "all letters."

We learned to type by using the phrase "The quick brown fox jumps over the lazy dog" because the phrase contains all the letters in our English alphabet. By practicing to type this one sentence, our fingers found their way to every key we'd need to type anything we'd ever want.

I took Rachel's words to mean this one verse said everything. In her mind, this was a summary of the biblical message.

The next words stunned me.

"Write this down. Write this down!"

This is a divine directive, so important we're told to write it down as though God was saying "tie a string around this verse. Commit it to memory. Don't forget it because some day you'll need this verse." I wept uncontrollably as the words washed over my troubled soul.

No more mourning, no more crying, no more pain, and no more death.

Finally, as I wiped the tears from my eyes, I was surprised to discover that beneath the words "biblical pangram" Rachel had written me a personal note.

"Rocky, if you're reading this, I want you to know there is a letter for you in the top drawer of my desk."

A chill ran down my spine. Immediately, I went scrambling into her office. There, after a little searching, I found an envelope taped to the back of her desk drawer with my name on it. As I opened it, several pictures fell out onto the floor.

I recognized some of them. Rachel had the habit of using pictures as bookmarks in her Bible, and these were some of those. I thumbed through them slowly, and together we went down memory lane. There was a black and white photo of the two of us getting into my old jeep outside the church on the day we got married. Another was up north in Michigan when she and I spent an afternoon cross-country skiing on the trails by Mission Point lighthouse. There was also a picture from the day Lucy was born, one from the open house we had for the office, and another from a crisp fall day when the two of us were picking apples at the orchards. I sat on the floor, with tears streaming down my cheeks. I looked at each picture, trying to remember the exact day they were taken.

We were so happy then. It was so easy to take it all for granted. Finally, I unfolded the note. As I did, I could smell the faint lingering of her perfume. In her beautifully crafted script, she wrote:

Dear sweet Rocky,
You were truly my rock in all of this. I could not have fought this fight without you. But if you are reading this, I know we have lost the final battle. I also know my death will be hardest on you. No one loved this body of mine more than you. I want you to know your touch, your strong embrace made even the worst days better. You, my love, held me through the good times and the tears. I love you for that. But now you must learn to let me go. For a while, I know that will be hard. There is a part

of me which is glad about that, but my heart breaks to know your heart is breaking. For this reason, I want to release you, my love, so you might love again.

God appointed a Rocky and Rachel time, and we fit together like peanut butter and jelly, like love and marriage, and like God and grace. But now the love we had must be put on hold for a while. I promised you I'd be waiting for you inside heaven's gate, and I will, but I cannot bear the thought of you being alone until then.

Perhaps that's what Jesus meant when he said, "At the resurrection people will neither marry nor be given in marriage; but will be like the angels in heaven."

Maybe we will love everyone deeply and completely like you and I love each other now. I really don't know. All I know is my love for you is stronger than anything, even death. Our love was a gift from God. Nothing will ever change that. So please, Rocky, don't be afraid to fall in love again. Dare to go where your best thoughts take you. My only hope is you will make someone else as happy as you've made me. And don't worry, my love. No matter what might happen on earth, I know in heaven you will be mine forever."

Eventually I made my way to bed, but I didn't sleep much. I was continually agitated by my restless thoughts of Rachel—and by Gunny snoring in the guest bedroom.

chapter 44

RECONSIDER

He is no fool who lets go of what he cannot keep to grab hold of that which he cannot lose. —Jim Elliot, *The Journals of Jim Elliot*

True to his word, Gunny stayed two days. He left early in the morning of the twenty-third of December. Later that day, Lucy and I drove up to Suttons Bay to spend Christmas with my family. This was the heart of winter in Michigan—the air bone-chilling cold, trees naked and bare against a gray and cloudy sky. The world lay dormant under a thick blanket of white snow. Even the strongest pine branches bent low by the weight of it. Like us, cars filled with packages and people were going over the river and through the woods to grandma's house.

Lucy was excited to see her cousins and to open presents. I felt better just knowing I was going home. My dad and my brothers would take me skiing early Christmas morning—our holiday tradition. Then we'd come home to the feast and the festivities. For a while, I could hide from my pain. At some point, I knew my mom would come over, put her arm around me, and say what she always says.

"It'll be all right, Rocky, it'll be all right." Even if it wasn't true, hearing her say the words made them true for a little while.

As usual, the hum of the motor slowly put Lucy to sleep. I looked at my iPhone. Not yet five o'clock but already dark. Just north of Ludington, I was alone once again with my thoughts. Gunny had traveled back home. We were traveling north. The whole world was on the move. I couldn't help but remember something Paul said when I asked him if he ever got tired of all the traveling.

"We're always so eager to get somewhere," he said, skirting my question for the moment. "We act as if the goal of life is to arrive at some appointed destination, but life is about the journey. If we don't take the time to enjoy the journey, we'll end up missing the blessings God has hidden for us along the way."

Driving silently in the moonlit night, I realized Paul was right. The earth is thick with God's handiwork. As I drove along the lakeshore, I knew why people call northern Michigan "God's country." Huge snowflakes danced in my headlights. They almost looked like falling stars against the dark denim sky. Northern Michigan is a breathtakingly beautiful place, a winter wonderland.

There was a part of me that wanted to take Paul home with me for Christmas. I wanted to share all this with him. I'd grown quite fond of the guy over the last few months. Not that there wouldn't be room, my folks always made room for anyone I ever brought home, and not that he wouldn't be welcome, either. My family would welcome anyone to their table who was hungry. My problem was I wasn't sure what I'd say.

Hi, Mom—hi, Dad. This is my friend Paul from work. He's a homeless schizophrenic who thinks he's the apostle Paul. To be honest, some days I think he might be, but he's probably not, definitely not, well, okay, maybe.

In my more rational moments, I've tried to find out who he really is, and I have narrowed his identity down some. For a while, I believed he was Gabriel Shalhoub from the other side of the state, but I was wrong. Now I vacillate between believing he's a Canadian priest named Father Paul Aboud or an Israeli archeologist named Dr. Avrehim Laubstein. Unfortunately, all I really know is that his story and my story intertwine, a lot. I know, this sounds a little bizarre, but don't worry, I don't think he's dangerous.

Some stones are better left unturned. This was one of those. I decided to let Paul celebrate Jesus's birth with his friends at the mission. Truthfully, if Jesus was going to be anywhere this Christmas, he'd probably be there, eating pork and potatoes with Paul and Leo and the widow ladies from the Wesleyan church. I chuckled at the thought but sobered a bit when I remembered I still had to write my report for Judge Summerdyke's court when I got back home. For all my sessions with the man, his identity remained a mystery to me.

We drove three hours from our house in Holland to my family's farm arriving there a little after six. We put our stuff in the bay cottage, and Lucy went up to the main house to help Frankie with dinner. They're serious about food at the farm. Most nights they have meat, potatoes, vegetables, and dessert, usually pie. Tonight was no exception.

Nobody makes fried chicken like Mom does. As usual, I ate too much including a big slab of apple pie with ice cream. After dinner, Lucy went to spend the night with her cousins, and I went back to the bay cottage alone. I lit a fire, sat in Sea's leather recliner, and picked up the *New York Times*, one of the few daily newspapers left in our digital world. Sea always read the *Times* after dinner. He liked to keep up on what was going on in the world. This was one of the many things we had in common.

As I flipped through the international section, a headline three-quarters of the way down caught my eye.

"Injured Israeli Archeologist Returns to Syria."

"What," I said, out loud, "how could this be?" Until that moment, I was almost certain Paul was, in fact, Laubstein.

The article crashed the teeter-totter of my speculations in Aboud's direction.

> Dr. Avrehim Joseph Laubstein, professor of Jewish studies at Hebrew University in Jerusalem, will return to Syria in January with a team of UN archeologists. Airstrikes led by the US coalition have driven ISIS forces back across the Syrian border. Laubstein and the UN team are eager to see firsthand what was left of several religious sites terrorists had targeted.

It went on to explain how the professor had been critically injured a little over a year and a half ago. An IED went off at a shrine marking the spot where the resurrected Jesus confronted the apostle Paul on his way to Damascus. The explosion injured Laubstein and killed his wife Marta and two others. The article said he felt the best way to honor their memory was to finish the work they'd begun together.

"Death and the forces of evil cannot have the last word," he said. "The work must be resurrected. The middle east hungers for a little Easter."

His words grabbed me by the throat. Suddenly, I realized Paul could not possibly be Laubstein. In so many ways, I knew no more about his identity than I did the first night I met him in a Holland Hospital. Like it or not, I was almost back at square one. My mind was whirling with all the old questions. Who is this man? Where did he come from? How could he know so much about the apostle Paul? Could he possibly be who he claimed to be? Of course not. Don't be ridiculous. He must be the priest.

chapter 45

WRESTLING

Jacob wrestled with God for the blessing. He wrestled
with Esau for the blessing. He wrestled with Isaac for the
blessing, with Laban for the blessing, and in each case he
eventually prevailed. He wrestled because he recognized
that the blessings were worth the struggle.
—Jonahan Safron Foer, *Here I Am*

Like Jacob at Jabok, sometimes I wrestle with God after
dark, and we took to the mat again that night. I hardly
slept. I couldn't stop thinking about Paul. A swarm of
unanswered questions buzzed around like bees inside
my brain. Unfortunately, insomnia is familiar territory for
me—a consistent condition I know well. I also know where
sleeplessness leads. Darkness begets darkness. Soon, an
angry gang of thoughts marched across my mind, and once
again, I found myself missing Rachel. Memories have a way
of sneaking up on me, and suddenly one grabbed me by the
throat.

It was just about a year ago, I thought, when I finally
began to admit to myself that she might not survive.

Her first surgery was at Holland Hospital. We were
hopeful, but when the cancer came back a year later, we went

to the University Hospital in Ann Arbor. The melanoma was aggressive and had gone to her lymph nodes and her lungs. The doctor was somber when he came in to talk with us after the surgery. He was young—in his late twenties—and an older colleague stood behind him holding a clipboard. While the younger doctor evaluated Rachel, the older doctor evaluated him. The young doctor's nervousness indicated this was the first time he had delivered news of this nature.

"Dr. Goldberg and I did what we could," he said, shifting his weight from one foot to the other. Then he looked back at his mentor. After an approving nod, he continued.

"We took the tumor and considerable margin as well, but I'm afraid the growth had already spread beyond that. This is a very aggressive type of cancer. We'll try chemo and radiation. You can do that back in Holland if you'd like, but the prognosis isn't good. I'm sorry to say this. My advice is to go home and put your affairs in order."

"Thank you, Doctor," Rachel said, putting his needs ahead of her own. "I can't imagine how difficult your job must be at times like this. You were very compassionate."

I could see she was trying to make this as easy as possible for him.

"Thanks," he said, smiling slightly. Then he and the doctor with the clipboard left us alone to try to make sense of the prognosis.

That was in September. We were in the middle of the second round of chemo by the time the holidays rolled around. Treatment had been a bumpy road. She felt weak. Food lost its taste, and she had trouble keeping anything down. Then, one morning just before Thanksgiving, her long amber hair started coming out in clumps. During the whole ordeal, she rarely cried or complained, but that day she cried uncontrollably. I tried to console her, but my feeble efforts were in vain. She'd bottled up her tears for too long, and once they started flowing, they wouldn't stop.

A few days later, after shaving what little hair remained on her head, we went to Grand Rapids and got a wig. She never liked it. Most days she defiantly tied a silk scarf around her head like an outlaw biker. Other days she just went bald and beautiful. Christmas Eve was one of those days.

The pain was piling up, and we were crumbling under the weight. At least I was, for sure. I didn't want Lucy to see us struggle, so earlier that week I sent her up to Sutton's Bay to spend the holidays with my family. I spent the next few days at the hospital with Rachel. In the late afternoon of Christmas Eve, Rachel went down for radiation. This gave me a chance to go home and get cleaned up and get a change of clothes. I took a long, hot shower. The warmth felt good. I was driving back to the hospital in the dark when a cold thought began to chill my soul.

"What am I going to do if Rachel dies?" I whispered to myself. My heart was racing. I hadn't dared ask that question before. Every now and then, for a fleeting second, I thought about her possible death, but I'd bury the question as quickly as I could. I hoped if I didn't think about the possibility, maybe the cancer would just go away. Miracles happen, right?

The preacher said miracles are like raindrops. They fall on the just and the unjust, and sooner or later, we all get one. So, we prayed, pleaded, bartered, and begged. But looking back now, we were carrying an umbrella to the desert.

Christmas lights budded like little luminescent tulips on the trees along River Avenue. I took my time driving back to the hospital, trying to get in the Christmas spirit. An inflatable Santa danced in the wind on the lawn across the street from the Emergency Room entrance. Like everyone else, I had a wish list, but mine was only one word long.

"Remission," I whispered silently, asking God to conform his will to mine. "Drive this cancer back to hell where it belongs."

The day was gray and cloudy. Dirty snow piles lined the streets. Winter has a way of working on you if you're not careful. I was not going to let that happen. For Rachel's sake, I was going to be upbeat even if it killed me.

"Maybe we'll go to church tonight," I told myself. "She'd like that. Maybe church could take her mind off things for a while. Mine too, maybe."

When I got out of the car, I pulled a $100 bill out of my money clip and tucked the C-note under the driver's license in my wallet, just in case they took an offering. In hindsight, I was probably hoping to buy Rachel a little more time. I was bargaining with God, or at least trying. The problem is that he wasn't playing. He rarely does.

The ER was around the back. There was a small parking lot to the north where the staff and clergy parked. A gaunt, gray-haired woman with sunken cheeks rang the Salvation Army bell just outside the door. I shoved a twenty into her kettle.

"God's blessings be with you, good sir," she said, giving me a toothless grin.

"And also with you," I replied, hoping her prediction would come true.

When I walked into Rachel's room, the lights were off. I could barely see her lying there in the green glow of the machines that were keeping her alive. The blankets were all scrunched up at the end of the bed. She had part of the sheet draped over her midsection. Her arms dangled lifelessly off either side of the bed, and she had an IV tube sticking out of each wrist. Her legs were crossed, and a drainage tube was sticking out of her side.

For a moment I panicked, but then her chest expanded ever so slightly as she took a breath.

Thank God, she's only sleeping.

The chemo treatments had slowly robbed her of her strength and her appetite. She was terribly gaunt. This was the first time I'd seen her naked in quite a while. I was crushed by her condition. She looked like one of those Catholic crucifixes that still has Jesus spiked to the cross. I sat down in the chair beside her bed, and for the first time in a long time we slept together.

About an hour later she woke up, smiled at me slightly, and said she was hungry.

I rejoiced in my mind. *Hallelujah, she's getting her appetite back. The chemo must be working.*

Some friends from Hope had stopped by earlier. They brought us a meal of chicken soup and homemade banana bread. I had stopped at deBoer Bakery on my way back to the hospital and got her a half a dozen *kraklingens* and a ring of frosted *banket*. The first is a very light and airy pretzel-shaped sugar cookie. The second is a golden-brown puff pastry dough that's filled with almond paste. The Dutch treats were Rachel's favorites. This was the best Christmas dinner we could have had under the circumstances. Afterward, the two of us exchanged gifts. She got me a navy-blue Patagonia down vest. I got her diamond earrings.

"You're the most beautiful woman I know," I whispered as she put in the earrings. And I meant it.

"You just have a thing for skinny bald chicks," she said, smiling.

"Yeah, that's it," I said, reaching over and holding her hand. For a while, the two of us were lost in our love for each other.

Only two theologians would have this kind of a talk in the cancer ward. Strangely, our conversation seemed quite natural to us. The hospital had piped Christmas music through the hallway. We could hear the faint sound of Phillip Brooks' "O Little Town of Bethlehem." For a few minutes, we closed our eyes and let the music take us someplace else. Then she broke the silence.

"In Dante's Inferno," she said, "there's a sign above the gates of Hell that reads 'Abandon all hope, ye who enter here.'"

I wasn't sure where she was going with all this, but Rachel quoted the sign not to inform me as much as to remind me.

"Christmas stands in contrast to that," she continued in a whisper.

Then she softly sang a line from the familiar Christmas carol.

"The hopes and fears of all the years are met in Thee tonight."

"Yes," I said, "we can never give up hope."

"Hope and fear," she said. "Those words describe the knife's edge between eternal life and eternal death. They stand between the promise of hope and utter hopelessness."

I nodded my head in agreement.

"I guess I've always known the truth in my heart," she continued. "but with the possibility of death on the horizon, I think I finally can resonate with the words of the apostle Paul. 'For to me, to live is Christ, and to die is gain.'"

"I get it now," she said softly as she gazed out the window at the darkening sky. "Like him, 'I am torn between the two—I desire to depart and be with Christ, which is better by far,' but for your sake it is better I go on living."

She looked up at me for a moment to make sure I was listening, then she continued her sermon.

"Death is the end of all weakness and pain, and I long for that. To escape sin and temptation and the Evil One's influence is more attractive to me than ever. I understand now the apostle was trying to choose between two really great things—living *for* Christ or living *with* Christ. At the same time, I also realize those who have the greatest desire to leave this world behind also have the greatest responsibility to stay behind and try to change it."

"I already told you that you have to stick around for a while," I said, a little frustrated with the direction the conversation had gone. "Besides, do we really have to talk about death on Christmas Eve?"

"Yes," she said, tilting her head and looking at me with the tiniest smile on her lips. "You know the melanoma is stage four now, and short of a miracle ..."

I interrupted her before she could finish the thought.

"Then we just won't settle for anything less than a Christmas miracle," I said. "And that's all I've got to say about that." The last line was from one of her favorite movies, which caused her to laugh out loud. I hadn't heard her laugh in so long, even sarcastically. For a moment, I was encouraged to see the fire of cynicism in her eye again.

"Well, okay then," she said. "Let's just pretend everything is going to be just fine."

"Now you're talking," I said. "I believe in miracles, don't you?"

She nodded her head in agreement. For a moment, we danced to the tune of our faltering faith, waiting for Jesus to perform another miracle. I grew up believing in Christmas miracles. And in that moment, I knew God loved me so much he'd have to answer my prayers.

I crawled up on to the bed beside her, and she laid her head on my shoulder. For a little while, the world was as it should be again. There was one lone star hanging low in the western sky like that first Christmas. A sign from God? I could hope.

On that silent, holy night, I wished on the star with all my might.

chapter 46

GOING HOME

You have been made for a person and a place. That person is Jesus, and the place is heaven. Until you're tapped into that knowledge, your heart will be restless.—Levi Lusko, *Through the Eyes of a Lion*

Even then Rachel knew better.

"Absent from the body," she whispered in my ear as I lay down beside her and held her tired, frail body. "Present with the Lord."

"Not yet," I whimpered back in the dark. "I'm not ready to let you go."

"God is calling me home," she said quietly. "And it's a wonderful thing. He will hold me in his arms until you can come and hold me once again."

"Someday, maybe, but not today," I said. "Today I'll be the arms of God for you."

"I'll be waiting just inside *the gate*," she said, making a reference to a book we both loved—a novel about a man who got to visit heaven for a while. For reasons left unexplained, he's allowed to stay in the guest cottage, and each night someone he's loved and lost comes to make him dinner. As the two share a meal, his guests also share the hidden secrets of how to live a life that matters.

"When you come to visit me," Rachel joked, "I'll make you a fresh ham roast with cabbage, corn, and mashed potatoes."

"If only there was such a gate," I said, "I'd use it every night until God decides to dismantle the universe and make a new one, star by star."

"That's the promise," she said. "And I intend to hold him to it. God promised that he'd give us a new heaven, a new earth, and an eternity together to make up for the few days we'll be apart."

"I'm not ready for us to be apart," I said. "Neither is Lucy." Immediately Rachel's face fell. Her eyes blinked rapidly, and a tear slowly rolled down her alabaster cheek. She'd come to grips with the possibility of leaving me for Jesus. But she couldn't bear the thought of leaving Lucy. For a moment, I wished I could take back my words.

"Okay," she said, too weak to argue and too tired to want to. "Okay, I'll keep fighting for another day."

"That's my girl," I said. "All I really want for Christmas is one more day, one more day every day, until eternity runs out of days. That's not too much to ask, is it?"

"You'll have to talk to God about that one," she said.

"Oh, I do," I said. "I pray every night for our days not to end."

Truthfully, even then a part of me wondered if I was asking too much. I dismissed the thought as quickly as it came. After all, what could one more day matter to the God of eternity? Then again, maybe he's asking, 'what could eternity matter to a man who's asking for one more day?' Such are the thoughts one has late at night in the cancer ward. Thankfully, Rachel was asleep in a matter of minutes, and I wasn't far behind. Later that night, her fever spiked and never came down. The doctors diagnosed the flu and said her immune system was just too compromised from the chemo to fight it. Life can change so fast.

A month earlier, we were celebrating Thanksgiving with my family in Sutton's Bay. The two of us had taken a walk in the orchard on a beautiful day. We stopped on a hill overlooking Grand Traverse Bay. Try as I might to deny it, she knew what was coming.

"I want to make it until Christmas," she said.

All I could say was "of course, you'll make it to Christmas." Then I quickly changed the subject. If only I'd let her talk.

She beat her goal by three days. The doctor pulled me aside a little after six on Christmas night.

"She's in quite a bit of pain," he said. "But she's fighting for your sake. There's really no reason for her to suffer anymore. I'd really like to up her morphine. Is that all right with you?"

"Sure," I said. But inside I was screaming, "No, no, not more morphine."

I knew she'd start to drift away when they increased her pain meds. An ugly thought, I know, but I was selfishly trying to hold on to her as long as I could.

"Is there anyone I can call, a pastor maybe?" said the doctor.

"No," I replied. "We're both pastors. We've already said whatever needed to be said."

The morphine did its job. Rachel slept peacefully after that. My brother brought Lucy by for a while. When she bent down and whispered in her ear, Rachel stirred slightly and smiled, but she never opened her eyes.

"Is Mommy with the angels?" Lucy asked as she was leaving.

"Not yet," I said, "but she will be soon."

One by one, other friends and family paraded through the door to say their goodbyes. Gunny came to do the deathwatch with me. For the next couple of days, he slept at our house, and every day he came and sat by her bed for a little while. Like Lucy, he whispered in her ear. I couldn't hear what he said, and he kept his thoughts to himself. Still, I could see he was reliving Tika's loss every time he walked into the room.

On the morning of Rachel's death, Gunny came by again for a few minutes. He stood by her bed pressing his index finger to his lips as if he was holding back his words. Then he finally spoke.

"She looks peaceful, don't you think?"

"Yes," I said, "she's at peace, and she has no pain."

"That's good," he replied, wiping a tear from his eye. "That's all we can ask."

On his way out of the room, he stood silently in the doorway with his head bowed for the longest time. I wasn't sure if he was praying or crying. Maybe both. After a while he began to shake his head ever so slightly from side to side, as if the emotions of the moment had stuck a nerve of discontent somewhere deep inside his soul. When he looked up, there was an anger burning in his eyes, and his words suddenly turned raw and brutally honest.

"This isn't right," he said. "It just isn't right. If I ever do make it to heaven, God's going to have some serious explaining to do."

I wanted to respond, to somehow defend God's honor, but I couldn't find the words. Gunny was right. Only God knows why this was happening.

Then, as if someone had flicked a switch in his heart, his mood changed again.

"I guess if anyone knows what it's like to watch your child die it's him," Gunny said. "I'm sure when he watched them nail his boy to the cross everything inside him said 'This isn't right, it just isn't right!' But it was right. It was the most righteous thing anybody's ever done."

Then he walked over and gave me a bear hug that almost took my breath away.

"I'm praying for you, Son," he said. "God knows I'm praying for you."

"I'm praying for you too, Gunny," I said softly, and then he walked out without saying another word.

A couple minutes later, he appeared again in the doorway. Then suddenly he spoke the words that were buried in his heart.

"I love you, princess," he said. "I love you." And then he walked away moaning and sobbing like a man who'd lost his only child.

I wanted to run after him and tell him that everything would be all right. But I knew better. There was nothing right about this. After that, I held his daughter in my arms and cried for us both.

An hour later, a nurse came in to give her another dose of morphine. Her nametag said she was Sally. The name fit her. She was a large woman in her sixties with a kind smile. As she pushed the fluid into her IV, Rachel got the tiniest smile on her face.

"She's dreaming," Sally said.

I hoped she was dreaming of me.

Sally took out all her IVs but one. Then she disconnected her from a couple monitors and gently washed her face with a warm cloth. I could tell this was not her first encounter with death. She was familiar with the workings and words of the cancer ward. I was glad for that.

"She's going home," Sally said softly. "And we want her to look beautiful for the angels."

All I could think was she'd never looked more beautiful to me.

When Sally left, she shut off the light. I lay down on the bed next to Rachel and covered us both with a blanket. As I held her in my arms, I could feel her heartbeat in perfect rhythm with mine.

The Bible was right. The two have become one flesh.

My mind went back to Holly Hill and the day of our wedding.

"Repeat after me," the preacher had said.

I did so without thinking.

"For better, for worse," he said softly in his eastern drawl. "For richer, for poorer, in sickness and in health, 'til death do us part."

When you promise to love someone 'until death do you part,' you never really think about the death part. You just think about living your lives together, forever. One day falls into another, and after a while your lives just sort of get all tangled up together. They become a part of you, and you become a part of them. Like the Bible says, 'The two become one flesh.' But then one cold, winter day the fairytale ends, and you're supposed to just untangle it all and go back to being single. But you can't. Once your lives get all tangled up you never really get untangled, at least not totally.

Looking back now, I realize we were young and innocent when we got married, as innocent as Adam and Eve in the garden. We knew nothing of life or loss. We lived in a world where the sun always shined until one day it didn't.

At the time, the idea never occurred to me that our life together would end. If I didn't run out on her, and she didn't run out on me, sooner or later, time would run out on us both. The end was inevitable, and death would tear us apart like a piece of bread.

And now, the end of our time together was happening, and I could do nothing. I was on the last leg of my deathwatch. In the silence, I listened to the sound of each click of the clock. Rachel was straining to breathe. Each breath was longer and lower than the last. Her lungs made that heavy wheezing chirp baby birds make when they fall from the nest. Her life was slipping away. In the swirling holiness of the moment, I also realized my life would never be the same again. Finally, I said the words I'd been dreading to say.

"It's all right, honey," I whispered through my tears. "It's all right. I know you're tired. You have fought the good fight, but you can stop fighting now. It's all right."

The words stung like acid on my tongue.

Sometime after midnight, I fell asleep praying she'd wake up in heaven. When she did, I wanted to take back my prayer. Why does God answer some prayers but not others? I don't know. All I know is as the wind howled in the hungering night, she quietly slipped from my arms into the arms of Jesus. Death took her life, but Jesus took her home.

Perhaps the old apostle said it best.

"Absent from the body, present with the Lord."

There, in the shadow of death, I continued to hold her bony body in my arms. A half hour later, nurse Sally came in and forced me to face reality.

"She's gone, Dr. DeVos," she said in a soft, almost pastoral voice. "She's home now. You can let her go."

"I know," I said. "I've known for a while. I'm just not ready to say goodbye."

"We're never really ready," Sally whispered. "Sometimes, the hardest thing to do is to let go of what we can't hold on to."

She read my thoughts. That's exactly where I was. I was stubbornly refusing to let her go, but in my heart, I knew she was already gone.

"Come with me," said Sally, grabbing my hand and leading me to a small waiting room down the hall.

There were papers to be signed and phone calls to be made, and I did what I had to do. At times like that, you go through the motions without really thinking about what you're doing. The next hours were a blur. I know I called my brother, Seth. I remember that clearly, but I don't remember much of our conversation. He and his wife Jamie were staying at my house with Lucy. He said Lucy was sleeping, so I told him not to wake her.

"I'll be home soon," I said. "I want to tell her myself."

Nurse Sally quietly gathered up the notes, photos, and personal belongings from Rachel's nightstand and brought them to me in a large plastic bag. I made my way down the back stairway and out the Emergency Room door.

As I was leaving, I saw the Salvation Army kettle unattended. For a moment anger and compassion went to war in my soul. Finally, I emptied my wallet and shoved all the loose bills I had through the slot.

"I guess I better help them, Father," I screamed through clenched teeth. "Lord knows you won't."

Then in a fit of rage, I kicked over the kettle, scattering the coins and the bills across the parking lot.

The security guard came running out the door behind me shaking his nightstick and yelling.

"Hey, buddy," he shouted, "what do you think you're doing?"

I walked to my car as he picked up the money. A mixture of sleet and snow pelted me like buckshot, and the wind screamed in my ear.

Under my breath I whispered, "See what you made me do, Lord?"

I was as disgusted with him as I was with myself, and the words of Job echoed in my head.

"Surely, God, you have worn me out; you have devastated my entire household."

chapter 47

CONTROL

Anything under God's control is never really out of
control.—Charles R. Swindol, *Insight for Living*

I drove home slowly, trying to figure out how to tell Lucy
her mother was gone. Life was spinning out of control. She
wouldn't understand everything, but she was old enough
to know the finality of death. That hurt me most of all. As
soon as I said what I had to say, our lives would never be
the same again.

I wanted to answer her questions as honestly as I
could, but I didn't want to pretend I knew things that were
unknowable. As I walked into her room, she already knew
what I was about to tell her. She sat in bed, holding on to
her stuffed dog Rufus and watching the snow blow through
the naked trees outside her window.

"Mommy is with the angels, isn't she?"

"Yes," I said, sitting down beside her and slipping my arm
around her shoulder. I knew how difficult this would be for
Lucy, so I tried my best to be strong for her sake. Whenever
anyone asked me what to tell their children about death,

my answer was always the same. "Saying too little is better than too much."

"So, she's with Jesus," Lucy said, forcing a smile. "And with Grandma Tika too, right?"

"That's right, Mommy's with all of them in heaven now."

"I'm glad she's not alone." Lucy said.

"Me too," I said. "Me too."

"I heard Aunt Jamie talking on the phone," Lucy said, looking down as if she were a little embarrassed about eavesdropping.

"She said her and Uncle Simon couldn't stand to see Mommy in so much pain, so they were praying God would take her home soon. Were you praying for that too, Daddy?"

"No. I didn't want her to go, but I'm glad her pain is gone. We're all glad for that."

She nodded as if she was also glad that her mother's suffering had finally ended.

"My Sunday School teacher, Tonya, said heaven is up there somewhere beyond the clouds," Lucy said, looking up inquisitively. "Does it take a long time to get there?"

"No," I said, "not really. You know how sometimes you fall asleep watching TV in the living room? And then the next morning you wake up in your bed."

"Yes," she said, smiling. "You carry me to my room while I'm sleeping."

"That's right," I said. "Going to heaven is kind of like that. You close your eyes here on earth, and when you open them again, you're in heaven. God carried you there in his arms."

Lucy put her elbow on her knee, rested her chin on her fist, and stared out the window again, trying to make some sense of the mystery of death. She looked so tiny sitting there on that big bed in her princess pajamas. For a time, I hugged her, and she hugged Rufus. Lucy was only eight when Rachel died. Third graders aren't supposed to bury their mothers.

"This isn't fair, God," I said under my breath, wanting to hurt him for hurting my only child. "She's just a little girl. Way too young to have to deal with all this."

I blinked my eyes, desperately trying not to cry, but as I watched Lucy struggle, a single tear dripped down the corner of my cheek.

When she saw it, Lucy reached up with her little finger and wiped it away.

"Miss Tonya says that there are no tears in heaven. Is that true, Daddy?"

"Yes," I said, sniffling a bit, "no tears."

"But is it okay if we cry a little down here?" she asked. "Because sometimes I really feel like crying."

"Yes," I said, "we can cry." Then Lucy's eyes puddled with a thousand tears. For the next several minutes, I held her in my arms, and we cried so hard we almost drowned poor Rufus with our tears.

Finally, when we were both about cried out, I looked at Lucy and tried to explain.

"Crying is okay, Honey," I said. "Our tears tell the world how much we loved her. So, whenever you feel like you need to cry, you just call me. I'll come and cry with you. Okay?"

"Okay," she said, snuffling. "Does that go for hugs too?"

"Yes," I said, "hugs too. I'll never run out of hugs for you."

"I love you, Daddy," she said, putting her little hands on either side of my face.

"I love you too, Lucy," I said. "Always and forever."

I reached over and gave her and Rufus a hug. She hugged me back really, really hard. And for those few moments, we both felt a little better.

"Daddy," she said, finally breaking the silence. "I wish I could tell Mommy I love her too."

"Don't worry, Honey," I said. "She knows how you feel. She lives with God now, but there's a part of her that still lives in your heart, so she knows. Besides, do you remember what Mommy used to say about the wind?"

"Yes," Lucy said, smiling slightly, "she said whenever the wind blows, God is whispering, 'I love you.'"

"Well," I said, "since Mommy's with God now, maybe she can do the same thing. In fact, I think that wind outside your window might be her. Shhh, listen, do you hear that?"

For a few moments, we sat there listening to the wind howl outside her window. The blowing seemed to grow in intensity with our silence. And then, as quietly as I could, I whispered the words on my heart.

"I love you," I said. "I'll always love you."

And deep down in my soul, I hoped that somehow Rachel could hear me too.

"I love you ... more," Lucy whispered back. Her words fell like salt on my broken heart. Rachel responded the same way whenever I told her I loved her.

Lucy smiled. Like me, she'd heard her mother and me say those words many times. For a few moments, we bounced the phrase back and forth like a ping-pong ball. As we did, I could almost feel Rachel's spirit in the room. To be honest, it was one of those rare, holy moments you sometimes have with the people you love.

When we had soaked up all the love our hearts could carry, Lucy got dressed and the two of us went downstairs and made some hot chocolate.

We had Rachel's funeral at ten o'clock in the morning on New Year's Eve. In some ways I suppose this was fitting. Rachel would begin her new life with God, and we would begin our new lives without her. Clearly, she got the better end of the bargain. Still, for her sake, I was politically correct enough not to offend anyone with my anger. I smiled politely and tried my best to hold myself together on the outside, but inside, I silently cursed God and his preacher.

In seminary, we were given a template for doing a funeral. We could choose various parts and pieces to include, such as opening salutations, Scripture lessons, confessions, words of committal, prayers, hymns, and a benediction. The template was intentionally generic—even including the words 'insert the deceased's name here' at various places. I cringed as Ben read the perfunctory pieces inserting Rachel's name as he went.

Inside my head I was screaming.

This isn't right. You knew her, Ben. Shame on you.

"We may not know what they are, but we do know God has his reasons for taking Rachel home," he said. "And we also know she's in a better place."

"The Lord gave, and the Lord has taken away," Boonstra said as he stood in the pulpit in his black robe and scarlet stole. "May the name of the Lord be praised."

In his mind, that seemed to settle the matter, but of course, *his* wife wasn't lying dead in the casket.

You never know what you believe about death until you put boots on your faith and walk it into the funeral home to view the body of someone you love. Until then, your beliefs are just wishful thinking and theory. As I stood in the shadow of death, the fabric of my faith felt flimsy and threadbare. To be honest, I was afraid I might unravel emotionally at any moment.

Do you remember the dream you had when you were a kid where you were sitting in school and suddenly, you realize you're naked? That's where I was. With Rachel gone,

I felt naked, exposed, and vulnerable. I was alone in my own garden of Gethsemane, wrestling with my God and my grief. And worse, inside I knew the agony and the emptiness were only starting.

In that moment, any respect I had for Ben Boonstra evaporated. He quoted Scripture as if he were an actor reciting the lines of a play. Act one the gospels, act two the epistle, act three the psalms. All I could think of was Solomon's words from Ecclesiastes. "Meaningless! Meaningless!" says the Teacher. "Utterly meaningless! Everything is meaningless."

Ben might be able to win a game of Bible trivia, but the words were just words. He was as lost as I was. After the service, he came up to me and wanted to have a conversation. I wasn't in the mood.

"We should get together and talk about all this, Rock," he said. "Maybe we can go out for pizza, or a game of golf. Grieving is natural—there's a time to weep and a time to mourn—but eventually your heart will heal. You're a young man with a lot of life left in you. You must pick up the pieces and move on. I think I can help you with that. I know what you're thinking, but if you won't do it for yourself, then do it for Lucy. A young girl like that needs a mother. Like the Book says, 'it is not good for the man to be alone.'"

He may have meant well, I don't know, but I didn't want his help. The only things he knew about death came from a book. I'd read those same books in seminary, and they weren't helping me much. I wanted to say, "call me when your wife dies, and then we'll get that pizza," but I didn't. Instead, I clenched my teeth and swallowed my words, and walked away shaking my head in disbelief. I knew if I said anything, there would be an argument, and I didn't want that, not there at least. Besides, sometimes silence is the best argument. My mom taught me that.

"Too often," she'd say, "we waste our words on people who only deserve our silence."

"The clergy are supposed to be the messengers of God," an old seminary professor I had used to say, "but, alas, so many have forgotten the message."

Maybe I'd forgotten too. That night I drank more cider than I should have, and I watched on TV when the ball dropped in Times Square. While the rest of the world sang "May old acquaintance be forgot," I vowed I would never forget. I knew loving Rachel was worth the pain of losing her. Given the chance, I'd do it all again in a heartbeat.

As I sat there, I asked myself the nagging question that had haunted my soul since I'd left the hospital.

"Do I still believe in God?" I whispered under my breath. Then I answered my own question.

"Of course, I do," I said. "Only a fool would be this angry at someone he didn't believe was real."

I got in bed and wondered if I would fall asleep or fall apart. I fell apart. Eventually, after questioning God's fairness for the thousandth time, I drifted off into an uneasy sleep, begging him to never wake me up again. Like so many others, this prayer also went unanswered.

The next morning, I saw Rachel's devotional on the nightstand next to her side of the bed. I'd dropped it there last night, along with a stack of sympathy cards. Almost without thinking, I turned to the reading for the day. Matthew was recounting "The Slaughter of the Innocent." The words captured the moment perfectly. Under my breath, I cursed at God for his calloused heart.

"This just isn't right," I said. "Why would you allow such evil to exist? Why would you allow someone you love to die right before your eyes? Speak to me, God. Is your heart made of stone?"

His silence spoke volumes to my soul.

chapter 48

RECREATION

The creation of the world did not take place once and for all time, but takes place every day.—Samuel Becket, *Proust*

Over a year has passed since Rachel died. I'm learning to cope with her loss, but I still struggle whenever I'm alone. I know I need to do things to keep busy. With school out for the holidays, I also know keeping busy will be difficult. So, before we left for Sutton's Bay, I dug out the stack of sympathy cards we'd gotten a year ago and put them in my suitcase. I thought I'd read them all again, have a good cry, and then burn them in the fireplace at the lake house.

That's exactly what I did.

I started a roaring fire, made myself a cup of coffee, and sat down in Sea's chair. One by one, I read the cards out loud, each an outpouring of sympathy and love. People had promised to pray, to bring a meal, and to be there for Lucy and me. Looking back now, they've kept those promises. I am blessed with family and friends. As I expected, the process was emotional, but also cathartic. Toward the end of the stack, there was a note from an old friend at Hope College.

Dr. Rene Huizenga taught Old Testament. He lived it too. The card was homemade. Rene had a passion and a talent for fashioning beautifully handwritten notes with his calligraphy pen. Across the front, in his large bold elegant rolling script, he'd written the word, "Resurrection." Inside the card, his heart and his faith spilled out onto the page.

"Like Jesus, sometimes the best we can do is to wade through the heartache and the hell and hold on to the promise that God is still in the resurrection business."

I vaguely remember reading his note a year ago. What I hadn't noticed before, however, were the folded sheets of paper tucked inside the envelope. They'd been torn from a yellow legal pad and were dog-eared and faded. As I looked more closely, I realized they were the notes from a chapel service Huizenga had led during my college days.

This was so like Rene. Little things often had a deeper meaning with him. He was one of my favorite professors at Hope. He had a habit of giving little personal mementos to his students. A fountain pen maybe or a book or a handwritten note, but the gift always carried some hidden significance. Once he gave me a tattered copy of Abraham Heschel's, *The Prophets*.

"If you're ever going to appreciate the depth and richness of the prophets," he said, "you will need to feel their pain."

Reading *The Prophets* was one of the reasons I decided to go to seminary.

Huizenga grew up the son of Dutch immigrants in North Carolina. His parents came over in their early thirties wanting a better life for their only son. His mother died a few years later when Rene was nine. Whenever he mentioned her name, his face revealed he still carried the pain of her death. His father was a cabinetmaker in the furniture industry, and he worked long hours to make ends meet. Rene quickly realized education was his best ticket out of poverty. His father continued to speak their native language at home, so Rene had the slightest hint of a Dutch brogue. He also had the slow elegance of a southern drawl which made him fun to hear.

Huizenga graduated Cum Laude from Duke and then received the same honors when he finished his doctoral work at the Free University in Amsterdam. After a few years as an assistant professor at Trinity College in Palos Heights, Illinois, he took the position at Hope. He would be there for life. Rene was in his fifties when I was a student there.

He combed his wispy blonde hair straight back. Tortoise shell glasses sat on the bridge of his nose, and he sported a neatly trimmed gray goatee. Being from the south, he never cared much for cold weather. He always wore a heavy collared cardigan or a tweed vest of some kind. His rumpled white shirt opened at the collar, and his loosened tie pulled off to one side.

One Friday a month, he had what he called the *Ma'amat*—a Hebrew word meaning something like "the confrontation." For that one hour, his students could ask him anything they wanted. At times, things got quite heated. Students would ask about things like God's wrath, the ethnic cleansing of the Canaanites, polygamy, the biblical status of women, and a host of other things.

Toward the end of one Ma'amat, I asked him about creation.

"The writer of Genesis seems to think creation happened sequentially in a week of twenty-four-hour days," I said from the back of the class. "But I'm having a hard time imagining God being bound by the limitations of a wristwatch."

"Is there a question in there somewhere?" the professor asked in a sober tone.

"Yes," I said, feeling the hint of condemnation in his voice. "As I understand, God is outside of time. You said so yourself. So, tell me, professor, why would the One who inhabits eternity bind himself to the calendar for the week of creation?"

"Mr. DeVos, I'm afraid you have mistakenly strapped that wristwatch of yours on the sacred writer," he responded in his slow Dutchy drawl. "Your question is one that is only asked by those of you who read the Bible in English."

"In the Book of Beginnings, the Hebrew word you refer to is *yom*. The root of this word has to do with temperature. Literally, the word would best be rendered in English as 'the warm time.' For this reason, yom is often translated as 'day.' However, a couple chapters later in Genesis 4:3, this same word yom is translated simply as 'time.' The same thing happens again in Isaiah 30:8. In 1 Kings 1:1 and 2 Chronicles 21:19, this word is rendered as 'year.' As is often the case with Hebrew, because this word has several different meanings, definition becomes the translator's choice. In other words, the context defines the word."

"Remember your Bible, my son. The Psalmist tells us that 'A thousand years in your sight are like a day that has just gone by.' So in reality, the scriptures imply that only God knows how long creation took. And if you pressed them, you'd find the best scientists would say the same thing."

With that the bell rang and we never finished the conversation.

A few weeks later, however, he seemed to take up our conversation again in his chapel message.

These notes were from that talk. In them, he tried to explain the connection between the creation and the resurrection. I remember hearing this talk and being impressed with the depth of his thought, but I'd forgotten about it until I saw his notes again.

"The only problem was that mortal man was, well mortal. Like everything God had created, sin had tainted humanity,

288

and every one of them has an expiration date at birth. They would be born, they would live, and they would die, returning once again to the earth from whence they came. And with every death, once again, God apparently moved on to something new.

"But like I said, one of the mysteries of God is just when we think he's moved on to something new, he surprises us by breathing new life into something old.

"Resurrection always catches us by surprise. The human mind simply cannot totally understand resurrection. For this reason, we often use the language of poetry, music, and metaphor to describe resurrection. Even so, our methods don't make resurrection any less true. The truth is resurrection is so true mere words are inadequate. For this reason, like all truth, we must simply take resurrection on faith.

"You must decide for yourself," Huizenga said, "but as for me, I cling to hope like a dog with a bone. And nothing will take hope away from me, not hardship, not suffering, not even death. I know in my heart the apostle Paul is right.

"'I believe our present sufferings are not worth comparing with the glory that will come.'

"Even if nothing else in this world is true, I want that to be true," Huizenga said. "Don't you?"

With that question, he stepped away from the lectern. A student began to clap, then another joined in, and finally the acoustics of Dimnent Chapel echoed with applause. He ended his lecture with my question about creation just hanging there. Each of us must decide how we'd answer it for ourselves.

As I sat in Sea's chair at the Bay Cottage, I knew I wanted the Scriptures to be true more than ever. I guess you could say faith was slowly having its way with my heart. The thin space between "what I could prove" and "what I believe" was smaller now. That space also has a name—hope. I'm hopeful. I believe Huizenga was right. Better days are on the horizon.

Sometimes the best we can do is to wade through the heartache and the hell and hold on to the promise that God is still in the resurrection business.

That night I slept better than I had in months.

chapter 49

Desires

That is part of the beauty of all literature. You discover that your longings are universal longings, that you're not lonely and isolated from anyone. You belong.
—F. Scott Fitzgerald, quoted by Sheilah Graham, *Beloved Infidel*

The next day, I woke early and went up to the big house for breakfast. After that, I walked up to Angel's Perch and remembered Rachel for a while. I spent the rest of the day with my dad and my brothers. Being with them was just what I needed. Working with them reminded me a farmer is always at God's mercy.

"Pray we get some rain," my dad would say as I sat down for breakfast as a kid. "If we don't, the cherries will shrivel up like raisins."

Then the next year, he'd say the opposite.

"Pray this rain stops soon, or there won't be much of a crop this year."

A farmer's kid soon learns "rain falls on the righteous and the unrighteous," but you pray anyway. Not so much because praying guarantees we'll get what we want, but because praying reminds us God is in charge and we're not. My dad and my brothers understood that, so they all just seemed to take life in stride. They trusted God in the good times and the bad. Being around them reminded me I could do better. Late in the afternoon, I went back to the bay cottage to shower. Then for a while I sat at the table alone with my thoughts.

"What do you really want from God?" I asked myself, already knowing the answer. I wanted Rachel. I loved her like a wild fox loves grapes. She was my addiction, my heart's desire. But was wanting her so desperately destroying my life?

In my work, I'd watched a lot of people pray for things that ended up ruining their lives. They let some competing desires become their heart's desire. When they did, someone or something became their god. Maybe the desire was for money or power or sex or drugs or alcohol. Regardless, they believed having their heart's desire would fill the void in their lives.

That's where I'd been for the last year.

I kept thinking, if only Rachel were here, she could fill this emptiness in my heart. Now, inside, I knew that was impossible.

As I sat in the bay cottage, I realized I would have to make peace with God before my heart can be full again. Jesus may stand at the door of our hearts and knock, but he won't force his way inside. He waits to be invited. I'd been pushing him away for over a year.

I'd worked with a lot of addicts, and the truth is most of them didn't have a drug problem, a pornography problem, an alcohol problem, or a gambling problem. They had a soul problem. Until they addressed that, any satisfaction they might find would be temporary. In my case, my heart's desire was to have Rachel back, and I clung to my desire like a dog with a bone.

In Ecclesiastes, Solomon lets us in on a secret. "[God] has also set eternity in the human heart."

He meant we all have this longing, this hunger for something that simply can't be satisfied with the things of this earth. Built into our DNA is this God-given desire to have a deep abiding relationship with him. Apart from that, life will never make sense. Satisfaction will always be just out of our reach, no matter how hard we strive.

I sat in the chair while my thoughts and emotions unraveled inside my spirit like the ribbons of a maypole until Lucy came bouncing through the door.

"Daddy," she said, "We're waiting for you. This is Christmas Eve, and everyone is up at the big house already. Frankie said if you're not there pretty quick, they're going to start the party without you."

"We can't have *that*," I said, grabbing my coat. The two of us walked hand in hand through the snow toward the house I grew up in. Like every Christmas Eve, we would eat a magnificent meal, open our presents one by one, and then head off to Orchard View Church for the candlelight service. I wanted Lucy to love every bit of that as much as I did.

As we finished opening our presents, my dad reminded us church would start soon. "Time to go to God's house," he said, "to celebrate the birth of his son."

As we drove through town on our way to Orchard Hill, we rode by Saint Michael the Archangel, and Lucy started unpacking my father's words.

"That's a church, right, Dad?"

"Yes," I said, "that's Saint Michael's Church." The stone structure has been the gathering place for Catholics in Suttons Bay since 1873.

A little farther down the road she asked her question again.

"That's a church too, right?"

"Yes," I said "Immanuel Lutheran is almost as old as Saint Michael's. Everybody's celebrating Christmas tonight."

I could see that she was deep in thought.

What are you thinking, child? Tell me what's on your mind.

And right on cue, she did.

"Why does everyone call their church the house of God if God doesn't really live there?"

"It's just a figure of speech."

"What does that mean?"

"A figure of speech is something you say when you're comparing two things that aren't exactly the same but they do have some things in common."

"I don't understand."

"Let me see if I can explain figure of speech a little better. When someone says life is like a rollercoaster, they really mean that, emotionally, their life has been up and down. And when people call their church 'God's house,' they mean church is the place where they go to talk to God or hear from God or feel closer to him. Does that make sense?"

"I guess so," she said. "If someone is looking for God, church is where they go to find him?"

"People who are searching for God often go looking for him at church," I said. "Sometimes they find him in a sermon, a song, or something they find in Scripture, but sometimes they also find him in the beauty of a summer sunset, the leaves of October painted in all the colors of fall, or the sparkling eyes of a newborn baby. God can be found anywhere if we look hard enough."

As I explained it to her, I remembered how often Scripture says that those who seek God find him. I had been doing the opposite, running away from the One I wanted to find. I silently wrestled with that revelation until Lucy brought me back to the moment.

"I wish God had an address," she said. "If he did, then we could go to his house and see Mommy."

"I wish that too," I said. "I wish so too."

chapter 50

CHRISTMAS EVE

Then the Grinch thought of something he hadn't before!
What if Christmas, he thought, doesn't come from a store.
What if Christmas ... perhaps ... means a little bit more!—
Dr. Seuss, *How the Grinch Stole Christmas!*

A thick snow fell from the northern sky as we drove up to the church. A candy-cane spiral with evergreens wrapped the four white wooden pillars of the front porch. A large wreath with a red-checked ribbon hung against the clapboard siding a few feet above the church's two massive front doors—just like a Christmas card. I recognized my mother's touch—another part of my family's holiday tradition to decorate the little white church at Christmas.

The slow, haunting, melodic sound of Jamie Harrison playing "Away in a Manger" on the soprano saxophone greeted us as we walked through the door.

The sanctuary looked like a Christmas card too. White lights exquisitely lit a ten-foot tree, roped greens swooped from rafter to rafter, candles flickered in the windows which lined both sides of the church, and a lifelike baby doll wrapped in swaddling clothes lay in the straw-covered manger. For a moment, I was a child again. Christmas was awash with wonder.

"The decorations are beautiful, aren't they, Lucy?"

"Yes," she said, smiling, "Mommy would have loved them."

I nodded in agreement and tried to hide my emotions. Holidays are hard on those who mourn. Everyone else's happiness only magnifies the heartache. Lucy leaned toward me and stabbed me in the heart.

"Daddy," she whispered, "that's not really the baby Jesus in the manger—just a doll, right?"

When did you become so cynical, my child? I was so hoping you'd hold on to your innocence a little longer. I'm afraid my doubts were stronger than your faith.

The irony of the moment burned a hole in my soul. As I was finding my way back to faith, Lucy was losing hers.

Oh my God, what have I done? I've polluted the only pure thing left in my life.

"You're right," I said blinking back my tears, "Just a doll."

For a moment, she looked up at me and smiled as if she had just discovered a secret. I smiled back in silence. I wanted to say something more. I wanted to tell her not to be so quick to let go of her innocence, but then Ed Hartman tapped his director's baton against the music stand, the lights dimmed, and the choir began to sing "Silent Night."

The Christmas Eve service was always special. Even more so this year with Jake Lankheet back in the pulpit. Reverend Harland Vandyke had been the pastor there since Jake's retirement twelve years ago but never quite filled his shoes. Now that Vandyke had taken a call, people were talking about calling a "young Jake." For now, the old Jake would do just fine.

As always, the service started at eleven o'clock sharp and would end with communion at midnight for the packed church. Lankheet was both punctual and powerful. I looked forward to hearing him again. We arrived late enough we had to sit two rows from the front—no hiding there. Martha Hayworth played Christmas carols on the organ as we slid into the white painted pew.

After singing a handful of carols, we listened to Katie Wierenga sing "Mary, Did You Know," a cappella. Then my brother, Simon, read the Christmas story from Luke's gospel and said a prayer. As he sat down, the lights dimmed, and Jacob Lankheet climbed the steps and stood to the right of the pulpit. He was dressed more casually than usual. He wore a black turtleneck sweater and gray plaid wool trousers. His silver hair picked up the light from the Christmas tree, and he smiled like a man who was about to share a secret. Everyone in the room knew this would be a good sermon.

"This is Christmas Eve," old Jake said with a twinkle in his eye. "You know the story, or at least you think you do. You all have big plans for tomorrow, so I'll be brief. Let me read you one very familiar, but very telling, verse again. As you listen, try to put yourself in the story. Slide into Joseph's sandals for a few minutes. Feel the fear, the uncertainty, and the doubt that he must have had."

In his deep voice, Jake quoted Luke's gospel from memory. "Joseph went up from the town of Nazareth in Galilee to Judea, to Bethlehem the town of David."

"And now, just to give you some perspective," Jake said, stiffening his back and standing to his full six feet. "That's a distance of a little over seventy miles, like walking from here to Manistee. Had Caesar Augustus not issued his decree, they never would have made the trip. This was not part of their plans. Try to get your mind around the fact that for Joseph, Bethlehem was plan B. Originally, he and Mary wanted to have the baby at home. They wanted this to be a family affair, but God had other plans.

"Trust me," Jake said, "this was a major inconvenience for them. But the trip took them to exactly where God wanted them to be as foretold by the prophets that the Messiah would be born in the city of Bethlehem. So, for Jesus to keep his date with destiny, Joseph would have to take his pregnant wife out for a seventy-mile walk."

He paused for a moment hoping what he was saying would sink in with his audience. The skeptic in me had always challenged the concept that Creator and caretaker of the universe would bother to manipulate the affairs of our lives to accomplish his purpose, but as Jake spoke the idea seems so natural. He who creates all things controls all things. *How could I have missed that?*

"There are two famous Josephs in the Bible," Jake continued, reminding us of what we already knew. "There is Joseph in his coat of many colors and the Joseph in his carpenter's cloak. The two men had a lot in common even though they were separated by over fifteen hundred years."

Jake did this kind of thing a lot. He liked to teach something new by connecting the dots with something old. In this way, he reminded us God was always up to something. I smiled slightly as he pulled us into the story.

"Both Josephs had a father named Jacob," he said. "Both of them had their hearts broken by people they loved. Both left their homes and went to Egypt. Both of their lives were profoundly influenced by dreams. And finally, both had to walk a path they didn't want to walk to end up where God wanted them to be.

"So, like I said," Jake continued, "for a few moments try to put yourself in Joseph's sandals. Ask yourself the questions he had to be asking.

"What do you do when your world is turned upside down? What do you do when you pray, I mean really pray, and the answer you get isn't the answer you want? What do you do when the people you love the most suddenly let you down?

"This is painful stuff," Jake said, now pacing back and forth and motioning periodically with his hands. "No one ever grows up thinking someday they'll fall head over heels in love and then have their heart stepped on. But it happens. Maybe you can relate to that. Maybe you can imagine all too well exactly how Joseph must have felt. Maybe you remember that painful day when you finally realized life wasn't going to work out like you expected."

He made a point not to look directly at me. In that moment, I knew who he wrote this sermon for. A seminary professor of mine used to say, 'If you preach to the broken-hearted, you'll always have an audience.' Jake meant this for me.

"I know you grew up believing the Christmas story was for children," he said. "It isn't. This is rated PG-13. This is for adults. This isn't a fairy tale. This is life in its coldest and harshest reality. This is one of those 'go-to' Scriptures you can pull out when the doctor says 'cancer,' or when your boss says 'we're downsizing,' or when the person you love says 'I don't think I love you anymore.' This is a good place to camp out for a while when whatever you thought would never happen, happens.

"You see, pain is often the lightning rod that connects us to God. Whether we're believers or not, we always drag God into our pain. We start praying.

"'How could you let this happen, God?' we ask. 'Why didn't you stop it? And why does it have to hurt so bad?'"

"That's where Joseph was.

"Ask away if you want," Jake said, looking around the room. "But don't really expect God to answer. He rarely participates in that kind of discussion. You see, if we really want to get God involved in our lives, we need to do what Joseph did."

He took what preachers call a dramatic pause so we could catch up with what he just said.

What exactly did Joseph do, Jake? we all asked in the silence of our thoughts. Then he answered our question.

"Instead of asking questions, Joseph asked for directions." Jake spoke in that Dutchy drawl of his, reeling us in like a fish on a line. "Instead of telling God what he wants, Joseph listens to what God wants. Instead of demanding something from God, Joseph obeys God's demands. That's what we need to do. We need to ask God to show us the plans he has for our marriage or our career or our kids or our future. That's Christmas. That was Joseph's prayer. And that's the kind of prayer God loves to answer."

As Jake walked down the steps to the communion table, Katie Wierenga sang *God Rest Ye Merry Gentlemen*. Then one by one, we walked to the front and took communion, which was being served by intinction, that is, we each tore a small piece of bread from the loaf to dip into a common cup. I hadn't taken communion since Rachel died. As the usher dismissed our row, I made my way to the front and found myself looking into Lankheet's deep blue eyes.

"The Son of God was sent to earth for you, my son," he said.

And in like fashion I responded,

"And also for you."

As Jake gave the benediction and sent us on our way, hot tears streamed down my cheeks. My time with Paul these last few months had pulled me back into the fold of God like a lost lamb. Jake's words shut the door of the sheep's pen. I was home. That night my prayer was a simple one.

"If your plan isn't my plan," I whispered, "then show me the way you want me to go, Lord. I'll do my best to follow."

Jake was right. It's a good prayer.

When I tucked Lucy in bed that night, she said her prayers, and then I asked her if she had a good day.

"Oh yes, Daddy," she said, "a wonderful day. I think maybe I finally understand Christmas now."

"Tell me," I said. "What do you understand?"

"Well," she said, "Christmas isn't about presents or trees or dinner with the family. Christmas is about the baby Jesus."

"Yes," I said under my breath. "Teach me, child. Pull me into the wonder of what you see. Tell me what Christmas looks like through your eyes."

"People can call church 'the house of God,'" she said, "but the building is not his home. Heaven is his home. That's where he belongs, and that's where we belong too. Somewhere along the way, we got lost and now, we can't find our way home. So, God sent Jesus to show us the way home. I think that's what Christmas is all about."

"I think so, too," I said.

"I kept wishing that Mommy could come home for Christmas this year, but then tonight, I realized she is home, she's really home."

"Yes," I agreed, "she's home."

I kissed her goodnight and sat down in Sea's chair. Maybe for the first time in my life I understood Christmas. Out of the mouths of babes.

chapter 51

ANSWERS

I call it an Aha! Moment. It is when the answer travels from my heart to my head and says, "This is so." No questions follow, no objections interrupt; just the recognition that I must listen and follow.—Sharon E. Rainey, *Making a Pearl from the Grit of Life*

Three days later, I drove back to Holland by myself. Lucy wanted to spend the week up north with her cousins. The plan was for her to ride back to Holland with Simon on New Year's Eve. So, once again, I was home alone. I got up the next morning and went downtown early. I was eager to talk to Paul. The temperature hovered just below zero, an unusually cold day. The west wind blew in from Lake Mac. I could feel the tips of my fingers and ears tingling from the cold. As I walked down Eighth Street, I pulled my stocking cap down over my ears and put my hands in my pockets. I crossed River Avenue, turned north, and headed toward the Lighthouse Mission. That's when I ran into Leo. He was standing in front of the Clock Tower looking a little lost.

"What are you doing out here this morning, Leo?" I asked.

"If you're looking for Paul," he said, ignoring my question, "you're too late. He, Stewie, and Atticus O'Malley all left earlier this morning. The three of them all said they had unfinished business to tend to. I guess I do too, but maybe mine will have to wait. I can't afford to just go running off like that."

"Running off?" I said. "What are you talking about?"

"Well," he said, leaning his elbow against the brick wall of the mission, "What happened is kind of hard to explain. I'm not sure you'll believe what happened. To be honest, I'm not sure I believe it, and I was there."

"Try me," I said.

"I guess the whole thing started with Stewie. He got a phone call two days after Christmas telling him his brother-in-law, Bud, had died. Somebody shoved a knife in his ribs outside the Sparrow Bar in Lansing.

"From what Stewie's told me about Bud, he probably deserved it. He was a bully. He tormented Stewie. The man picked on him unmercifully. And what's worse is that Stewie's sister, Nellie, just let it happen. Who knows why she did what she did? Maybe she was afraid of him, maybe Bud abused her like he did Stewie, or maybe she just didn't care. I don't know. All I know is that as soon as Stewie heard about the knifing, he felt like he needed to go and be with Nellie.

"'Not forever,' Stewie said when he came by to tell me he was leaving, 'but for a while, for as long as Nellie needs me.'

"You know how he is," Leo continued. "He sees the good in people even when there's no good to be seen. I guess what they say is true, blood is thicker than water. Nellie will probably take advantage of the boy, but when he heard his sister was hurting, there was no stopping him. Paul's been filling his head with all that talk of forgiveness, and I guess Stewie took it to heart. He's easily influenced like that."

"And Paul," I asked, "he went with him?"

"Sort of," Leo said.

"What do you mean 'sort of'?"

"Well, Paul said he had arranged to hitch a ride with some trucker headed east, and Stewie could ride along as far as Lansing if he wanted to."

"East?" I said, "With a trucker? I don't understand. Where exactly is he going?"

"I don't really know," Leo said. "You know Paul. He talks in riddles. Sometimes he's kind of hard to figure out. He said something about God wanting him to take on the powers-that-be and bear witness before the council in Rome."

"Rome? You mean like Rome, Italy?"

"Maybe. Could be. I don't know. I didn't take him literally. I thought he was talking about going to Washington and testifying before Congress or something. But now that you say that, I guess he could have meant Rome, Italy."

"Well, when's he coming back?"

"I don't know that either," Leo said, looking down at his shoes. "Honestly, I'm not sure he is coming back."

"Sure he is," I said, more for my sake than Leo's. "He has to. He wouldn't leave without saying goodbye."

"Maybe," Leo said softly, "but I don't think so."

To be honest, I was a little frustrated with Paul. Maybe hurt is a better word. If he was leaving, I thought he at least owed me an explanation. But one thing was for sure. Leo's words confirmed what I'd been thinking for quite a while. Paul was the Catholic priest, and, misguided or not, now he was on his way to Rome.

I was so self-absorbed with the thought of Paul leaving I hardly noticed Leo's big, brown canvas duffle bag sitting on the sidewalk.

"You going somewhere too, Leo?" I asked.

"I'm thinking about leaving." Leo said, looking down at the floor. "Ever since Paul showed up, a lot of things have changed in my life. I quit smoking, and I quit drinking too. I haven't touched a drop. I even promised God I'd stop taking things that didn't belong to me. I'm trying real hard to keep that promise too. Like Paul says, 'followers of Jesus are supposed to act like Jesus.' A lot of people say stuff like that, but Paul actually does act like Jesus. And I guess some of him has rubbed off on me.

"I don't know what it is about Paul," Leo continued, "but the more you're around him the more you want to be like him. You know what I mean?"

"Yes," I said, "I know exactly what you mean. The man has a way of making you want to be a better person."

"Exactly," Leo said. "Exactly. Even if he hardly knows you, he treats you like you were his best friend. And the thing is, he treats everybody like that. He makes you feel special, like you're somebody, like you mattered. I can't explain it."

"You don't have to," I said. "I know what you mean."

"I was going to go with them," Leo said. "I really wanted to go, but Paul said no. Since I'm sober now, he thought maybe I should thumb-it down to Kansas City and look up my boys. I'm not sure I'm ready for that. Worse, I'm not sure they even want me to come. But Paul was persuasive, and I've never been to Kansas City. So, I don't know. I guess maybe I'm going to go tend to a little unfinished business of my own. I figure with a little luck I can hitchhike my way down there in a couple of days."

"Sounds like a good idea to me," I said.

"Well, that settles it then," Leo said. "I wasn't sure. I was having some second thoughts. But if you and Paul both think finding my boys is a good idea, then okay, I'll try."

I offered to give Leo a ride out to the highway, and he accepted, less because he enjoyed my company and more because the cold was blistering, and the wind was biting.

My car was parked in the lot behind my office on Eighth Street, so we retraced my steps with Leo's duffle bag in tow. When we turned the corner, I hit the remote, unlocked the car doors, and Leo tossed his stuff in the back seat. Inside, the warm air from the heater felt good.

As Leo rubbed his hands together, he reminisced about his life and his family, and we kind of connected. I realized, like Paul, this drunken thief was also my brother. We'd both lost people we love, we both lost our way, and we were both trying to find our way back.

For some reason I found myself offering to buy Leo a train ticket to Kansas City. At first, he protested—said he didn't mind hitchhiking.

"Besides," he said, "costs too much money."

I told him not to worry about it, that I could afford it. Besides, "followers of Jesus are supposed to act like Jesus," and that's what he'd do. After that, Leo graciously accepted my offer.

When we got to the train station, I went in with him and bought a ticket from Holland to Chicago, and then to Kansas City—$96.75. Once again Leo protested.

"That's too much," he said. "I can't let you do that."

I told him about the hundred-dollar bill I had tucked under my driver's license.

"The money belongs to God," I said. "I've carried that bill around for over a year now waiting for him to tell me what to do with it. And I'm pretty sure he's telling me to spend it on your train ticket."

Leo turned and looked at me inquisitively.

"Do you talk to God, Doc?" he asked.

I told him that, for a long time, God and I weren't really on speaking terms. But lately we'd been talking some again.

"Well, okay, then," Leo said. "I'm sure not going to argue with God."

That sort of settled the matter for him.

"If the Spirit is on the loose," he said, "you best not get in his way. Paul taught me that. There's no stopping God when he's up to something."

The two of us sat in the station and talked about Paul and God, and how both were hard to understand sometimes. About twenty minutes into our conversation, Leo started to unload some things that were weighing on his heart.

"Hey, Doc," he said, in a tone that told me he was serious. "I want to tell you something. Right before Paul and Stewie left, things got a little weird. Unexplainable things started happening."

"Like what?" I asked.

"Well, like I said, for some reason Paul and Stewie were going to meet up with some trucker out by the Byron exit of I-96. They were going to walk out there and then catch a ride with him."

"That's not so strange," I said. "Paul's always enjoyed walking."

"Ya, I get that," Leo said, "but that's not the strange part. When the two of them came to say their goodbyes, Atticus O'Malley wasn't there. Somehow, he got wind they were leaving, and he got all upset. He said he wasn't much for goodbyes, so he went out back to the alley for a smoke.

"When Paul heard what happened, he went out back looking for him, and Stewie and I tagged along behind. When we got outside, Paul yelled across the parking lot at O'Malley.

"'Come on, Atticus,' he said. 'Time to go. We talked about this. You know you want to. You've got some unfinished business of your own.'

"'I can't,' Atticus said, brooding and feeling sorry for himself like he does. 'I told you, I'm not going down the aisle in this chair.'

"'Then leave the chair behind,' Paul said. 'That girl's not going to wait forever, you know.'

"'I can't,' Atticus said, 'and you know it.' You could tell the boy was angry with Paul for taunting him like that.

"Then Paul and Stewie walked over to where he was sitting. I couldn't really hear what they were saying until I went a little closer, but Atticus was crying. Paul took the cigarette from his hand and crushed it on the ground.

"'Time you quit that too,' he said. Then Paul knelt on one knee in front of Atticus's wheelchair, so the two of them were eyeball to eyeball.

"'We talked about this,' Paul said in a very soft voice—I could barely hear him. 'You can do anything you want to, but your faith needs to be stronger than your excuses. God believes in you. Bonnie Jean believes in you. We all believe in you. The only one who doesn't believe in you is you.'

"For a moment," Leo said, shaking his head in disbelief, "the two of them just looked at each other in silence, and then Paul reached out his hand toward the man.

"'Come on," Paul said. 'You'll never get out of that chair if you don't try.'

"That's when it happened," Leo said. "Almost as if they'd rehearsed, Paul and Stewie grabbed Atticus by the arms, and together, they lifted him to his feet. Then, with a very determined look on his face, Atticus took a stumbling step.

"I watched them," Leo said, "but I couldn't believe what I was seeing. He started hobbling around on those spindly, spidery legs of his, and all I could think was, 'Atticus O'Malley is walking. The cripple is walking.'

"The three of them began limping and laughing their way around the parking lot," Leo said with a furrowed brow. "Atticus twisted and shuffled his way along in a jerking motion, and his legs seemed to get stronger with every step.

I'm telling you it was like a scene out of a movie or something. Atticus looked like a little baby taking his first steps. In some ways, maybe he was."

"After a few minutes, Stewie must have figured that Atticus had practiced walking long enough.

"'Are we going or not?' he said.

"And with that, Paul, Atticus, and Stewie looked at each other like they had a secret or something. Then the three of them started walking arm in arm toward Eighth Street—like the scene from the *Wizard of Oz* where the lion, the scarecrow, and the tinman are all dancing down the yellow brick road.

"'Wait a minute,' I said. 'Are you sure this is a good idea? You'll have a thirteen-mile walk out to the freeway."

"'We'll hitch when we get out of town,' Stewie said, holding up his thumb.

"I felt like a bride left at the altar," Leo said. "After that, I went back inside, cleaned out my locker, and put all my stuff in this bag. That's about when you showed up.

"I know this sounds crazy," Leo finally said after catching his breath. "But as sure as my name is Leo Raphael Rodriguez Jr., I swear it's the God's honest truth. I saw it with my own eyes. What do you make of all that, Doc?"

"I'm not sure," I said. "What do you make of it, Leo?"

"I don't know," Leo said softly, shaking his head, "I just know there's something special about that man Paul. He's got a way of bringing things out of you you didn't know were inside you, and I'm going to miss him. The truth is I'm missing him already."

I agreed. Like Leo I was missing the man. But then, for some reason, my mind flashed back to something Rachel had said the first time we met. I turned to Leo.

"Did you say your name was Leo Raphael Rodriguez Jr.?"

"Ya, so what?"

"Was your dad a trumpet player?"

"I don't know," Leo said. "My parents abandoned me when I was a baby. I grew up in an orphanage in Jersey."

"You better sit back down, Leo," I said. "I have something to tell you."

Then as gently as I could, I explained how Rachel had met his mother in the hospital.

"Your mother's name was Esther," I said. "She was a dancer. And your dad played trumpet with the Jimmy Dorsey band. He didn't abandon you, Leo. He got drafted and died in Korea. After that, your mom started drinking heavily, and when she found out she was pregnant, she just couldn't stop drinking. Social Services took you away from her in the hospital."

"'She wasn't fit,' they said, but she never stopped loving you, never."

I told him the whole story, and when he heard it, Leo cried like a baby. As he did, I sat in the train station and held the big man in my arms.

"You are like the arms of God for me," he said and wouldn't let me go. Finally, when his train came in, he tried to compose himself. Eventually, we said our goodbyes. I watched and waved as Leo went off to Kansas City. Later that afternoon, I went back to my office at Hope. With all that fresh in my mind, I sat down and tried to write my final report for Summerdyke's court.

"First," I said, "I want to reiterate what I said earlier. I do not believe Sha'ul Ben-Andronicus, case number 1761-5SBA, aka Paul, presents any danger to himself or to anyone else. In fact, the opposite seems to be true. He extends an uncommon kindness to anyone he meets.

"Secondly, I see no reason for the courts or for me to see him again."

Such was my belief, but not my hope. Somehow, I wished our paths would cross again. I still had a lot of things to say to him and even more to ask. But honestly, I didn't really think I'd ever get the chance.

He was still a mystery, but maybe I had started to put some of the pieces of the puzzle together. Then again, maybe not, who knows. I don't know. I just don't know.

I remembered how Paul sat in the Holland Hospital garden and talked into the silence of Emma Higgins' life. How he spoke to her as if she could hear him clear as a bell. Then I remembered how he waved to blind old Tobin Welch sitting on Eighth Street with his dark glasses and white cane. And then memories of Paul fell like dominos. Scratch Weinstein and his psoriasis, Stewie Overbrook and his shyness, Leo Rodriguez and his thieving ways, Atticus O'Malley and his spindly legs, and of course—me. Our encounters with Paul were different, yet in another way they were the same. We all experienced healing of some kind in his presence.

My mind was playing hopscotch with the possibilities. Eventually, I was so overcome with emotion I started to cry. As I sat there weeping, Rachel's song from Isaiah kept playing in my head.

> "say to those with fearful hearts,
>   Be strong, do not fear.
> Your God will come,
>   he will come with vengeance;
> With divine retribution.
>   he will come to save you."
> Then will the eyes of the blind be opened
>   And the ears of the deaf unstopped,
> Then will the lame leap like deer,
>   And the mute tongue shout for joy.

That night my study of psychology and theology began to converge in my mind.

In 1969, the Swiss psychiatrist Elisabeth Kübler-Ross wrote a book entitled *On Death and Dying*. She revolutionized the way we think about death. She suggested the terminally ill, and those who love them, go through five stages of grief. First comes Denial, then Anger, Bargaining, Depression, and finally, Acceptance.

We know now, of course, that no one grieves by the book. Death is messy. Kübler-Ross was right and wrong. We go through her stages, but not in any defined order. We're angry one minute and then fall back into denial the next. We accept the reality of what's happening, only to turn around and shake our heads in disbelief.

"This can't be happening," we say, "it just can't. I won't let it. Not yet, not now."

When death comes calling, we hopscotch our way through Kübler-Ross's stages wishing, hoping, and praying for something more. Thankfully there is something more. Her work was incomplete. There is a sixth stage. The one she missed is called Resurrection, and that's where theology comes into play.

Like it or not, life is full of irreconcilable contradictions. Loving someone can be both wonderful and painful. A good God somehow allows bad things to happen. In helping others, sometimes we find the help we need. And we long to live with certainty, but faith—true faith—'is confidence in what we hope for and assurance about what we do not see.' Accepting that reality helped resurrect my faith.

Like I said, life is full of little Easters, and the truth of that is evident if we have an eye for it. Every day, miracles happen somewhere in our world. Failed marriages are mended. Broken hearts and lives are made whole again. Unbreakable addictions are broken. And the dead are welcomed through the gates of heaven. God is faithful. He just doesn't always follow our timeline. As Christians, we gather in the shadow of whatever crosses we have to bear and remind each other Easter always comes on the heels of tragedy. That's my story. That's your story. And that's where our stories connect with God's story too. Perhaps Paul said it best.

"For I am convinced that neither death nor life, neither angels nor demons, neither the present nor the future, nor any powers, neither height nor depth, nor anything else in all creation, will be able to separate us from the love of God that is in Christ Jesus our Lord."

On New Year's Eve, on the last hours of the last day of the year, I sat in the living room in front of a roaring fire. The back-porch light opened a tiny window into the night. I looked out as the waves of winter crashed against the frozen beach. Wisps of wind and snow blew in off the lake and disappeared into the shivering pines on the side of the house. The lake and the sky merged in a sea of darkness. God's cathedral was vast and foreboding. I felt tired, small, and alone. A part of me thought about going to bed, but I didn't.

"Too early—not even seven o'clock," I said to myself. "If I go to bed now, I'll just end up tossing and turning for most of the night."

I decided to get myself a sandwich and a cider and watch *60 Minutes*, which I'd taped.

The tick-tock of the *60 Minutes* stopwatch flashed across the screen. As the stopwatch counted down the seconds, I heard Scott Pelley's familiar Texas drawl.

"Father Paul Aboud," he said as the priest's picture appeared, "the Catholic priest who mysteriously disappeared after our report aired on the secret practices of the Catholic Church, has finally resurfaced. He's in Rome working for the

Vatican alongside Cardinal Francesco Giuliani, who many believe will be the next Pope. For the past several months, the two of them have headed up the papal investigation into over one hundred priests who've been accused of sexually molesting children. That story and more next on *60 Minutes*."

"What?" I whispered. "Several months, how could that be? Paul has been here in Holland for the past eight months."

Postlude

THE LETTER

A letter is always better than a phone call. People write things in letters they would never say in person.
—Alice Steinbach, *Educating Alice: Adventures of a Curious Woman*

Two weeks later, as I went up the stairs to my downtown office, I saw a manila-wrapped parcel with my name and address sticking out of the mail slot of the door. There was no return address or postmark, and that understandably piqued my interest. I fumbled to open the package. Inside, I found a small leather satchel made from a single piece of tanned calves' skin neatly stitched up both sides. The back flap of the pouch folded over the front with laces that tied. My heart raced as I read the handwritten note inside.

Paul, a servant of him who brings comfort to the broken. Grace to you and peace from God our Father and the Lord Jesus Christ.

I thank my God whenever I think of you. My heart broke when I had to leave so abruptly. We have some unfinished business between us. I was hoping to explain more in our final session, but he who calls us all had called me. For this reason, I ask your forgiveness for not taking the time to say goodbye. I knew you would understand.

I remember all too well the suffering you have had to endure and the unfairness of what has happened to you. Still, I would remind you that faith is not intended to keep bad things from happening but rather to keep us when they do. For this reason, I implore you to trust in God and his grace.

I earnestly pray that you will find your way in the Lord, even as I know you will. For your progress is evident to me as I'm sure to you also. Meanwhile, I extol you to continue encouraging those around you who struggle and to share what you have already learned. For I am confident that he who has begun the work of reconciliation in you will see it through to completion.

Until then, every day we're apart from those we have loved and lost only brings us one day closer to our reunion with them. He who never breaks a promise has promised to give us an eternity of unending days, and so we pray the thin space between heaven and earth will soon be no more.

For this reason, I implore you to be about the business of the Lord. Comfort others even as you yourself have been comforted, for he is coming soon.

People say time heals all wounds. I disagree. Time merely scabs over the wounds. Only Jesus can heal all wounds, so we long for his return. On that day, time won't matter anymore. We'll stop counting. Knowing that, the founders of our faith had a favorite prayer.

"Come, Lord Jesus," they said, "Come quickly." Some of us are still saying it and praying it.

About the Author

DANN STOUTEN (DMin, Western Theological Seminary) is the pastor of Leadership and Teaching at Christ Memorial Church in Holland, Michigan. Dann has always been a lover of stories. He believes if we write about hope, it's because we have found hope. If we write about tragedy, it's because we have experienced tragedy. If we write about love, it's because we have been loved well or want to be. If we write about faith, it's because we have wrestled with our doubts and come out on the other side. Doubt is the enemy of faith and nothing stirs up doubt like death.

When we lose someone we love, our faith is either strengthened or strangled. That death will drive us closer to God or drive us farther away. We find ourselves in *The Thin*

Space between wanting to believe and wondering if we do. For a time, faith and doubt play tug-o-war with our souls. In the end, whether we chose to believe or not is often decided by the stories we're told. My prayer is that my words might bring people comfort and bring them closer to God.

Dann's first novel, *The Gate,* is also available in book stores and online.

Scriptural Index